Up From the Grave

Marilyn Leach

Up From the Grave

Contact Information: titleadmin@pelicanbookgroup.com

All scripture quotations, unless otherwise indicated, are taken from the Holy Bible, New International Version[R], NIV[R], Copyright 1973, 1978, 1984 by Biblica, Inc.™ Used by permission of Zondervan. All rights reserved worldwide. www.zondervan.com

Cover Art by *Nicola Martinez*

Harbourlight Books, a division of Pelican Ventures, LLC
www.pelicanbookgroup.com PO Box 1738 *Aztec, NM * 87410

Harbourlight Books sail and mast logo is a trademark of Pelican Ventures, LLC

Publishing History
First Harbourlight Edition, 2013
Paperback Edition ISBN 978-1-61116-270-7
Electronic Edition ISBN 978-1-61116-269-1
Published in the United States of America

Dedication

To Andy and Lillie Harris whose generosity, support, and humor have opened the way for my appreciation of the English culture and proven English friends are family.

Praise for Marilyn Leach

Praise for Berdie Elliott Mystery, *Candle for a Corpse*:

"This is an engaging mystery with likeable and interesting characters. I hope we'll be seeing more of Berdie and friends. ~ Liz Carey's Library

You will not be able to put the book down until you're finished. ~ Cindy Loven, The Borrowed Book.

Prologue

In the dampness of the English spring night, the woods at the edge of Aidan Kirkwood could trick the imagination into believing something or someone moved amongst the ancient twisted trees and through the upstart arbors.

The man shivered and searched the wooded landscape. How long had he been walking? Pale light from a half moon fell across his facial features and exposed the sheen of his black satin dressing gown. A sharp pain on the sole of his foot woke him to the uneven woodland floor beneath his moist bed slippers. It wasn't until that moment he realized he still wore his nightclothes.

The black wooded recesses etched his own murky dilemma deeper into his consciousness.

"What am I doing?" The man lifted his mortified voice into the darkness.

In a silvery flash, he caught another glimpse of movement. It wasn't his frenzied vision playing games. It was definite movement. His wildly pulsing heart urged him forward to get a fuller view.

A shadowed figure emerged from the trees not more than a few yards away. Both men started, coming to an abrupt halt.

The figure was only an outline, but his widened eyes were just visible below his woodsman cap. Moonlight glinted off the edge of a pointed spade hugged close to his side. A pungent odor of freshly upturned earth penetrated the night air. The stranger's eyes ran the full length of the night-clothed male.

The gulf of silence between them became an uneasy space.

"Why are you on this property, woodsman?" The man hoped his words weren't filled with the anxiety that gripped him.

"Why are ya about the wood in your bed clothes?" the stranger retorted.

The man swallowed hard. "Perhaps it's best if we agree to forget this chance meeting."

With an awkward vigilance, the woodsman's eyes stayed squarely upon the oddly clad male. "So be it." He stepped back into the black of the protective trees and moved on.

The man pulled his robe tighter. "Where am I now?" he questioned the darkness. He took several steps forward where he could just make out the edge of the wood. There it stood. The outline of an ancient edifice, a moonlight-edged church prevailed solidly against the night as if wearing a halo.

"God sees all." He placed his hands over his face. This was a dark night despite the moonlight, and he would never be able to erase the memory of it.

1

The jolly bell that hung on the door of the Copper Kettle Tea Shop sounded its farewell in Berdie Elliott's ear. None too soon, she stepped from the shop. Laden with white boxes stuffed with fresh, warm scones, she was attended by Lillie Foxworth who also balanced several full boxes in her arms.

"Step lively, Lillie, we need to get these to the vicarage as quickly as possible." She took a deep breath, inhaling the fresh aroma of the scones mingled with the refreshing spring air. She turned her bit-more-pudgy-than-lean body to stride up the High Street, and Lillie followed along.

"I do believe, Lillie, there's enough hot air in that tea shop to stir up gale force winds in the North Sea."

Lillie gave a quick grin. "And would you expect any different where people of a small village gather?"

"Not really I s'pose."

"I take it, then, you did hear comments made over tea about our parish council chairman."

"I did indeed."

"You were ear wigging."

Berdie half grinned. "And you weren't? As I said, gales of hot air."

"Well, you must admit, Berdie, Grayson Webb is rather flash and glam."

"He's not flash. He's just progressive."

"Still, not always the best feature for a small

English village. Progressive means change and that's seldom welcomed."

Berdie's eyebrows, which she had delicately shaped just this morning, escalated above her glasses. "Who wouldn't welcome a small floral feature with a calming pond in the back garden of the church?"

"Oh the village loves the plan for the garden feature. It's all the ado Grayson has made of this mystery benefactor who's to appear at the ceremony that they don't like."

"What did you hear, Lillie? Or should I say overhear?"

"On one side, many think gifts to the church should be private. And then on the other side there's Dudley Horn who's set up a 'Guess the Benefactor' betting pool at the Upland Arms."

"Oh yes, he asked my Hugh if he'd like a go." Berdie couldn't help but smile.

"And did he?"

"He told Dudley he'd have five goes if the proceeds all went towards the church garden scheme. He suggested"—she lowered her voice to mimic her husband—"'that way everyone in the pool could all attend the fête as surprise benefactors.'"

"Good show, Hugh."

"Grayson Webb may be causing a stir, but then who in Aidan Kirkwood doesn't own a very large spoon?"

"True enough."

Berdie exhaled and let the controversy swirling round the parish council chairman depart into the easy warmth of the afternoon.

She took in the shops and businesses that called this street home in Aidan Kirkwood and thought back to only a year and a half ago when this was all new to her and her husband, Reverend Hugh Elliott. It was Hugh's first pastorate, having chosen to enter 'the Lord's army' upon retirement from Her Majesty's Royal Navy.

Now, the familiarity of this tidy road felt like the warming spring sun. The whole of the parish was in the midst of the Lenten season with a keen eye to the Easter celebration that followed. And Berdie was the hostess.

"You know, Lillie, I think I've discovered Villette's recipe for her rhubarb sponge tartlets." Berdie gave a quick nod towards the tea shop now behind her.

"She's a bulldog concerning her recipes," Lillie declared. "How'd you do that?"

"I told her I had tried making some tartlets like hers with that fine almond flavor, but I added too much almond extract. 'No, no,' she said, 'never use almond extract.'" Berdie moved a short red-brown wisp of bobbed hair behind her ear. "So the next time I saw her, I told her that I used almond flour in the mix. 'Oh my,' Villette said 'that had to make the tartlets quite dry.'"

"I don't remember you making these tartlets," Lillie challenged, her hazel-green eyes in a bit of a squint.

Berdie tipped her head and formed her lips into a coy smile. "But don't you see, that means she grinds her own almonds for the little cakes."

Lillie shook her head of dark natural curls. "But you don't like rhubarb tartlets. Indeed, you aren't that keen in the kitchen."

"That's not the point," Berdie countered impatiently.

"Now that is a feat!" Lillie teased. "Why yes, the former highly regarded investigative reporter from a large city newspaper has ferreted out the best rhubarb sponge tartlets recipe in the wee village, and she has no intention of ever making or eating them." A quick laugh and Lillie's thin tawny face all but lit up like a spring dawn. "Snap!" Lillie stopped dead still on the narrow walkway and focused on her friend of over twenty years. "Bernadine Abigail Elliott, you're bored."

"I should say not." Berdie could feel the pink rise to her cheeks even while moving forward.

"You haven't had any desperate crimes to solve in over a year and you're bored!" An impish grin spread across Lillie's attractive face. "Come on, Berdie. Admit it."

Berdie halted. She spun round so quickly to face Lillie it sent her tortoiseshell glasses on a slight cascade down her nose. "I love working with Hugh in the church."

"You do a fine job."

Berdie adjusted the unruly spectacles with one hand while balancing the scones in the other. "And Aidan Kirkwood is a wonderful place to live despite the fact it can get a bit *close*."

"Indeed!" Lillie tapped her fingers on the top box she held. "Go on then."

Berdie pursed her lips. She looked her friend directly in the eye. "Well, I wouldn't use the word bored. Maybe"—she searched for the right expression—"a bit rusty."

"Wire wool. That works well on rust." Young David Exton, the editor of the Kirkwood Times, zipped by with a quick nod to both the women. "See you later at the fête," he quipped.

"Yes," Berdie called after him. Then she fastened her gaze again on Lillie. "And keep your voice down."

"A-ha!" Lillie shook her head again. "Your intuitive gift for sniffing out and fixing trouble needs a rigorous workout." Her dark thick lashes made her now wide eyes appear even larger. "Our talents are never allowed to go spare. I shouldn't wonder if something big is brewing. Yes indeed, but what?"

"Now you're being silly." Berdie recommitted herself to charging up the street. "First of all, my fine husband feels that involvement in crime solving distracts from my church duties."

"When has that stopped you before?" Lillie took several fast steps to keep astride her comrade.

"Secondly, the biggest thing that's going to happen is to successfully complete a simple welcome tea this afternoon along with a modest sod turning ceremony. Hardly a catastrophic agenda."

"Is that all you have to say on the matter?"

Berdie didn't respond. She simply redirected the conversation to a topic she knew to be close to Lillie's heart. "Is your handsome Loren coming to the festivities today?"

The jolly Lillie went quiet. A seldom seen tightening of the jaw loosened just enough to speak a stark. "One should think."

"Another interrupted dinner date last night, then?"

"Oh yes, another," Lillie answered abruptly. "Another lonely cab ride home, another egg and chips for one in front of the telly." She huffed. "It's been weeks since we've made it through an entire evening together without his mobile crying out for him to return to work."

"He's a pathologist, Lillie. His work is demanding, and his hours are often higgledy-piggledy."

Berdie could see Lillie's frustration and at the same time felt the need to quickly get to the vicarage. She nudged Lillie's arm and began rapid steps forward. Lillie moved with her.

"How can the dead make so many demands on the living?" Lillie spewed the words. "If you please, a cold figure down in the lab seems preferable to a living one at his side."

"Stuff and nonsense."

"The saddest part is that when Loren asks me to dinner again, I'll go."

"I dare say."

Lillie lifted her chin. "Well maybe not this time. Maybe we'll just see."

Berdie glanced at the clock nestled near the roof line of The White Window Box, a gift and garden shop. Knowing the clock was accurate only seventy percent of the time at best, she hoped it was now fast. "Is that the correct time on the Window Box clock?"

Lillie peeked at her watch. "It looks as if it's seven minutes slow."

"My dear Lord have mercy," Berdie yelped. And both women doubled their speed.

They flew past the shops with their simple windows of displayed goods, where owners swept the walkways enveloped by the warm afternoon sun. Berdie and Lillie greeted the people who chatted in the office entries and treaded the walkway. Despite being in a mad dash, Berdie admired the fresh daffodil blooms that decorated the terraced homes along the way.

Finally, at the end of the High Street on the front end of a wooded area, Saint Aidan of the Wood Parish Church sat elegantly awaiting all who wished to enter. Like a large tree offering shade in the heat of the day, this building made of ancient stones held peace and restoration for the pilgrims of this mortal earth just as it had for eight hundred years.

The moment Berdie and Lillie entered the pathway towards the vicarage, just a hundred yards from the church itself, a voice from across the front garden swelled.

"Mrs. Elliott."

Berdie stopped short causing Lillie to bump into her.

It was Ivy Butz. Her rotund figure moved quite quickly towards the two women. Her brown hair was banded by a pretty yellow ribbon that matched her pinny. And her usual jolly full-moon cheeks danced at the end of each corner of her upturned mouth. Not one of her six children was in tow this time round, but she held the elbow of Cherry Lawler and nearly tugged her along. Cherry's twenty-two-year-old visage and attitude contrasted greatly to Ivy's. The petite young woman's body reluctantly bounced along with Mrs. Butz. Cherry's lowered eyes peeked out from behind the blonde fringe of her pixie haircut, her lips set.

When they arrived at Berdie's side, Ivy urged the young woman. "Now tell Mrs. Elliott the problem, Cherry. She's ever so good at finding solutions." Ivy glowed expectantly at Berdie.

"Thank you for your confidence, Ivy. I only hope I can help. What is it, Cherry?"

The young woman lifted her pointy chin. Her slender fingers twisted the long sleeve of her jumper.

"It's just that we have two extra guests from the Golden Season's Tour, and we just haven't an inch of room left at our bed and breakfast. That is to say, my Jeff said we can't possibly fit any more in unless they want to sleep standing up."

"I'll take them," Lilly offered energetically.

"Could you do?" Cherry brightened.

"The garret flat at Swallow Gate is available," Lillie offered. "It's very comfortable."

"That's brilliant!" Cherry smiled, but her eyes still held a sense of distress.

"Now go on," Ivy urged. "Tell the vicar's wife the other thing—you know."

Cherry Lawler's thin bottom lip began to quiver. "It's a bit personal."

Ivy flashed a not often seen frown towards Berdie. "My uncle Wilkie, Cherry's granddad, can be a daft old sort. And that's all I have to say on the matter. I'll see to the tea preparations, Mrs. Elliott." Ivy hijacked the scone boxes from Berdie. "Take good care of my cousin here." Ivy gave Cherry a pat. "I'll leave you to it."

"Yes, must get the women's chorus in form for the ceremonial performance." Lillie, choir director extraordinaire and understandingly discreet, excused herself as well.

"I don't mean to be a bother Mrs. Elliott." Cherry apologized and swallowed.

"Not a bother." Berdie put her hand on Cherry Lawler's arm. "Please, go on."

"It's just that, well, you know my grandfather."

Berdie nodded.

"He's against this whole church garden scheme."

Hugh had told Berdie about Wilkie Gordon's explosive reaction at the parish meeting where the garden expansion was approved. Something about dismantling God's green earth as she recalled. "Yes, I've gotten word."

"He says that the money could be better spent on people in need, and the church is being irresponsible."

"Oh. Well, we do give generously to many charities and missions of course."

"Yes, Mrs. Elliott. We all know that. He knows that. But he insists the whole affair diminishes both the church and God's honor."

Berdie knitted her brow and shook her head. "That seems a bit extreme."

"Mrs. Elliott, I'm afraid he's going to do something daft, and it's creating a great deal of tension in our family."

Berdie noticed the moisture building in Cherry's generous eyes.

"How daft, exactly?" Berdie asked cautiously.

"Who can say? I've never seen him this angry before."

Berdie could see a silent plea in Cherry's face.

"I wish someone could help my grandfather see sense."

Berdie became instantly aware who 'someone' meant to Cherry Lawler. "Would you like my husband to have a word?"

Cherry wore relief like a lavish Easter bonnet. "Could he? Oh, that would be brilliant…and before the ceremony?"

"I'll give Hugh the message straight away. You have my word. I'm sure he'll be glad to help. He'll speak with your grandfather as soon as possible. Don't trouble yourself on the matter anymore."

"I'm grateful," Cherry tittered with relief. "I'll just

go catch Ivy up." With a decidedly lighter step, the young woman departed.

Berdie made haste for the church. She wondered why Wilkie Gordon was going on so. He had been the church gardener for several years but had quit the position just a few months before Berdie and Hugh arrived. It seemed, Berdie reasoned, he should be one who would delight in a water feature for the church garden. But she didn't have time to think about it now. She not only had to greet the Golden Season Tour guests who were to arrive soon and help service the tea for them; but she was also the greeter for the ceremony proceedings. Now she needed to have a quiet moment with her husband before the sod turning.

"And I'm already late," she announced to the warm sun.

❧❦

"Watch your step." Hugh Elliott assisted an elderly woman from Golden Season Tours down the large coach steps. "Welcome to Saint Aidan of the Woods Church."

Berdie eyed her tall husband. Even after twenty-seven years of marriage, he held a magnetism that pulled Berdie like an arrow to due north. His military bearing, a leftover from his former career, enhanced his clerical collar and couldn't hide his kind, keen interest in people. And then of course there was his rugged build, silvery hair, and striking blue eyes.

"Hugh, may I have a word?" Berdie asked.

"Of course, love. Can you first attend to our guest?" Hugh smiled, and Berdie recognized his lifted left eyebrow as his gentle reprimand for being late.

When the woman he was assisting reached the ground of the church garden, Berdie took the old dear by the elbow.

In a whisk of impatience, a man alighted from the coach and pushed through, nearly knocking the frail pensioner over. Berdie felt the woman's weight against her but caught the visitor in a firm grasp that held the woman steady as the fellow passenger moved across the garden towards the terrace near the woods.

"What a boor!" A woman wearing a broad orange hat voiced her annoyance.

"Sir!" Hugh's voice commanded respect that all could clearly hear.

The man stopped short and turned. "Pardon." He offered little penitence towards the woman Berdie had by the hand. Then, once again, he continued moving towards the back garden.

"Sir." Hugh made it sound more a command than a title. "Please attend to your meeting inside the church if you will. The tea on the terrace is still in the ready."

The man stopped and angled his body towards Hugh. With a sullen nod, he retrieved his steps and entered the front door of the church.

"I say"—fired the orange hat female—"so rude and all!"

Berdie made sure her little guest was steady. "Are you quite all right?"

The white head made an uneasy nod.

"I'm Mrs. Elliott, Reverend Elliott's wife."

"Here now, I'll see to her." Miss Orange Hat took the woman's arm. "Come along now dear." The vocal woman looked at Berdie. "Are we going to hear a sermon?" she asked baldly.

"Oh, no." Berdie grinned. "Mathew Reese, your

tour organizer, will inform you about the particulars of your stay here, quick as you like. Then it's tea."

"Oh, tea!" A large smile spread across both visitors' faces as they made for the door.

Berdie excused herself and turned just in time to observe the huge coach pull away, wheezing black diesel smoke like a cottage chimney. It took to the road like a giant on its way down an elfin lane.

She glanced back toward the church, but Hugh was not in sight. "Oh, dear." She thought to go find him but then spotted Ivy scooting across the garden with a tray of yellow dafs in little posies. Just the thing to add a touch of spring to the tables being laid for tea.

"Have you by chance seen my husband?" Berdie called out to the busy woman.

"Sorry, no. Did all go well with Cherry?"

"It did," Berdie assured. "And all will be set when I find Hugh." She watched Ivy try to manage the tray while placing the posies. "Do you need some help?"

"Oh, yes, please."

Just a twinkle of time, and all was in the ready. Berdie noticed guests beginning to trickle from the church door towards the tables.

The slate terrace was just large enough to seat the crowd at tables for eight and still have a bit of leeway for the servers. The goods in place, the tea commenced.

Berdie was grateful for the ideal weather. Mostly blue sky, the sun felt warm. She wondered if its brightness on her hair betrayed the enhanced red highlights resulting from the recent trips to Michael's Coiffure in Timsley, the bustling market town not thirty minutes away.

"Lovely today." Berdie poured hot liquid from a bright yellow teapot into awaiting cups that held splashes of milk. She found herself at the table where the little woman she assisted sat with Miss Orange Hat and several others.

"'Tis lovely," spoke Orange Hat. "But I rather hope that one, Mister Rude-and-Unfriendly, has curdled milk for his tea."

Berdie followed the woman's gaze to a table where the impatient gentleman sat with the youthful Mathew Reese. The middle-aged man appeared rather non-descript—regular features, salt and pepper hair combed flat, medium build, moderate clothing.

"Even though it's Lent, all our milk is fresh," Berdie offered with levity.

Orange Hat bypassed the well-intended humor. She brought the dainty teacup to her lips and took a rather voluble slurp.

With a courteous nod, and smothered giggle, Berdie moved to the next table where she glanced round searching for Hugh, but he wasn't to be found.

In the midst of pouring tea, Mathew approached her.

"Mrs. Elliott, may I speak to you a moment?"

The tall and remarkably handsome golden haired university student cum tour director had grown up a parishioner of St. Aidan's. Though currently attending university some distance away, he returned often. And now his special course project, organizing and leading a Senior Lenten tour, brought him back to his home parish. The tour, almost a pilgrimage really, visited several of the larger cathedrals. The few days in Aidan Kirkwood were to be a quiet respite in the midst of the travel. Mathew took Berdie aside.

"The business end of things I do brilliantly, but I'm desperately poor at making artful conversation. Do you think you could give it a go, artful conversation, I mean?" He made a quick nod towards the now solitary man with whom he had been seated.

"I'll do my best Mathew." Berdie was none too confident the guest would be keen on speaking with her.

In a moment, she was offering to top off the gentleman's tea. Berdie lifted the yellow pot and smiled. But the stranger waved her off. Not deterred, she set the pot on the table and proceeded. "I do hope you'll enjoy the next event. It's our sod turning for a new water feature in our church garden."

The gentleman blinked and at last directed his gaze towards her.

"I'm the vicar's wife, Mrs. Elliott. Welcome to Saint Aidan of the Wood."

"Groundbreaking, you say?" The man was suddenly alive and not especially gracious.

"Yes." Berdie pointed towards the edge of the wood on the far end of the church garden. "Just there where the wild geranium grows."

The man's brow made a deep furrow. "By the Lenten roses?" His voice became animated. "You're digging a church garden pond by, what I presume to be, a protected wood?"

"Just at the edge, and it is church property." Berdie suddenly found herself on the defensive.

The man thrust his hand towards the trees. "What real benefit is a garden pond? Leave the flora and fauna as intended." His voice grew fiery and none too calm. "That wood is the heritage of our great isle. We've all but destroyed most our forests. You'd give that up for a church pond?"

Eyes across the terrace settled upon Berdie and the

loner who had become molten lava. She sat and pulled her chair close to the fellow.

"It's all quite legal. We have appropriate approval." She spoke in hushed tones. "The wood will hardly be touched. It will not be exploited; there is an eco-preservation scheme in place. Our parish council has crossed all their *T's*."

Berdie wondered how the man would carry on if he knew Grayson Webb's primary interest for creating the pond: to build church attendance. She rested her hand on the man's arm. "You can be assured it will be well looked after."

The gentleman stiffened, and his eyes expanded. As he did so, Berdie sensed that she had seen him somewhere before. He glanced at her hand on his arm and cleared his throat. Berdie quickly removed the comforting gesture.

"If you pardon me, sir, have we met before?" She couldn't help but ask.

"Most certainly not." The disgruntled male, face turning pink as a spring sunrise, arose.

Berdie watched him walk swiftly towards the front garden and hoped he didn't rally the Green Army to Saint Aidan's little church garden. Realizing that silence had draped itself over the gaping onlookers, she stood confidently with great grace, smiled, and moved on to the next table. It was a signal that the crowd could return to their fairy cakes and conversation.

Ivy approached. "I say, what was that all about?"

"You know, I'm not quite sure, Ivy. But I have a sense that today's sod turning could be a bit lively."

"But it's only a wee little water feature," Ivy replied.

Berdie pursed her lips. "And Emperor Napoleon Bonaparte was only a wee little man."

2

In what seemed to Berdie a skip of time on the heels of the tea, the physical arrangements for the groundbreaking ceremony were in place. And very timely at that. Villagers were arriving. Spectators' chairs were positioned across the back garden. A single row of seats faced the audience. They were for Hugh and the parish counsel and included a chair, decorated with white and gold ribbons, next to where Mr. Webb was to sit. There it was, Berdie perceived, the spot reserved for the mystery guest who engendered rumors, betting pools, and questioning of values.

The beautiful wood was an enchanting backdrop to the whole arrangement. A large spray of flowers near the line of chairs added a sense of decorum and also signaled the spot where the women's chorus would stand to perform.

In the tranquil yet festive setting, Berdie greeted parishioners who found their way to seats.

Ivy, having finished tidying up the tea, was joined by her husband, Edsel, and all six children.

Ivy cradled the newest member of the Butz family, seven-month-old Dotty Elizabeth, in her arms. "The tea went splendidly, didn't it Mrs. Elliott? I mean apart from that odd 'tree' fellow." Ivy glowed.

"Splendidly." Berdie smiled at the two oldest Butz girls. "Hello Lila, Lucy,"

Lila looked just like her mother, but for very large

eye glasses. She nodded her fifteen-year-old head shyly.

Lucy, the first-born, was in her sixth form with an eye on technical college. The sixteen-year-old sported enough lip gloss to fill Boots Pharmacy. "I hope this isn't too long. I have a study date after."

"Only the time needed to dignify the event," Berdie assured.

Preteen twins Martha and Milton filed past Berdie in their usual nonchalant manner.

"Where's little Duncan?" Berdie quizzed. The two usually had their four-year-old brother in tow.

Milton threw his thumb towards Mr. and Mrs. Raheem. Sharday, her sari flowing, and Hardeep both clutched Duncan by his pudgy hands.

"We're keeping the eye on him as family friends do," Mr. Raheem informed.

"Have you shut up shop, then?" Berdie asked the green grocer.

"Oh, yes, we don't want to miss this surprise." Mr. Raheem nodded towards the mystery chair.

Berdie smiled. "I dare say that's the reason most everyone's here."

"My money's on Mrs. Flora Preswood"—Edsel whispered Berdie's way—"in a manner of speaking."

"Ah. That manner of speaking wouldn't have to do with Dudley Horn at the Upland Arms, would it?"

Edsel laid his finger aside his nose.

Berdie was fond of this man with his big barrel chest and easy laugh. He and his toolbox had intervened in a time of danger for Berdie, and she would be eternally grateful.

"Oh, no sooner said." Edsel grinned and discreetly pointed his shoulder in the direction of the arriving

Preswoods.

Berdie spied Colonel Randal Preswood, his thin body stick straight and shoulders back. He appeared quite uninterested coming alongside his wife, Flora, who chaired the county Family Heritage Circle. Classically dressed as befitted those of rank, they were the current Preswoods that resided at Bampkingswith Hall, or Swithy Hall as known by locals. The handsome estate had been held by Colonel Preswood's family for just over two hundred years. He was still considered the village squire by some.

"I see they have a nose for curiosity as well," Berdie confided to Edsel.

This was a rare appearance for the Preswoods who really had no true regard for the church but felt a sense of obligation to keep astride village dealings.

"Good afternoon, Colonel, Mrs. Preswood." Berdie nodded.

The colonel simply grunted, but the well dressed and nicely coiffed Mrs. Preswood spoke, her distinctive chin moving rhythmically. "Rosalie's singing in the women's chorus today you know."

Their niece, Rosalie, was more a daughter than a niece, really. Berdie had a certain respect for this couple simply because they were surrogate parents for both Rosalie and her twin, Roberta, or Robin, as most called her. The girls had come to the Preswood household at an early age.

"Robin, dear." Mrs. Preswood sat and patted the chair next to her.

Roberta Darbyshire scooted past Berdie just bumping her shoulder. The twenty-five-year old bestowed a quick glance with her aqua eyes and gave her short dark hair a quick toss.

"Excuse me," she offered in a rushed manner and went to the chair next to her aunt.

Berdie politely tipped her head. Robin, in the past three years, had spent most of her time near London. And it would appear that London was now spending time in her.

Mrs. Preswood, dressed in linen, laid her hands in her lap, and directed her words towards Berdie. "Robin inherited my father's keen business acumen. Now Colonel Preswood is grooming her to become managing director of Preswood Enterprises." She smiled, then the expression went a bit limp. "Rosalie, it seems on the other hand, took after her mother in that she is gifted with vocal abilities. My sister, Rose, had a brief professional musical career."

Singing in the follies at Blackpool is what Berdie recalled being said somewhere. "Rosalie has a fine voice. We enjoy her being a part of the choir," Berdie confirmed. "I'm so glad you came to hear her perform."

"Mrs. Elliott, hello," Jamie Donovan called. His handsome face, rimmed with black locks, beamed as he approached the row behind the Preswoods. In his muscular arms, the young man held his first born, ten-month-old Katy, christened Kathleen Grace after her two dearly departed grandmothers. She had her father's dark hair and her mother's grey eyes, all shown off nicely by a dainty pink dress.

"Good afternoon," Berdie greeted. "And hello little precious one." Berdie made a cooing noise that made the baby giggle.

"Happy as she goes." Jamie shook his head.

"Quite fussy actually," corrected Cara Graystone Donovan, the beautiful wife and mother whose arm slipped around her husband's elbow.

The long blonde hair that usually cascaded down her back was caught back in a twist. The shapely shoulders that once held a beauty contest banner now carried a strap attached to a bag of baby goods. "Of course when her father's about, she's an angel."

"Isn't that the way?" Berdie laughed. "It was the same with my Clare."

"And my father is spoiling Katy pitifully," Cara said under her breath.

Preston Graystone stepped close to his daughter. His angular features and salt and pepper hair fit his surname quite well. Berdie had to grin at the sophisticated village solicitor who handled all the residents' legal matters, as he now carried a small Paddington Bear and a pink sunbonnet. He gave Berdie a polite nod.

"Hello Randal, Flora," he spoke to the couple in the row forward. He gave a deliberate nod to Mrs. Preswood who responded with what seemed only a furtive glance.

How odd that she didn't respond to him.

Mr. Graystone took a deep breath then proceeded to the chair next to his daughter. He gripped the baby wares like a holiday hare unwilling to give up its carrots.

"Graystone's quite smitten with his granddaughter, I should think, and rightly so." Young Dave Exton, the newspaper editor Berdie saw earlier on the High Street, stood near her. "Though it is hard to believe the old iceberg has a warm spot in that arctic heart of his."

"Everyone has a warm spot in their heart," Berdie replied. "It just sometimes takes a bit of defrosting to find it."

"Including that one?" The editor pushed his trendy glasses against the bridge of his nose and thrust his chin towards the village constable, Albert Goodnight.

Oh that one! Berdie didn't voice the thought. "Yes, well, with a good blasting furnace at hand, indeed he does."

Berdie wasn't sure if it was so much a matter of finding the amiability of Albert Goodnight's heart or just the need to see him demonstrate some genuine competence in his line of work.

The editor drew near the large constable who hung at the edge of the crowd. Goodnight's rotund stature made youthful Dave Exton look absolutely willowy. The constable's uniform showed large gaps between the buttons, and his sleeves were just short of his wrists.

Albert could probably sweep the village roads with that large unkempt mustache.

Nonetheless, Albert Goodnight was the law in Aidan Kirkwood, as Hugh had pointed out to her on more than one occasion.

Berdie continued her meeting and greeting exercises until the parish council lined up and took their seats without great fanfare. Hugh and Mr. Webb sat first. Mr. Webb was next to the enigmatic empty chair. Lillie, in her choirmaster robe, led the way for the women's chorus who came to rest behind the flower spray.

Hugh arose wearing his pastoral duties like a royal scepter. "Good afternoon. As your parish priest, I welcome all, parishioners and visitors alike, to this festive sod turning for the new water feature of Saint

Aidan of the Wood Parish Church. Following the turn of the spade, we will pronounce a blessing."

The crowd clapped vigorously.

"I will now turn the ceremony over to Mr. Grayson Webb, our parish council chairman."

The applause was not quite as vigorous.

Mr. Webb's expensive clothes, slightly over-the-top for the event, fit him well and enhanced his fashionable hairstyle and tanned features. With his usual flair, undaunted by the lukewarm response, Mr. Webb launched into his oration. "Today we celebrate the expansion of our church grounds, a great opportunity to 'enlarge our tent' as the Good Book says. To begin our joyful gathering, I now ask our wonderful women's chorus to raise their voice in song."

With that, Lillie lifted her slender hands to direct and at the first down beat, the women's voices broke into sweet harmony.

Berdie wondered if the disgruntled coach tour man she spoke to earlier at the tea did indeed stay for the fête. And then she wondered if he might present a fuss if he was here. She hadn't seen him, but while the choristers sang the second and third verses of All Creatures of Our God and King, she unobtrusively surveyed the crowd from her second row chair on the edge of the seating. Berdie recognized most of the coach tour visitors and then she spied him, the distressed gentleman.

He stood in the very back of the audience along with a few others who seemed to simply be skulking about, taking in the fanfare. However, the man's former anger had apparently eased. He was motionless, his eyes fixed intently on the women's chorus. No. Rather he was transfixed. True, the women were singing with great expression, but the hymn was one sung prolifically in churches and concert halls all across England.

Let all things their Creator bless, And worship Him in humbleness, O praise Him, Alleluia!

Berdie saw a hint of moisture in the fellow's mellowed eye.

Praise, praise the Father, praise the Son, And praise the Spirit, Three in One!

The cool grey man appeared to take on the color of spring. Something was stirred deeply within him. *A nature lover indeed*, Berdie thought. Or perhaps this song had a special memory in his life. And it appeared his resolute displeasure that the church was turning earth to create a pond had quite melted.

"Good," Berdie whispered.

Then she spotted something unusual. A black limousine halted in the road by the front church garden; and there emerged a silhouette, much like a film star, wearing sunglasses. Her soft tan skin looked fresh against the pink linen tailored dress and pomegranate-colored shrug she wore. Her very first step, though unnoticed by the crowd, announced her arrival eloquently. She swept silently along the side of the engaged spectators. Mr. Webb, with broad smile, tipped his head towards the empty chair upon seeing the woman. With demure movement, she made her way to the seat creating a great stir amongst the onlookers, which put Lillie, who gazed at the surprising figure, off her form thus ending the musical presentation in an understated manner.

"Who is she?" Berdie whispered to the One Who always hears.

Almost immediately, Mr. Webb and the men seated up front were on their feet. A quick nod from the woman gave the gentlemen permission to resume their seats.

The creature's upswept hair, though dark, gleamed in the sun creating the sense of a natural tiara. After a quick greeting between Mr. Webb and the woman—a kiss on both cheeks, "Ah, European," Berdie quietly noted.

Without delay, Mr. Webb gripped the large nearby spade and stepped to the microphone with great pomp. "Thank you, chorus," he acknowledged without even looking in their direction. "Ladies and gentlemen, I present to you a very special and generous friend to Aidan Kirkwood. Countess Carlotta Santolio, who, amidst her demanding schedule, will assist in turning the first spade of soil to our new garden scheme."

Berdie heard a loud tone above the murmur of those gathered. Perhaps it was those who said goodbye to their money in the betting pool.

"What has a nobbily countess we've never heard of have to do with our church garden?" Wilkie Gordon gave voice to the question everyone probably wanted to ask.

Berdie turned to see Mr. Gordon rise from his seat. Stretched to his full five feet and seven inches, Mr. Gordon's bald head took on a pink cast while his face appeared as pomegranate red as the contessa's shrug. The bushy white beard that edged his visage outlined the crimson. He raised a clenched fist.

"Missus, you are about to do a great evil. If you must splash out, give your alms to the poor, unnoted and in quiet. Go and take your money with you. Leave our church garden be."

Berdie felt red heat all across her cheeks. *Oh no, Wilkie Gordon! I forgot to ask Hugh to speak with him.* Berdie closed her eyes as if to shut out her empty promise to Cherry, and reopened them quickly. "Oh my," was all she could muster at the moment.

A flurry of head turning accompanied by a collective inhale of the afternoon air was followed by undistinguishable verbal patter, which hopped around the audience like a young rabbit.

"And furthermore," was all Wilkie managed to get out when another booming voice interrupted.

"Wilkie Gordon, do sit down." The tall and commanding Colonel Preswood was on his feet, shoulders squared and jaw tight, spitting the words in the old dissenter's direction. "For heaven's sake, man, get a grip." Though his suit was nicely tailored and pressed, his broad features were sour as he addressed the crowd. "Our guest can do whatever she chooses with her money. Now let's get on with what we're here for."

In haste Mr. Webb half-whispered words of reassurance to the countess. "Don't pay any mind to them." He pushed the spade handle into her palm, pointing to the ground. "Now!" commanded the harassed council president.

Berdie watched Hugh who had also risen to his feet. She knew he'd put things in place and restore the calm. But before he could speak, the contessa pushed the polished tool up to the hilt into the soil. Despite her spike-heeled shoes, and with some labor, she turned its contents over. The woman's face went pale. A voluble shriek escaped from the pink shimmering lips of Contessa Santolio.

All heads, as if observing a tennis match, moved

from the Wilkie Gordon-Colonel Preswood drama to the elegant woman who threw down the large spade with such force it almost made a direct plant on Mr. Webb's Italian leather shoe.

The head of council peered into the newly made hole. His face became morose.

Berdie watched Hugh place himself delicately to take a peek at what was causing such a reaction. Indeed, half the audience was now straining forward as if to catch a glimpse. The very proper Mrs. Plinkerton, a respected member of the parish council seated closest to the cavity, peered into the soil.

"Bones," she screeched. Her aging face whitened, and she fell back against her chair, sending her large pink hat on a tumble.

"Bones?" Berdie said aloud.

The council members next to Mrs. Plinkerton grabbed the hat and worked furiously to fan her.

Hugh raised his hands calmly. "Let's keep our sensibilities. First, Edsel, would you please get Mrs. Plinkerton a glass of water?"

Edsel Butz made way to the church.

Hugh's voice was clear and strong. "All our lands are open grazing. It's very likely nothing more than the remains of a sheep."

"You've desecrated a grave," someone yelled in the crowd.

"Let's not rush to judgment," Hugh cautioned.

Berdie sensed someone bending towards her.

"What's going on?" Dr. Loren Meredith's voice could melt butter. "I just arrived. Looks a bit of a mad house."

With Lillie's love interest, the pathologist Dr. Loren Meredith, being so near, Berdie became aware of his unique scent. It was a combination of fresh scrubbed soap and a touch of mountain air. What a shame, she thought, that the rest of the afternoon wasn't as pleasant as Dr. Meredith's presence.

"I'm afraid the whole affair has gone a bit pear shaped," Berdie responded. And not just before Constable Goodnight poked his considerable finger into the doctor's shoulder.

"Need your services if you please," he grumbled through his mustache. "Come along."

The handsome physician followed Goodnight to the gouged earth.

The constable bellowed forth making his rotund shape heave. "Everyone sit down, or I'll arrest the lot of ya."

The boom sent baby Katy Donovan into a great crying frenzy, which soon became a chorus when Dotty Butz and several other infants joined in. Few paid attention to Goodnight's command.

Dr. Meredith bent close to the earth and pushed aside additional dirt revealing more remains.

Berdie's curiosity got the better of her, and deftly she stepped to the sight the doctor examined.

"Human, a little one," the pathologist said discreetly and stood.

"Well I never," Berdie exhaled, "of all times and places."

"Quite," the animated voice of Mr. Webb sounded. "Surely, there's been some mistake."

Goodnight, standing next to Berdie, grunted, took a deep breath, and trumpeted across the crowd, "I'm declaring this a crime scene. You lot go home now."

"Albert, is this really necessary?" Mr. Webb's disgust was in sharp contrast to his smart dress.

"Do pigs grunt?"

"Reverend Elliott, Wilkie Gordon's collapsed," a voice cried out.

Berdie caught her breath as Hugh, quite fit for a man his age, nearly hurdled the chairs to get to Mr. Gordon. A small group had gathered round.

"I appreciate your concern, but please stand back, give him room to breathe," Hugh ordered.

Edsel came next to Hugh and moved people along as Hugh attended to the old gentleman.

"I said go home!" Goodnight bellowed like an evening foghorn.

Whipped by the swirl of events and Goodnight's volume, a mad migration of people took flight for the front road. Chairs tipped and children were swept up. Mr. Webb hurriedly escorted the contessa back to her limousine, and Dave Exton, who seemed to relish the action, went snap happy with his camera.

Dr. Meredith turned his attention to Hugh and Mr. Gordon. He took a step.

"Stay right here, Doctor. Vicar's doin' a fine job," Goodnight growled.

"Are you mad, Goodnight?" Dr. Meredith frowned and moved quickly to Wilkie's side.

Berdie took in the policeman. "Shouldn't you be doing something to help Mr. Gordon, Constable Goodnight?"

"More important I keep an eye on this." The law officer stabbed his thumb in the direction of the skeleton. "I shall be calling the Yard in on this."

Berdie could see that her husband and the doctor were taking care of the old fellow. Nonetheless, she felt constrained to be close to Mr. Gordon. After all, would his outburst have been prevented if she had gotten

Hugh to speak with him?

When Berdie got to him, the bit red Wilkie was sitting up and breathing regularly as Loren checked his pulse. Ivy was at her uncle's side.

"I'm fine. Leave me be," the man said weakly.

"Mr. Gordon, I believe you and I are going to make our way to Dr. Honeywell's office," Hugh decreed.

"As a physician, I must say it really is the thing to do immediately." Loren examined Wilkie's eyes. "Yes, should do."

The home of the village doctor, George Honeywell, wasn't far.

Wilkie Gordon blinked and squeezed his lips.

"Please, Uncle." Ivy's voice was kind but firm.

"What about my Mary? She's by herself."

"I'll see to Aunt Mary. Now off you go." Ivy shooed them away with a wave of her hands.

Hugh and Dr. Meredith helped the man to his feet.

Berdie put her hand on his shoulder. "Your Mary would want you to see Dr. Honeywell."

Wilkie gave a tiny nod. "But don't let on what happened here." He turned to Ivy. "None of it. Just tell her I'm momentarily with the Reverend. Promise me."

Ivy was somewhat befuddled. "But…"

"Promise me." His raised voice sent his face scarlet again.

"Yes, yes, Uncle Wilkie, I promise." Ivy placed her hand on her uncle's back. "Please calm yourself."

"I'll get the car then." Hugh was off to the vicarage drive almost as quickly as he had hurdled chairs.

Berdie stood at Wilkie's side, and Loren steadied the fellow. Ivy was to the off, heading in the direction of the Gordon's home.

"Please," the oldster had a tone of desperation, "don't tell Mary. She's so ill, she needn't have more concern."

"Not to worry," Berdie assured him. She was already keenly aware that his wife had been undergoing special medical treatments in Timsley.

Hugh brought the car round. He and Loren settled Wilkie in the vehicle.

"Do you need me to come with you?" Berdie whispered circumspectly to Hugh.

"Thank you, love, but I need you to see to matters here." Hugh glanced quickly at the constable.

"Oh I'd love to give that 'matter' a right ear full, frightening the children and causing havoc."

"Berdie," Hugh cautioned as he arched his left eyebrow, "mind how you go."

"I'll try to be as civil as possible," she promised her husband and watched the auto trundle down the road.

Taking deliberate steps with Dr. Meredith toward the upturned earth, Berdie took in the full scene of the mad scramble: the disturbed earth, the guardian constable, and Wilkie's toppled chair.

"It's quite mad," she declared then stopped to question the pathologist. "Does Goodnight have just cause to call this a crime scene? People have been buried in church yards for hundreds of years."

Dr. Meredith tipped his head. "We need to examine it a bit more, but those are not ancient bones. Human remains in a shallow grave with no apparent vestige of burial, yes, we need some investigating." Loren put his broad shoulders at attention. "I dare say Albert Goodnight has not handled the situation appropriately, but that doesn't discredit the law entirely."

Berdie smiled. "Well said."

Lillie approached, appearing quite shaken. "Had a film writer created this whole event I wouldn't have believed it." With a bewildered look in her eye, she gave her hand to the doctor who caressed it gently. He pulled her near and placed a kiss on her cheek.

"Are you all right?" he asked.

"Far better than Mr. Gordon, I dare say."

"Hugh's taken him to Honeywell's," Loren assured.

"How are you fairing?" Lillie, Berdie knew, could read her uneasiness.

She looked at the ground. "Frankly, I feel a bit responsible for Wilkie."

"You?" Lillie questioned with a wrinkled brow.

"I made a promise to a parishioner concerning him, and I didn't follow through. Perhaps he would be home with his Mary now instead of being dashed off to the doctor had I done my part."

"Stuff and nonsense." Loren's voice was soothing. "You can't be responsible for another person's behavior, promise or not."

Lillie nodded, her eyes expressing the kindness best friends share.

"As you say." Berdie understood the doctor's point. Still, she'd let Cherry down. Perhaps a few words from Hugh could have settled Wilkie a bit. But that now was a moot point.

"Moving on then." Lillie looked expectantly at her love interest. "What did you think of our musical performance?"

When he didn't respond her smile left with the silence.

"Ah, I see. Some desperate corpse needed a rush liver dissection I shouldn't wonder?" Lillie had a splash of cold rain in her voice.

"Something like that." Loren took her other hand and focused his full attention on his beautiful woman. "This has all been a bit of an ordeal. Lillie, why don't you go home and take a moment. I'll be there in a tic to take you out for dinner." The doctor's smoldering brown eyes searched Lillie's face.

"Right," she responded and looked sheepishly at Berdie. Then she directed her eyes to Loren, one hand on her hip. "Hopefully, no needy corpse will interrupt this time. Perhaps we'll actually complete our meal?" She was curt.

"Shortly then."

Lillie released the doctor's hands and made for the road.

"It's not just today's upset that's troubling her, is it?" Loren observed out loud.

"No," Berdie offered honestly thinking of the conversation she and Lillie had earlier in the day. "But that's a discussion between you and her."

"How long could investigating something like this take?" Goodnight, still standing by the dig, called to the doctor.

Berdie and Loren moved next to the constable.

"We're quite busy in the lab. Short a person," Dr. Meredith responded.

Goodnight addressed Berdie. "You can run along home now, Mrs. Elliott. The vicar's wife don't hang about crime scenes."

"Constable, I was an investigative reporter. Crime scenes were everyday fare."

"Yes, but that was then. You're with the church

now, aren't you?"

"Mrs. Elliott could be a grand asset for you, if this indeed truly is a crime scene," Doctor Meredith protested.

"Of course it's a crime scene," Goodnight sputtered. "I've declared it so." The constable's bushy brows knitted, making him appear to have one large swathe of hair above his eyes. "Snoopy vicars' wives have no place in the law." Goodnight turned his attention to Berdie. "Now don't you have to Hoover your sitting room rug, get it good and clean for the next women's jabbering session?"

Berdie bit her tongue. Her jaw tightened like a lid on pickled eggs.

"I say," the doctor's voice had a distinct sound of dismay. He took Berdie aside.

"I'd love to put a flea in his ear." Berdie spit the words.

"Don't let Goodnight get up your nose. It only gives him more power. Go on, I'll stay here and look after things for the moment. It may calm the beast."

"Of course you're right," Berdie reasoned. "Oh, but what about Lillie?"

"If I'm a bit late, she'll understand," the doctor assured her.

Perhaps not, my doctor friend, but Berdie kept her peace.

"I'll keep you informed on all that goes on here." He cocked his head toward the constable.

Berdie nodded. "Thanks, Loren."

She walked towards the vicarage, thoughts tumbling through her mind. The warm sun and rosy scent of spring brought fresh serenity. She took a deep breath as she started to calculate just what all this falderal could mean. The garden scheme, at this point in time, would surely not go forward. The crime scene area, whether a real crime was committed or not, would be impassable until the investigation, which Goodnight had set in motion, was concluded. Lillie and Loren were apt to have a row, a grand disagreement, at a time when they most probably needed concerted understanding in their relationship. And the entire community would be buzzing like warm season bees about the whole affair: mystery guest, Wilkie Gordon, bones, crime scene. Worst of all, what if there really was a crime committed? Would it forever be connected to the lovely grounds of St. Aidan in the Wood Parish Church?

Berdie entered the quiet hall of the vicarage where only the ticking of the station clock in the nearby library gave an assuring rhythm.

A ring from the vicarage phone split into the quiet.

"I'm not home!" Berdie pronounced to the polished oak wood that plated the walls. She reluctantly picked up the receiver. "Vicarage, this is Mrs. Elliott."

"Berdie," Hugh was on the other end. "Oh good, you're in. How is it with Goodnight?"

"Loren's seeing to him."

"Have you an extra meat pie in the freezer?"

"Whatever for?"

"It's just that Wilkie isn't feeling at the top of his form, and with Mary being too ill to cook, could you see your way clear to provide dinner for the Gordons? Meet me at their home, number twelve Oakwood Gardens, say, in an hour."

"Of course, love, just after I Hoover the sitting room rug," Berdie answered.

"What?"

"I'll be there in an hour, dinner in tow. See you then," Berdie promised and hung up the phone.

"Meat pie," Berdie mumbled. "Can't vouch that it will delight the pallet, but at least it's a promise I can by all means keep."

3

Berdie clutched the white wicker basket that held dinner for the Gordons: hot meat pie, brown gravy, spring greens, and lemon pudding for afters.

During the brisk quarter mile walk to number twelve Oakwood Gardens, three different villagers stopped her. One asked if Mr. Gordon was all right. Widow Sheridan wanted to know what an Italian was doing in our village when they weren't our ally in that horrible war. And someone who wasn't even at the event asked if the body was recognizable?

"Not a body, simply bones," Berdie said aloud now as if to reiterate once again.

She turned the corner that opened onto Oakwood Gardens, a pleasant road where stone block terrace houses, attached on their sidewalls, sat in a row like British soldiers trooping the colors. Though all the same design, each home had its own natural embellishments. Spring green hedges hugged stone walls, door urns declared Easter greetings with multi-color tulips, while the scent of freshly upturned soil hinted of floral delights yet to come. Berdie breathed in the earthy odor that promised a new season of growth.

Number twelve had well-trimmed ivy displaying new leaves. It twisted up the stone block above the wooden door and across the upper edge of a broad window. A rock planter was home to dancing daffodils, frilly pink hyacinths, and naturalized ground-hugging white aconites. A testament to Wilkie's gardening skills, Berdie observed. She stepped directly in front of the door and rapped lightly.

The noise of a barking dog was accompanied by a rapid whoosh of the door opening. Ivy Butz stood in the doorway and held a desperately squirming Dachshund the rusty red of HP Sauce.

"Hello Mrs. Elliott," Ivy beamed holding the creature against her ample body with both arms. "Ignore him. He's just trying to prove he's more than a wee sausage," she jested.

"Don't speak ill of my Fritz." Berdie heard Wilkie's voice in full throttle.

Ivy winked. "He's better already," she said quietly. "Please come in."

Berdie stepped into a tiny entry then straight way into the cozy sitting room. It was simply dressed in papered walls that displayed shelves of porcelain plates, and the furnishings were plain but comfortable. Hugh sat in one of the large upholstered armchairs just across from Wilkie, who rose from the coffee-colored sofa. The man teetered a bit to one side.

"Oh, please sit down. Thank you." Berdie caught her husband's eye as she spoke. Gordon sank back down as Hugh rose and took the basket she held.

"Thank you, Berdie," he said tenderly as he gave up his chair for her.

"Let me take that through," Ivy offered.

Hugh seated himself in another comfortable armchair while Ivy put the wee sausage dog down and took the basket to the kitchen.

The dog sniffed all about the floor near Berdie's feet with brief lifts of his wiggly nose in the air as if torn between sussing out this newcomer and guzzling the delicious smelling meat pie.

"Fritz!" Wilkie beckoned the dog, who suddenly decided being near the pie was his priority. He dashed to the kitchen as quickly as his squatty legs would carry him. "He's not one to mind his manners," Wilkie apologized, "but we're quite fond of him. The little lad earns his keep." The old man smiled.

"And how's that?" Berdie chuckled. "I find the dear creatures loll about and eat more than their owners."

Wilkie blinked and rubbed his hand on the arm of the couch. "Well, he barks, of course."

"The great protector." Hugh relaxed his shoulders into the chair. "Busy little ones. Dachshunds were bred to chase prey and burrow after their victims, weren't they?"

"I believe so," Wilkie whispered with a short breath and then took a deep inhale.

Berdie became instantly aware of how taxing all the visitors and conversation must be for the recovering old gentleman.

"Here then, let me give my greetings to Mary and we're off." Berdie sent her gaze towards Hugh then stood.

"Capital idea," Hugh agreed.

"Mary's upstairs?" Berdie directed her inquiry to Mr. Gordon who tried to stand. "I can see to her," came between short breaths.

"Wilkie," Hugh advised, "let Berdie have a moment with her. She's quite good at cheering one."

When Berdie entered the small bedroom, Mary Gordon sat motionless in the bed, covered with layers of quilts. Her frail upper body was propped against double pillows that lined the iron rail headboard. The fact that Mary could sit upright was an improvement from the last time Berdie had visited. The woman's white hair was in a tangle and her dark, deep-set eyes had the mist of one visiting distant memories.

"Mary?" Berdie spoke in hushed tones. "How are you dear? It's Mrs. Elliott, from the church."

There was a spark of recognition and a faint smile.

Berdie stood by the bed and placed her hand on Mary's shoulder. "Is there any way I can help?"

"Help. Can anyone help me?" The woman's thin lips moved with effort. "Does God still love me?" Her sad eyes echoed the sentiment.

"Of course He does," Berdie assured. "I know things can get difficult, but nothing separates us from His love."

Mary raised her hand with great effort and feebly grasped Berdie's free hand. With as much strength as she possessed, she gave a squeeze. Berdie sat on the edge of the bed.

"And you know, Mary, that Hugh, Ivy, Cherry, indeed the whole church community, we all can lend a hand. We want to help."

"Do you?" she mumbled. She released Berdie's fingers. Her eyes redirected their gaze to a nearby dresser where a bottle of tablets stood next to a framed photo of an all-in-blue infant with chubby cheeks and a cheerful smile. Berdie studied the tablets. She arose and picked up the photo.

"Your grandchild?" Berdie asked.

"A treasure," a male voice responded.

Berdie started. Wilkie Gordon stood in the bedroom doorway. "Mr. Gordon," she said breathlessly and replaced the framed photo.

"It's time for my wife's medicine."

"Oh, I didn't realize. If you had only said."

The old man stood at the bed's edge. "Your husband waits for you," he mumbled, and then bent to tuck the quilts around his bride, obviously devoted to her comfort and care.

Berdie gave Mary an assuring nod. "Do hope you like meat pie. There's some waiting for you in the kitchen."

The sick woman nodded in return.

"Thank you, Mrs. Elliott," Wilkie clipped. "I think you best go downstairs."

Berdie momentarily paused outside the room.

"Love, I'm going to put the photo back in the drawer now and give you your medicine," Wilkie almost whispered.

Berdie moved quietly down the stairs and found Hugh standing at the door.

"Ready then?" he asked.

Berdie pursed her lips and nodded.

The jot to the vicarage afforded a stop at the Upland Arms. Hugh suggested getting take away. "After all, you've already cooked one full dinner." He winked.

The specialty of the day: roast chicken, mash, and cauliflower-cheese, was a favorite for both of them.

Berdie waited in the car while Hugh went into the local pub. She thought her husband truly brave to enter the establishment where surely tongues wagged with accounts both true and exaggerated concerning today's events.

Berdie glanced across the High Street where Flora Preswood and Preston Graystone stood near his solicitor's office. The well-off woman seemed in a rush when Mr. Graystone began a rapid pursuit. He caught

Flora by the arm, which was a bit too familiar for a lawyer and his client, Berdie reasoned. Flora yielded momentarily. Preston pulled her close and said something to the woman, which, by all appearances, created a fleeting surrender that turned quickly to anxiety. She wrenched her arm out of his grasp, furtively scanned for onlookers, and continued her quick pace. Preston Graystone looked after the departing woman with a woeful visage.

"How unlike him." Berdie had never known him to let anyone have the last word, let alone leave him wistful.

He made a quick sweep with his eyes for passersby, straightened his tie, and stepped along in the opposite direction.

"Now that would make tender fodder in the Upland Arms. Indeed it would," she breathed.

Just as she turned her mind to said events, to her surprise, Hugh returned. When he entered the car, Berdie inhaled the satisfying aroma that emanated from the carrier bags.

"I just witnessed a bit of an event."

"Oh, yes." Hugh seemed to have little interest in said event.

"Dare I ask how it was inside?" Berdie took the bags from her husband.

"I gave Dudley Horn a five pound note, said he was a fine publican, and told him to put a rush on. In terms of the rest of the lot in there, you can probably imagine."

"Let's see," Berdie made her voice hoarse and deep. "'Hey vicar, disposing of wayward parishioners in the church garden now, are ya'?"

"Along those lines, yes." Hugh displayed the

shadow of a smirk. "At least they're up front on the whole matter, and humor is a very acceptable way of putting dreadful things in order."

Berdie admired Hugh's ability to accept people just where they were. There were leaders in the church who would have found such comments deeply offensive. But her husband was not one of them. She popped a quick loving peck on his cheek.

"What's that for?" he asked.

"You still spend a few bob to impress your wife with roast chicken, of course," she teased.

When they pulled into the vicarage drive, police tapes were visible across the church back garden. An auto track on the grass lead to a white transit van displaying the word *Coroner* on the side. A small tent draped protection over the dig, and white-capped workers went about their business, but Berdie didn't see Dr. Meredith or Constable Goodnight.

Once inside the vicarage, sitting at the tiny wooden table in the gracious kitchen of Oak Leaf Cottage, it felt a tender sanctuary.

"For what we are about to receive we are truly grateful," rolled off Hugh's lips with a keen sense of appreciation. He gripped his fork and looked at Berdie with a sigh. "And I'm not half grateful that days like this one are rare in our parish."

Berdie nodded her head in agreement.

"A simple plan gone pear shaped."

"And a broken promise." Berdie felt the prick of guilt stab at her.

"How's that?" Hugh tucked his fork into potatoes.

"Cherry Lawler approached me this morning and expressed concern for her grandfather. I told her I'd ask you to see him before the ceremony. I lost track of you, and then I simply forgot."

"Ah." Hugh didn't seem upset. "Easy to do on such a busy day, and we have no assurance that anything I could have said would have helped." Hugh cut a piece of meat from the chicken bone. "One redeeming note: I'm so pleased Wilkie appears to be recovering."

"Mary seems slightly improved, too." Berdie drew her napkin across her lips. "Did Dr. Honeywell say anything to you about Wilkie's condition?"

"That information is strictly between the doctor and his patient, and you are fully aware of that. Wilkie did mention to me that he was out of his high blood pressure tablets. He was sure that was today's problem."

"Did he? That's odd."

"Doesn't seem odd to me."

"And the picture of their grandchild, that was off as well."

"Off?"

"Don't grandparents rabbit on when you view a picture of their grandchild?" She went on. "Well, neither did that. And they keep the photo in a drawer. Now that's off."

Hugh took a deep inhale. "Berdie, are you prying?"

Berdie sensed a bit of impatience in Hugh's voice. "Simply observing." She took another bite of mash. "And another thing, there was a full bottle of blood pressure tablets sitting on the dresser in the bedroom. His name was on it."

Hugh swallowed. "Wilkie's elderly. He probably forgot he had an extra bottle."

"Pensioners, don't have extra bottles of medication lying about."

Hugh lifted his left eyebrow, which was always the sign to Berdie that something didn't meet his pleasure. "Have you taken to rummaging through people's bedrooms?"

"Hugh Elliott"—Berdie's volume raised a decibel—"I should say not."

"Good, let's keep it that way."

Just as Berdie's lips formed a definitive defense, the vicarage phone in the hallway let out its holy bleating.

"I'll get it." Hugh stood and made hasty steps toward the hallway.

"Saved by the bell, that."

Berdie knew exactly what displeased her husband. It was in her nature to ask questions, to fill in missing pieces of the puzzle. He understood that. Often, he even appreciated it. He just wasn't fond of her muddling parish business with inquisitive designs, especially after the kind of happenings that took place today.

She crunched two cauliflower florets. "Rummaging indeed."

"It's Dr. Meredith." Hugh swung back through the kitchen door. "He wants to speak with you."

Berdie whisked to the hallway in double time.

"Loren?" Berdie wasn't quite sure what to expect, but she made herself ready to listen carefully.

"Do hope I'm not interrupting. Long to short, we're bringing in a forensic anthropologist. At the moment, all we know is that the victim appears to be a young child." His voice grew somber. "There are indications of trauma. Wish I had better news."

"Well, I dare say I know one person who will be happy as a sand boy."

"Goodnight will be unbearable."

"Well, thank you for the information."

There was a pause. "Lillie says to get the oil can out. I suppose you know what that means."

Berdie laughed. "Just a little something to do with an earlier conversation today about being rusty. You're with Lillie now then?"

"Dinner, yes."

"May I make a suggestion?"

"Put it out there."

"Turn your mobile off for the next hour or until your meal is finished."

There was a distinct silence. "You're not serious."

"As a heart attack. You'll be doing yourself a great favor if you turn it off."

"Thank you for the suggestion." He didn't sound even slightly convinced and returned to the initial subject. "I'll keep you abreast of developments in the case, on the Q T of course."

"Yes, thank you."

Berdie rang off. When she returned to the table, Hugh was picking at his food. Truly, her roast chicken, too, suddenly didn't seem quite as tasty.

"And so Loren informed you, as he did me, of the dark news?"

"Yes."

Hugh folded his napkin and sat it on the table. "Sad, sad business this."

"Indeed." Here sat her dear husband, who had been engaged in staggering active military warfare, now trying to comprehend the ugliness unearthed in his church garden.

"The police certainly have a great deal of work to do." Hugh directed his eyes keenly towards her. "Do you understand? *The police* have much to do."

Berdie nodded. She hoped the eagerness with which she wanted to dig into the matter was well concealed.

"And when it comes to it, I have work to do as well." Hugh's voice betrayed his disconcertedness. "There are a few things that need tending at the church."

"I'll have tea brewing when you return." Berdie squeezed his hand.

When Hugh departed, she watched out the library window to see the tall figure of her husband, in an uncustomary hunch, walk the hundred yards to the church.

Tidying the kitchen took no more than ten minutes. Berdie was looking forward to a nice soak where she would try the new rose-scented bath crystals Hugh had gotten for her just last week. Then she'd settle in with her latest Dorothy Sawyers read accompanied by a warm cup of tea. But, as she ascended the stairs, the front doorbell chimed. Berdie considered what kind of master plan to devise that would send whomever it was packing.

She retraced her steps and opened the door. "Mathew," she greeted in a less-than-warm tone.

"Am I interrupting?" The young man's face was flushed and his words clipped. "It's just that I need some assistance."

"Hugh's out but you're welcome to come in for tea."

"Thanks, but no time for tea. Where is Hugh exactly?"

"He's at the church." Berdie had barely made her reply when Mathew started for the house of worship. "You'll probably find him at the kneeling rail," she called after him.

"Dear me," Berdie said while closing the door. "Why so flushed?" But then, considering her Clare and Nick, what's youth if not a series of flushes?

The soft blue terry robe caressed her just-bathed skin. The scent of roses still lingered as she sat in her favorite Queen Anne chair near the hearth of the master bedroom and opened her book with enthusiasm.

Berdie had to make a concerted effort to keep focused on the reading material. Her thoughts drifted to all that had happened this day: the criticized Mr. Webb, the coarse coach tour gentleman, the unknown contessa, outcries against the construction of the garden, collapses, lost tablet bottles that were actually there, and then that child's photo.

It was just as she finished her second cup of tea and the last page of chapter four that the front door opened. She listened carefully to the steps of her husband ascending the stairs. His gait was his usual confident stride, although not as rapid as usual.

Hugh's quiet "I'm done in, love," as he entered the room prompted Berdie to fetch her husband a welcoming cup of tea. By the time she arrived back to the gracious bedroom, Hugh was already in his woolen robe, seated on the Chesterfield opposite Berdie's chair.

"Thank you, love." Hugh gratefully accepted the tea.

She hoped the refreshing liquid would add a touch of energy for her dear one. She ran her hand across the side of his cheek. "The weight of the world has gone a bit lighter?"

"God is still in His heaven." Hugh smiled. "Despite dozy vicars who momentarily forget that."

Berdie cuddled next to her husband on the couch.

"Speaking of lighter, Aidan Kirkwood has one less guest tonight." Hugh blew on the surface of the drink.

"How's that?"

"Mathew's woes," Hugh continued cooling the tea.

"He found you then."

"Indeed, one of his clients from the coach tour has gone missing."

"Gone missing?"

"Well, done a bunk really." Hugh took a swallow of the hot brew. "He signed in at the Lawler's B and B but never made dinner with the tour group. So Mathew went to rouse him from his room. The gentleman and his luggage were gone."

"Hard on Mathew, I shouldn't wonder."

"And Cherry Lawler was distressed, thinking something in the accommodations didn't suit. Mathew asked if the fellow may have said anything to you."

"Me?"

"Apparently, you had a conversation with him at the tea today?"

Berdie pursed her lips. "Oh, that gentleman, the surly one. He didn't have any problem expressing his disgust concerning what an environmental disaster the garden water feature would be. No, I'd say he's surely the type who would readily make known his dissatisfaction if that were an issue."

Hugh took another sip. "I told Mathew not to take it to heart. There were any number of reasons one would leave a tour without notice. I suggested he ring the fellow tomorrow and see if he could set things right. And then I encouraged him to apply himself completely to the people who didn't do a runner."

Berdie laid her head on Hugh's capable shoulder.

"Just a nightcap to the scramble of a day, I suppose." Hugh put his arm around Berdie. "Let's do hope tomorrow will be more even keeled."

"Yes." Berdie tried to make her voice sound resolutely in agreement while in her heart of hearts she courted an insatiable curiosity concerning the disappearance of Mathew's gentleman and just how it may play into the most peculiar puzzle taking place in their back garden. A copious grin spread across her face.

❦❧

The next morning, the lovely call of the church bell announcing Sunday worship sounded across the village, and Hugh was at its bidding. However, *scattered* was the best word to describe the attendance at church, Berdie decided, as she entered the nave.

She sat in a front pew, listening to Mr. Castle's rendition of "Christ is Made the Sure Foundation." Then he played it a second time, and a third. It was then Berdie realized something was missing. "Hugh," she whispered.

With haste, Berdie entered the sacristy. To her surprise, Hugh was talking to someone on the telephone.

"Hugh," she prodded. "Did you not hear the organ?"

Hugh nodded and silently pointed to the receiver

at his ear. "Yes, delighted," he said into the mouthpiece. "I am familiar, yes."

"Well?"

Hugh lifted his left brow. "I look forward to it, but I really must ring off now." He covered the mouthpiece with his hand. "I'll be right there," he whispered.

"There's no time to spare." She moved toward the door. "We're all waiting."

Berdie reentered the nave. Mr. Castle squinted his aging eyes and looked cross the nave for the absent priest.

The congregation, by this time, were fussing about and craning their necks up the church aisles.

Hugh bolted from the sacristy door like a horse loosed from his stable. He raced to where the acolytes stood, and the service officially began. The general tone of the congregants went from a fuddled unrest to an inestimable sense of well-being.

Hugh didn't skip a beat. Just as Berdie expected, he conducted the service with genuine grace and decorum, not a trace of hassled activity. When it was time for the sermon, he got right to it.

"With the events of yesterday filling our attentions, all the questions and emotions such a discovery can stir, it creates a certain amount of unease." Hugh had every ear, except Batty Natty whose chin rested on her chest in napping. "We need to be certain that said events do not steal away our focus on what Lent is all about. Remember God is greater than any unexpected event," Hugh told the congregation. "Not to take away from the seriousness of the unfortunate discovery, still we cannot let it deprive us of our season of preparation for Easter."

Some heads bobbed in agreement.

"Lent," he continued, "is the season of alignment. We all need sincere moments of self-reflection to make sure we are aligned with God's purposes."

Hugh used servicing an auto's engine as an illustration of the Lenten practice to heed the care of our soul.

Berdie noticed Preston Graystone fidgeting about at Hugh's words. But Lucy Butz, who just recently got her driver's license, was keenly attentive.

Hugh invited the congregation to be a part of the Lenten practice of special prayer. Early risers, he recommended, may enjoy taking part in matins. Or, he encouraged for those not up for morning prayers, midday Lenten prayers would also be taking place.

When, at the last, with sermon done and prayers prayed and hymns sung, the final notes of Mr. Castle's organ postlude sounded. Berdie and Hugh stood at the door of the church offering farewells. The entire lot of congregants were cheered and encouraged, save Mr. Graystone who had the same fidgety attitude that only allowed a tip of the head and a departing scowl.

The dappled sun peeked through large clouds as Hugh and Berdie finished their Sabbath duties and walked to the vicarage.

"I wonder if there will be rain this evening," Berdie mumbled, eyes to the sky.

Hugh stopped suddenly. "This evening," he whispered. He peered into Berdie's eyes. "Oh, yes, I haven't yet told you."

Berdie wasn't sure she liked the sound of those words.

"It was the Preswoods who rang me at the church earlier."

"Well, really. They must know that was a terribly

inconvenient time."

"I should think." Hugh's voice had no sense of impatience. He wrapped his fingers around Berdie's hand. "They've invited us to dinner at Swithy Hall this evening following evensong."

"Oh, Hugh, I hoped for a night in."

Hugh simply shrugged.

"I suppose they urged you. Really, the Preswoods ring you up, at the church, and in poor timing, because they want us to Sunday dinner?"

"Eight this evening, and, yes, they were quite insistent. Mrs. Preswood said they had something to discuss with us. And they want us to bring Lillie."

"We're to bring Lillie?" Berdie pulled her hand from Hugh's grasp. "Do they still consider themselves lord of the manor? They expect us to come at their beck and call."

Hugh used his clerical voice. "They may not attend church, Berdie, but they are members of the parish we're here to serve. And, yes, to a certain degree, they're still important and influential. We owe them the courtesy of attending just as we would any other family in the parish."

"Yes, well." Berdie knew he was right. "What do they want?" Berdie asked herself as much as she asked Hugh.

"At eight this evening, I dare say, we'll find out."

"Must we dress up?"

"I should think so."

Berdie sighed. "You know what that means." She and Hugh resumed walking. "An afternoon safari through the far reaches of my wardrobe."

Hugh just grinned and put his arm around Berdie's waist.

"Think of this evening as an opportunity to let someone else cook. What do you suppose the Preswoods will lay on for dinner?" Hugh asked playfully.

"I can assure you of one thing. It won't be humble pie."

4

Despite the quiet of an English countryside evening in spring, the crunch of the gravel drive beneath Berdie's feet assaulted her ears. And the rocky bits of it felt like boulders beneath her thinly soled evening dress shoes, which only made occasional forays from her wardrobe. The high heels made navigating her slightly robust body to the large front portico of Bampkingswith Hall a bit precarious. Berdie careened to the left, almost stumbling. She widened her eyes at the sense of impending disaster.

Hugh caught her elbow. "You all right then?"

Berdie curved her lips into an elfish smile, and she gave a quick nod to her husband.

"It wouldn't do for the vicar's wife to go head over backside in Colonel and Mrs. Preswood's drive now would it?" Lillie spoke what Berdie was thinking.

"Lillie, you mind your manners this evening." Berdie laughed.

"The both of you take care," Hugh admonished with a cheerful voice.

When the trio reached the front door, Hugh pulled the aged door chime, and a gentleman, smartly dressed in black, opened the door.

"Welcome to Bampkingswith Hall." His formal tone held just enough warmth to make it seem quite sincere. "Please come in."

Berdie contained her awe as she stepped into the

cavernous marble front hall.

Her former investigative reporter eyes scanned the room, observing it discreetly. There were two majestic Venetian mirrors, four Italian-styled chairs, with a similar small table between them, and a display cabinet brimming with glistening glassware, which stood at the bottom of a grand stairway. And over it all, a crystalline chandelier cast its silvery light.

Lillie, on the other hand, stood agape peering at the lighted sparkling display dangling overhead.

"Just like home, yes?" Berdie whispered unobtrusively to her friend.

The black clad butler waved his hand towards two large oak doors embellished with carved details. "If you please, make your way to the drawing room where refreshments are being served," he directed. "Colonel and Mrs. Preswood will join you shortly."

Berdie clung to Hugh's arm praying she'd make it across the polished floor without going "head over backside," as Lillie had put it. The trio's distinct clatter of footsteps on marble echoed as they made their way to the drawing room entrance.

The massive door swung open an instant before Hugh reached for it.

"I thought I heard someone arrive." Rosalie Darbyshire, the Preswood's niece, greeted them. The twenty-five-year-old's warm chestnut hair enhanced her green eyes and kind smile. "Vicar. Mrs. Elliot. I'm so glad you came. Lillie, you look lovely."

Rosalie was often seen at St. Aidan of the Woods Parish Church. She not only sang in the women's chorus but also was first alto in the church choir.

"And it's very pleasant to see you." Hugh tipped his head.

"Please sit down." The young woman picked up a tray of stemmed glasses sparkling with refreshment. "Raspberry Pimm's anyone?" She stretched out the tray towards Berdie.

"Oh, yes, thank you." Berdie took the Pimm's cordially, as did Lillie and Hugh.

"Raspberry Pimm's are one of Robin's favorites." Rosalie took a glass for herself and waved toward the grand sofa. "Please, do sit down."

All three seated themselves watching not to spill on the gold brocade.

"Where is that sister of yours?" Lillie held her Pimm's with both hands. "Someone said she's in from London."

"She is, indeed, but Robin went down to greet an overnight guest staying at the lodge this evening. She's seeing to their comfort and should arrive back in a tic." She paused. "Have things in the church garden quieted now? I mean, being a crime scene and all," Rosalie asked politely.

"A bit." Hugh cleared his throat. "We still have officials hovering about."

"I see." A wide grin spread across her light pink lips. "Did Aunt Flora tell you why we're gathering here tonight?" Her eyes beamed.

"Actually, no. Your aunt just said there was something of importance to be discussed with us and asked us to dinner."

"I see." Rosalie looked almost puckish.

"Perhaps it concerns the Easter Special number, something to do with new choir attire?" Lillie chirped with a note of hope.

"No, I'm afraid not. But I certainly don't want to spoil the surprise."

"Oh, I do love surprises." Lillie took a dainty sip of her Pimm's.

As long as they're pleasant. Berdie was not up to any unpleasantries. She eyed Rosalie's shoes, dark ballerina flat slippers. Now that footwear is sensible, Berdie thought, just as she felt a slight cramp in her left arch.

Rosalie wore a modest spring dress, and the shoes fit the style of it nicely. Her attire wasn't lavish, but it suited her. Rosalie Darbyshire didn't go in for all the trendy looks like Robin, her fraternal twin. Although Robin garnered all the beauty acclaim, Berdie decided that Rosalie, in her own simple way, was genuinely beautiful.

"What's this?" Lillie gestured to a large pink satin book lying on the small polished table next to where they sat.

Rosalie directed her gaze at the object. "Oh, Aunt Flora retrieved that from the library this afternoon. She and Robin were perusing the snaps."

"May I?" Lillie asked Rosalie.

"Of course. As long as you don't mind witnessing sun-kissed nine-year-olds displaying missing teeth and dripping lollies."

"Childhood pictures." Berdie enjoyed discovering what people were like as youngsters.

"A bit embarrassing really, but there it is." Rosalie had a merry tone in her voice.

"Our Clare hid the children's photo album one time, when she was thirteen," Berdie stated. "It took us weeks to find it."

Hugh chimed in. "Actually, Nick, he's our younger son, found it and brought it out for the entire world to see. Clare was embarrassed to the point of tears, and it caused a horrible row in our house."

"Not difficult to do amongst siblings." Rosalie gently laughed.

Lillie opened the satin book. "Look at those chubby little cheeks."

Berdie chuckled and pointed to a photo that displayed two toddlers smudged with mud head to foot. "You girls look ready for the bath. I see you found your way to a spring mud puddle no doubt."

"That's one of my favorite photos. It was taken one day after we arrived at Swithy Hall." Rosalie giggled. "Aunt Flora's not especially keen on it though. As chairperson of the county Family Heritage Circle, her two darling nieces looking a bit like lost waifs just won't do."

"Is that your mother giving you the glasses of lemonade?" Berdie asked of the young woman in the picture who held a laden tray.

"Good heavens, no, not lemonade and not Mummy. No, that was the domestic. The picture next is Mummy." She looked over Berdie's shoulder at the photo of the tall, shapely woman. Rosalie's voice went wispy as she continued to speak. "She was an entertainer, a dancer, and a cabaret singer. But she gave that all up for Robin and me. Wonderfully caring Mum, I loved her dearly." The young woman went on. "Of course Aunt Flora isn't especially keen on this photo either." Rosalie now whispered. "It was taken at Blackpool near the cabaret where Mummy performed, you see."

A chuckle rippled amongst the three women. They were aware that Flora Preswood took great pride in a family lineage of great distinction.

"She's an attractive woman," Hugh offered. "Where the picture was taken is of no matter. She was your mother and undoubtedly devoted."

There was that generous spirit for which Hugh was so highly regarded.

"Good evening, Reverend, Mrs. Elliott, Miss Foxworth." Mrs. Flora Parks Preswood had arrived and in full authority.

Hugh stood and the nearly six-foot woman stepped gracefully towards the group. Her coiffed hair, flawless makeup, and tailored dress declared her eminent urge for all to be neat and in appropriate order.

"Please sit down, Vicar. I see Rosalie is taking good care of you. Is everyone comfortable?"

"Yes," Hugh answered.

"Colonel Preswood received an important telephone call, business of course." Flora Preswood ran a well-manicured finger across her distinguishing chin. "If he's not in the London office, he's speaking to the London office. He'll join us at dinner."

She noticed the pink satin book open in Lillie's lap. "Rosalie, I'll look after our guests. Would you please get Charles? I believe he's reading in the library. Make sure he gets to the dining room."

"Right away, Aunt Flora. If you'll excuse me." Rosalie swept across the room and out the massive door.

"I see you're perusing the twins' photos." Mrs. Preswood's voice sounded more candid. "As you can see, there is precious little of them before they came to live here at the hall with Colonel Preswood and myself." She exhaled deeply and sat in a large brocade chair. "Rosalie showed you the ghastly picture of my precious but wayward younger sister, I'm sure."

Berdie, Hugh, and Lillie all nodded.

"She's quite pretty," Hugh said.

Mrs. Preswood raised a brow. "Yes, well, pretty though she may be, my dear sister never had the best judgment, frankly. Especially when it came to men. She married a loathsome con artist, John Darbyshire, who carried her off to Venezuela on some oil cache scheme that went terribly wrong. The girls were born there, you see. One morning, twenty-five years ago, I received a postcard from overseas in the morning mail from my sister. 'Dear Flora, you are the aunt of twins' was hastily written across the back." Mrs. Preswood took a deep breath. "At least Rose did have the decency to have the girls christened here the moment they set foot on English soil. When Darbyshire deserted Rose, leaving her desperately alone to care for the girls, she came to live with us. Shortly, she became ill. It was only a matter of months, and she was placed in hospital where she eventually succumbed. We assumed responsibility for Robin and Rosalie. We raised them as our own." The woman, as if just unloading a large basket of wilted flowers, sighed. "I do ask this information to stay in confidence."

"Of course," Hugh assured, "you needn't worry on that account."

She needn't worry, Berdie thought, *because everyone in the village, at least those at the Copper Kettle, are already aware of it anyway.*

The man in black stood in the drawing room doorway.

Berdie was expecting him to snap his heels.

"Dinner, madam." He bobbed his head, and Mrs. Preswood stood. She recovered the photo album from Lillie's lap. "To the dining room, shall we?"

The group made their way into the entry hall

where they found Robin eying herself in one of the large lavish mirrors.

"Robin, you're in." Flora Preswood stated the obvious.

The young woman's outfit, surely from Harrods, was the epitome of London chic, and it suited her model-thin body well. It was complemented by very Italian and, by the look of it, very expensive high-heeled sandal shoes.

Robin pushed a long black fringe back from her aqua-colored eyes, and it was then Berdie realized how flushed the young woman's cheeks were.

Robin turned to face them and shaped her satin lips into a smile. "Good evening," she said. "Sorry I wasn't able to join you earlier."

Robin ran her hand across the neckline of the stylish outfit she wore. Berdie thought she caught a sparkling glimpse flutter with Robin's movement.

"Come along, my sweet. We're just going to the dining room." Mrs. Preswood put her free arm across Robin's shoulder and placed a tender kiss on her niece's cheek.

Robin's smile went sour. "Oh, Aunt Flora, I thought you put that awful thing away." Robin grabbed the satin photo book from her aunt's fingers and held it tightly to her chest.

"Roberta! We have guests," Mrs. Preswood admonished.

"My point exactly." Robin looked piercingly at Hugh, Lillie, and then Berdie. "You haven't…"

"Oh, come, Robin, you were darling little girls," Lillie proffered.

"Still." She didn't smile. "How careless Aunt Flora," Robin scolded. The twin spun away from her aunt. Her jaw tightened and moisture appeared in the corners of her eyes, heavy with dark mascara. "These are quite personal, to say nothing of embarrassing. You should have returned them to their shelf. And I will not have them displayed on some mundane table at a whipped meringue wedding." Robin's tone was less than gracious. "I simply want to wed Charles. Not months away, I want to marry him now."

Marry who? Berdie questioned.

Mrs. Preswood's stern face softened. "Of course you want to marry Charles. I know all the planning is hectic my sweet. Be patient."

Robin clung to the pink satin book. She appeared to find no solace in her aunt's words. "I want to marry him now, Aunt Flora. Why should I wait any longer? I love him. He's everything to me." Robin nodded to Hugh. "Please excuse me."

"Are you okay, Robbie?" Rosalie's voice echoed across the hall.

Berdie turned to see Rosalie and a young man standing near the stairs.

Without a word, Robin moved briskly to the stairs and began a rapid ascent.

"What's going on here?" the young man asked. Though he looked to be just shy of Robin's height, he possessed a certain air. Both his hair and suit were a classic style. The tailored fabric clearly said moneyed.

"Well?" he asked.

"She's just a bit stressed, Charles. We've been working on plans for the wedding." Mrs. Preswood gestured toward the staircase. "A few moments to herself, and she'll be right as rain." She looked at Hugh. "Oh, do excuse me. Charles, this is Reverend Hugh Elliott, his wife Berdie, and our church choirmaster, Lillian Foxworth. May I introduce Mr. Charles Swindon-Pierce."

The young man stepped along to Hugh and shook his hand. "Vicar." He nodded politely to Lillie and Berdie.

Mrs. Preswood continued. "Mr. Swindon-Pierce is Robin's fiancé."

The man smiled and tipped his head courteously.

"They wish to marry here at the church. Isn't that wonderful, Vicar?" Mrs. Preswood continued.

"I see. It would certainly seem right to do so. Congratulations."

"We're so looking forward to it," Mrs. Preswood sounded resolutely confident.

Hugh went on. "You are aware I ask couples who wed at St. Aidan's to do two one hour pre-wedding sessions with me at the church? Wonderful guidance in navigating the waters of marriage. That's what I've been told by those who have done them."

Charles's mouth lost a corner of its smile. "Robin and I are doing just fine, thank you."

"Oh, I'm sure you are. No, I'm just saying that the couples who have completed the course found the information extremely valuable, a good footing."

"Robin and Charles are aware that a meeting with you, Vicar, is a prerequisite and are happy to oblige." Mrs. Preswood looked directly at her niece's future husband. "Aren't you, Charles?"

The groom-to-be simply lifted his chin.

"Well then." Hugh was warm but subdued.

"Yes. Well," Berdie added. Judging by the snapshot of the family dynamics so far this evening, she could clearly see the young couple needing every available advice to ward off shipwreck on those waters of marriage.

"And you'll be in charge of our music," Mrs. Preswood directed towards Lillie.

"How exciting." Lillie lit up. "It's all a very pleasant surprise. Oh, I do love weddings."

"Robin's over the moon," Rosalie piped and stepped next to Charles. "And I'm excited about having Charles as a brother-in-law."

Mrs. Preswood moved to the center of the group. "I had hoped to announce this properly with an appropriate toast at our special dinner. But it seems to have now gone by the wayside."

"A quick toast with the meal will do nicely, I should think," Charles presented as a peace offering on his fiancée's behalf.

Flora Preswood wasn't responsive.

"It's a happy occasion." Rosalie all but danced. "Let's enjoy it."

The gentleman in black reappeared. "Is there a delay for dinner, madam?" echoed across the great hall.

The disappointed Mrs. Preswood gathered herself. "No." She straightened her shoulders and resolutely led the party to the dining room of Bampkingswith Hall.

Once the aloof Randal Preswood arrived, the meal was served.

Hugh gave a blessing to which the Preswoods obliged. Colonel Preswood offered Hugh a stock tip, and apart from that, the meal was bereft of any truly stimulating conversation. Or any real discussion about the nuptials for that matter. It was a bit like the creamed cauliflower soup served as the first course: under-cooked and without true color.

Robin didn't even come to the dinner table until the dessert was served. And when the bride-to-be did arrive, her face was wan, and she clung to Charles like a climbing rose on a garden wall.

Berdie perceived a fat little elephant sitting squarely in the middle of the dining table but could not make out its composition or just exactly why it was there. This family, which worked at presenting themselves well, seemed to be trying too hard to do so.

The departure from this meal and Bampkingswith Hall came none too soon. Within twenty minutes of the last bite of strawberry mousse, Berdie, Hugh, and Lillie were out the door. Apart from the pleasant Rosalie, it had started with a foot cramp and went downhill from there.

As Hugh stood in the doorway finishing cordial conversation with the Preswoods, Berdie and Lillie were several yards down the drive waiting by the car.

"Did Robin Preswood seem more than odd to you this evening?"

"I think the bride should enter to the 'Trumpet Voluntary.'" Lillie nearly waltzed as she spoke. "What? Odd? Yes, well, my experience has been that brides do get testy when planning their big day."

"True," Berdie agreed, "but...No, there's something else going on there."

"Perhaps Dr. Avery could do a solo, yes, 'Come Down, O Love Divine.'"

"Lillie! Will you listen, please? There's a great deal of something else that surrounds the whole goings-on in that house, and it doesn't smell right."

"Indeed? A bit like the odiferous cauliflower soup." Lillie scrunched her nose.

"Well, something's off. I hear the trumpeting of a

large grey creature."

"You and your elephants." Lillie became more intrigued. "What sort of trumpeting?"

"Yes, if only I could put my finger on it."

"Knowing you as I do, my dear friend, you'll not put your finger on it. Rather, you'll lay on your entire weight and wrestle the creature to its knees until all is neatly sorted."

Hugh now joined the women at the car. "What needs sorted?"

Berdie gave Lillie a visual nudge to be quiet. "Deciding what time Lillie and I will meet for tea tomorrow." Berdie nodded her head as nonchalantly as possible.

"Elevenses, of course," Lillie stammered in an all-knowing kind of way. "At The Copper Kettle."

"Right." Hugh smiled slightly. "Why do I have the feeling you two are conspiring?" He pulled the car keys from his pocket. "I realize things in the Preswood home this evening were not perfect. Families seldom are. But it's up to the Preswoods to work it out for themselves. I should hope you leave things well enough alone."

"We're not ones to interfere." Lillie fluttered her dark lashes.

Hugh lifted his left brow. "That's like saying rain isn't wet," he countered and opened the car door for Berdie and Lillie. "If you try it on, everyone involved will be soaked through. Catch my meaning?" He looked very deliberately at Berdie.

"Eminently, dear," she replied and slipped onto the car seat.

Whether it was the dodgy cauliflower soup or the unstrung bits and pieces of recent events that played in her mind, Berdie was awake and restless when she should have been sleeping soundly.

She eyed Hugh, slumbering beside her, and thought again how grateful she was that his prolonged military jaunts here and there were no longer a part of their lives. No, now she just had to share him with every Tom, Dick, and Cherry in the parish, including the Preswoods. Even so, she was grateful for his presence.

She let go an easy sigh then arose. Putting on her dressing robe, she tried not to disturb the man with whom she delighted in sharing her bed.

Within minutes, she was in the kitchen and had the kettle on, navigating it all by the light of a small candle lamp that sat atop several stacked recipe books. She poured a cuppa.

Berdie felt compelled to wander down the dark hall to the library where she sat in one of the leather armchairs. She took a sip of the warm soothing liquid and let her restlessness melt into the stillness.

She noticed that the richly woven curtain on one of the windows facing the church garden was slightly open. Taking her warm cup with her, she thought to close it, but found herself peering up at the dappled clouds that played hide and seek with the vivid stars gracing the night sky.

There was something special about the wee hours when the world sleeps. The mad rush of conversation hushed, the frightful tear of spinning activity silenced. It was as if the beating of God's heart silently sent it's rhythm out to any who would take a moment to listen.

And Berdie readily took note.

She opened the curtain further and relaxed back into the gracious armchair where she could gaze into the beauty of the night.

She swallowed her tea slowly when her eyes fell to the ground of the back garden. Even the beehive of activity around the tented crime scene was now absent. One lone constable stood watch, slowly pacing, fighting against the tedium that made sleep so very attractive.

"Poor chap," Berdie whispered aloud. "I bet he'd love a cuppa." Just as she spoke the words, the solitary figure in the back garden commenced a great yawn accompanied by a stretch. "Tea it is."

By the time she prepared and poured the large Stanley flask, found Hugh's sizable torch that looked more a car headlight, put on her wellies, and buttoned her coat, several minutes had elapsed.

Once outside, the dark coolness reminded her that it was early spring.

She walked towards the taped-off area. But the constable wasn't pacing. In fact, he appeared to have become a big lump-of-a-thing in a piece of garden furniture. And not surprisingly, she heard a slight rattle-gurgle that sounded very much like snoring.

She started to rouse him then smiled and stopped. *Where's the harm? No one's about. I'll rouse him in a bit.* Berdie turned off the blinding torchlight.

She began to make a retreat but hesitated and breathed in the freshness of the English night. The stars were even grander now she was standing out in them, and she reveled in the moment.

She wasn't sure how long she had been basking in the glory of creation when she heard a sharp snap. A twig breaking? Someone was about. Thinking the constable had awakened, she spun to face the tent. But a muffled gurgle-sigh told her he was still slumbering. If she called out to awaken the guard, she would surely frighten off the intruder.

Silently, she inched her way along to the tented dig. She gripped the large tea flask, recognizing its value as a potential weapon. Her ears were on alert. She strained forward. Yes. There was a definite rustling. Indeed, someone was near at hand.

She raised the substantial flask, ready to strike, and set her thumb on the torchlight switch. In a lunge of energy she lurched forward, at the same moment turning on the torch that sent a blinding light, ripping away the dark of the crime scene. "Halt."

There he was, frozen at her command. Berdie recognized the intruder.

"Fritz!"

The stunned dachshund, eyes wide and ears perked, wore moist dirt about his pointy nose. He looked like a deer in the headlights until the constable, roused and suddenly aware, leaped from the garden chair, crashing it over in a heap.

The wee, now defensive, sausage scrambled in circles as his frenzied barks bit into the silence.

Berdie's apprehension melted into a foolish laugh.

"Freeze, don't move." The constable drew out his truncheon. Squinting, he raised his arm against the bright light of Berdie's torch as Fritz continued his barking.

"What goes on here?" the young man in uniform shouted trying to get his sea legs.

It was then Berdie was sure she heard a curt whistle from the wood. Instinctively, she turned the torchlight towards the trees, but saw only a quick movement.

Fritz gave a final nip near the constable's shoe and raced into the woods as fast as his stubby legs would take him, like a hound on the hunt, long ears flapping.

"Who goes there?" the constable asked, truncheon still in strike position.

"I'm Berdie Elliott, Constable, the vicar's wife." Berdie pointed to the vicarage.

"You really ought to keep your rascally dog on a lead, ma'am." The young man somewhat sheepishly returned his weapon to its proper place.

"Should do if he were mine."

"Why are you out here then?" The policeman eyed Berdie's wellies and dressing gown that hung down below the hem of her overcoat. He suddenly clasped his hands behind his back, trying desperately to appear very awake and very aware.

"It's just that I brought you some tea." Berdie smiled, and handed the former defensive tool, sloshing with hot liquid, to the guard. "Doing a double shift?"

The young man's face went a bit pink. "As a matter of fact, I am." He gave a quick nod and grasped the flask. "Ta."

"It's slightly sweetened. Does that suit, um, Constable…?"

"Daren. Tom Daren."

"Constable Daren?"

"Yes, thank you," he cordially responded.

"Well then, I'll go and brew a fresh pot for my husband." Berdie knew that if Hugh was not awakened by her stirring earlier, he certainly would now be.

The constable tipped his young head.

Berdie smiled and beamed her torch towards the vicarage. Despite the humor of it all, one menacing thought raced through her mind. What was Wilkie Gordon doing about the crime scene, and more importantly, why?

5

Berdie glared at the cloud dappled morning sun outside her kitchen window as if to send the possibility of showers retreating. The fact was, after the added affairs of last night, Berdie had more questions than answers concerning all sorts: Preswoods, Wilkie Gordon, coach tour run-away, and the inevitable bones.

It was almost time to meet Lillie at the Copper Kettle, and slogging through the rain certainly didn't sound a treat.

"Perhaps the weather will move on," Berdie spoke aloud at the exact same moment three watery drops hit the glass.

The spring shower tapped erratically on Berdie's taut umbrella as she ambled towards the High Street. By the time she spied the Copper Kettle, the dance had become a frenzied torrent. She felt the wet creep into the edges of her shoes.

The Copper Kettle's jingling bell sounded comfort and shelter despite the prospect of gossip flowing at high tide. Berdie shook the excess water from her umbrella and drew it closed.

There Lillie sat, looking a bit soggy herself, at a table with an awaiting chair and a brown betty teapot, steam rising from its spout.

"Remove your fins before sitting, please." Lillie swept her arm to the empty chair.

"That and all." Berdie sat right by the teapot.

Looking round, only one other table was occupied, unusual for this time of day. By eleven on most days, the Copper Kettle was at full throttle, but it suited her purposes that it was less populated. Suddenly, she appreciated the downpour. Very discreetly she pushed her wet shoes just off the heel, well under the table, of course.

Lillie poured a dash of milk into the cup closest to Berdie then added the hot, brown liquid. "Now, I can see by the wee lines beneath your eyes that you didn't sleep well last night, so lay it all out then." Lillie's tone had a gleeful edge to it, much like a child embarking on an Easter egg hunt. "Mustn't let the vicar overhear. That is why we're here."

"You are the impudent one." Berdie wore a half smirk.

"That's why I'm your best friend," Lillie retorted and took a sip of the hot tea in her cup. "Out with it."

Berdie leaned forward. "It's not just last night's visit with the Preswoods that's bothering me. It's a whole bag of peculiarities. This bones discovery seems to have unearthed, pardon the pun, a whole rash of odds and ends." Berdie added a spoonful of sugar and held the warm teacup in her hand. "The course man from the tour group, for instance. The moment he stepped from the coach he seemed to be set on going to the church back garden. Hugh actually had to strictly redirect the man into the church. I didn't think much of it at the time, apart from the fact he was churlish, but I dare say his desire for a soon-to-be-served tea was not a driving force. Why was he so interested in the back garden?"

"What we've seen of him, he didn't appear to be

especially social." Lillie tapped a finger on her chin. "Perhaps he just wanted a moment's peace away from the crowd."

"Precisely." Berdie took a large gulp of tea. "Now, why was someone of that makeup on a crowded coach tour to begin with?"

Berdie heard the clip-clop of sturdy shoes on the wooden floor. Villette Horn, the owner and operator of the Copper Kettle, was rapidly approaching the table.

Her long horseshoe shaped face made her inset eyes seem even smaller. Berdie always thought Villette's caramel brown colored hair looked as if it had been sprinkled with muscovado sugar.

"Good morning, Mrs. Elliott, Lillie. We've some lovely cakes this morning just out of the oven, also fresh treacle tart."

"Cakes, please," Berdie answered with haste.

"Right then, cakes it is," Villette nodded. "And have you heard more about the bones?"

"Not really," Berdie answered but her silence for a scant moment let the hostess know that this topic would not be pursued.

"Yes, well, cakes." Villette spoke with a slight tone of annoyance. She was not use to being denied any topic of conversation she chose to pursue. She turned abruptly and left the table.

"Now, continue while she's out of earshot."

"And there's our dear Wilkie Gordon," Berdie went on.

"Yes, poor Wilkie," Lillie agreed. "Just in the past year he's faced forced retirement as grounds manager at Swithy Hall and then his Mary's illness getting worse. How is he, now?" Lillie quizzed.

"Well, he's not short of blood pressure tablets."

"What?" Lillie absently blew on the cup's contents. "Poor Mary." She sighed. "She barely holds her own in the best of times."

"What do you mean?"

"She and Wilkie were years in the waiting before she gave birth to a child. There were some kind of complications along the way and, sadly, the child had to be placed in special care. Mary was never really the same after that. No one talks of it of course."

"At least not openly," Berdie corrected. She livened. "Perhaps that explains the picture of an infant I observed in their home, although Wilkie lead me to believe it was a grandchild. Yes." Berdie knitted her brow. "The picture looked to be a boy. But what about Cherry? Wilkie and Mary are her grandparents."

"Wilkie, yes." Lillie shook her dark curls. "Something about a previous marriage? No one talks about that either."

"Right." Berdie ran a finger on the edge of her cup. "Something is not quite right in the Gordon household. It appears Wilkie is, well, not forthcoming. His displeasure about the garden scheme ranged from doing harm to the environment to irresponsible church finance to distaste for rich Italians."

"He's grumpy." Lillie took another sip of tea.

"But it's as if he's grabbing on to any argument against the scheme that happens to pop along. At the council meeting, it was environmental. With Cherry, he argued church finances, and then he blasted the endowing contessa."

"Quite right." Lillie raised her cup to Berdie as if in congratulation. "Well spotted."

"Which indicates that the real reason he's against the scheme—"

"Hasn't truly come to light?" Lillie set her cup down. "So what is the real reason?"

Berdie took an abbreviated swallow of tea. "I'm not sure I can answer that yet, but I can tell you that he was about the crime scene last night."

"Really?" Lillie seemed genuinely surprised.

"Well, Fritz was about the crime scene, but I'm sure Wilkie was there as well."

"I should think."

"I heard his whistle beckoning his four-footed friend, and the creature responded like a child to sweeties. Think about it Lillie. Wilkie was the church gardener for several years."

Lillie's eyes widened. "Oh my, you don't think he knew about"—she barely whispered—"the bones?"

Berdie lifted her chin.

Then Lillie's face lightened, as if in realization of the full impact and what it implied. "Wilkie Gordon wouldn't be so vile." Her whisper was more energized. "He wouldn't hurt a fly." She placed her finger in the loop of the teacup and intently leaned forward, her hazel-green eyes widened. "Would he?"

"Cakes," Villette Horn's brazen voice announced. Lillie let go a yip and flipped the half-held teacup sideways creating a brown stream all cross the table and onto the floor.

"You're a fidgety one," Mrs. Horn all but yelled.

Berdie tried desperately not to laugh.

"I'm dreadfully sorry." Lillie's face went pink.

Villette smacked the cakes on the tabletop making it shift just slightly and sent more tea cascading to the floor. Then the woman turned. "Shells, bells, and little fishes."

While Villette had her back to the dripping mess,

Lillie snatched a colorful cotton serviette that sat astride her teaspoon. She made a quick dab towards the spilled tea.

"No." Berdie pushed the word out while still trying to smother laughter. "It will stain the serviette." She caught Lillie's hand just in time.

Lillie pulled it back and bit her lip as the corners of her mouth elevated. "If you make me laugh, I'll throw this napkin at you."

"Mind your feet," Villette clipped. Having returned, she began a vigorous swathing motion with the mop across the floor and under the table. "I say!" Her face went into a scowl. The swathing came to an abrupt standstill.

Berdie could feel the teashop operator's hard stare shoot under the table. Apparently, Lillie did too, because she bobbed her head to take a peak.

Quickly, Berdie scooted her heels back into the wet shoes.

"Have we no respect for this catering establishment?" Villette trumpeted.

Now Berdie felt the heat rise to her own cheeks. It was Lillie's turn to smother a laugh.

"I can assure you, Mrs. Horn, there is no disrespect intended." Berdie spoke loudly enough for the other group of occupants, who had become completely engaged in the goings on at this table, to hear clearly. It was for Hugh's sake, really, that she spoke for all to hear. "Absolutely no disrespect."

Villette tossed a terry cloth on the tabletop and it drank in the errant tea.

The bell tones of Elgar's Nimrod sounded from Lillie's coat pocket, and she made a mad grab to retrieve her mobile.

"I say, must we endure a third-party chat?" Villette's brow knitted, and she scrubbed the table in irritation. Berdie could see the woman was even more put-off.

"Good Morning, Loren," Lillie said brightly, then spoke to Villette. "I'll just step aside for a moment." She moved into a quiet corner where she continued her conversation.

"Mrs. Horn," Berdie said quietly, "thank you for all you've done, but I do believe we need to run along now. Do you mind putting our cakes in a take-away box?"

The hostess straightened, threw the dripping rag across her arm, and grabbed the cakes so quickly they nearly flew off their little pastel-colored plates. "Just as you say, Mrs. Elliott." She rushed in the direction of check out.

Berdie donned her coat, beckoned to Lillie, and made her way to pay for the treats. She opened her purse at the same moment Cherry Lawler, in her dripping yellow Macintosh, rushed into the teashop.

"It's cats and dogs out there." She stopped inside the doorway. "Oh, hello, Mrs. Elliott. Vi."

Berdie became suddenly aware that she never really apologized to Cherry for all that had befallen at the sod turning ceremony concerning the young woman's grandfather. "Cherry. Yes. Hello. Do you have a moment?" Berdie asked. "May I have a word with you?"

"Your buns, Cherry," Villette interrupted and thrust four large boxes into the arms of the petite woman who only just managed to hold them all. "Seven pounds ninety to you, Mrs. Elliott, for you and your friend,"

"Yes." Berdie counted out her money to the shop owner.

"Put the buns on the account," Cherry spoke quickly to Villette, and turned her attention to Berdie. "I must push off, Mrs. Elliott, coach tour guests stuffed into every corner, though they leave this evening."

"Of course."

"But I'm on for tomorrow. Come round, say half ten, for tea?" Cherry smiled.

"Lovely, see you then."

Using her free hand to pull the hood of the McIntosh over her head, Cherry Lawler clutched the precious parcels close to her body and exited as hurriedly as she had entered.

As she did so, Berdie caught sight through the open door of a large limousine pulling up outside Raheem's Green Grocer just cross the street. "I say," she barely whispered.

"I see even Italian aristos have to eat." Villette watched through the opened gingham-checked curtains at the shop window.

"I thought she had to push off after the ceremony," Berdie thought aloud.

"Didn't we all?" Villette dipped her chin. "She's taken up at Swithy Lodge, you know. Decided to spring holiday here in Aidan Kirkwood." The woman eyed Berdie as if waiting for some display.

No matter how badly Berdie wanted to arch her brows and declare, "Holiday here? Really? Now that seems odd," "Well," was all she offered the hostess.

Lillie finally joined Berdie at the counter. The best friend's countenance made Villette's vinegary face look positively sunny.

"It was Loren," Lillie growled in a voice quite

unlike the sprightly tone she used previously when answering the call. Villette wiped a nearby tray on the counter in a desperate attempt to look as if she wasn't listening.

"Shall we go outside into the deluge, Lillie? I have our cakes."

Lillie tersely nodded.

Villette sniffed. "You're bound to get soaked through. And do watch that limousine. Think they own the road, they do."

"Indeed, thank you." Berdie actually sensed sincerity in Villette's warning.

As she and Lillie stepped to the door threshold, the other occupants approached the counter to peer out the window at the large vehicle and join the tittle-tattle.

Berdie heard a rather high-pitched muted voice. "...hobnobbing, really. Exposed feet and whispered twitters with spilt tea. And she being a vicar's wife and all."

Berdie would have loved to put a flea in the ear of the woman speaking but instead bolted out the door with Lillie who seemed to be in need of her attention.

The rain poured so violently it nearly called for shouting in order to be heard. "Lillie, what's happening? Your face looks like a wet weekend."

"And I should think so, too, with the news I just received."

"And what's that?" Berdie leaned forward to hear Lillie respond and rammed her umbrella into Lillie's with such force it sent Lillie's vital rain protection skidding on the walk, accompanied by a gust of wind.

Lillie hopped-to like a mad rabbit chasing after the silly brolly, but the usual sparkle and humor Lillie displayed appeared as damp and wet as her whole being.

"I'm drenched," Lillie roared, repositioning the umbrella over her head.

Berdie heard a loud beep from cross the road. Hugh, in the church's people-carrier, had pulled in front of the limousine. He rolled down the window and beckoned. "My lovely ladies, do you wish to swim home, or may I offer you a ride?"

"Yes, please," Berdie shouted and dashed cross the road, Lillie behind. In a matter of seconds, umbrellas were down and automobile doors flung open.

Once seated, Berdie safely positioned the cake box and realized how truly wet she was. Then she ogled the dripping Lillie, who, once inside, slammed the vehicle's rear door with such force it sounded like a holiday firework.

"Sorry about the bump, Lillie," Berdie said carefully.

Hugh grinned. "I was passing. Just in time, too, I should say. You look utterly drenched. Actually, I'm off to Timsley."

"Are you now?" Lillie grumbled and ran her fingers through dripping curls. "Of course you would be."

"Interested?" Hugh asked somewhat hesitantly.

"Not so much interested as a calculated need." Lillie huffed.

Hugh glanced at Berdie who offered a quick shrug.

"Is that a yes?" Hugh asked Lillie.

"No." Lillie scowled. "Yes. Yes, I suppose it is."

"Berdie, are you coming as well?" Hugh looked at her and gave a gentle tip of the head towards the seat behind where Lillie sat wiping water from her chin.

Whatever was bothering Lillie, Berdie felt a compulsion to help her friend even though she wanted nothing more than to go home and get dry, feet first. Her glasses fogged, she pulled them down her nose. But still, she could clearly see Hugh's facial plea for her not to abandon him to a half hour ride with the off-color Lillie.

"I do need to stop at Sainsbury's," Berdie offered in an economical use of the truth. The moment she said it, the sunshine of relief showed itself on Hugh's face like a May afternoon.

Berdie turned to an unexpected tapping on her window. A water-logged Jamie Donovan was knocking. Berdie opened it just enough to make out the young man's voice.

"Sorry to bother, Mrs. Elliott." He was breathing hard. "Have you, by chance, seen Snowdrop?"

Snowdrop, Cara Graystone Donovan's white Highland Terrier, now Jamie's charge as well, was a bit too fussed over Berdie often thought.

"The little beast has taken to running off lately, and we can't find her. Cara's beside herself with worry."

"Sorry, no, Jamie, no sight of her." Berdie felt drops splashing through the open window.

"If we see her, we'll try to gather her and give you a call," Hugh offered from the driver's side.

"Cheers." Jamie nodded and began a trot down the doused street.

As Berdie closed the window, a prolonged horn blast emanated from the elegant vehicle behind.

"All right," Hugh spoke as if the driver would hear him. "We're on our way."

"Impatient lot." Lillie mopped her eyes.

Hugh pulled from the curb, and Lillie pattered on. "I mean really. Loren has a cheek. Could I meet him at the Timsley train station where he's greeting his arriving colleague? And he knows I have a voice lesson later this afternoon, and choir practice. 'I should think about it', I told him. Oh, but he goes on and tells me the real burner."

Berdie pushed her lenses back to their proper place and observed her dear friend glaring out the vehicle's window as if the village buildings were taking in every detail.

"And I'm sure you're going to tell us what that burner is," Berdie dropped into Lillie's tirade.

It was then Lillie appeared to become truly cognizant of the fact that two other people were present in the car. She leaned towards Berdie. "Yes, I'm meeting Roz, he says. As she's a forensic anthropologist, she's consulting on the bones case." Lillie blew out a spurt of air. "Of all the cheek."

"Roz." Hugh nodded his head. "Isn't she the university chum of Loren's we met in Northumbria?"

Lillie gave a terse bob of the chin.

"We never really met her, just saw her, really," Berdie reminded.

"Oh," Hugh cheered. "She was a great help on discovering the Livingston family, the key to unlocking the whole business with Miss Livingston, or rather Mrs. Avent. I'm sure she'll be of tremendous value to this case as well as to Loren."

"Oh, I see. Now she's wonder woman come to save the day." Lillie scornfully folded her arms.

"To be fair, that's not what I said." Hugh glanced in the rearview mirror at the sulking woman.

Berdie inclined herself towards Hugh and

whispered, "I should stop while ahead if I were you."

She turned herself as much as she could in her seatbelt to look back at Lillie. "Lillie, Loren's dealings with his colleague are simply professional."

"He calls her Roz."

"All right, Loren's dealings with Roz, albeit a friend, are simply professional."

"Oh, yes?"

"Look, Lillie. See sense. If he was carrying on with her, he'd hardly invite you to meet her at the station with him, would he?"

Lillie bit her lip and looked again out the window.

"If you permit me to interrupt for a moment," Hugh injected, apparently willing to take a chance.

Berdie took a deep breath.

"Speaking as a man, Lillie, let me remind you, that you are the person with whom Dr. Meredith has chosen to pursue romance. If he had wanted to have that kind of a relationship with Roz, he'd have had hundreds of opportunities to do so. The point is, she's an old university chum who happens to be in the same field as he. She's lending aid, and that's all there is to it."

"Well." Gone was the hard edge in Lillie's voice.

Berdie could see those devilish shades of green that can so easily rise at the thought of another woman being reasoned away.

"I suppose you're right."

Hugh, both hands gripping the wheel, glanced in the rearview mirror at his softening passenger and back to the road. "To be quite frank, Lillie, I have great respect for Roz's professional capacities, but she's hardly a film star is she?"

Berdie pursued the thought. "Her hair was right

out the bottle, brittle blonde. I'm sure her professional demands give limited time for personal care. Her wardrobe suits her job, but you could hardly call it flattering."

Lillie sniffled. "She didn't appear very warm."

"No," Berdie reaffirmed with an all-girls-together tone.

Hugh raised a palm from the steering wheel. "All right, before this turns into a feline frenzy..."

"I don't see anyone growing claws," Berdie boldly interjected.

Hugh continued, "Before this turns into a feline frenzy, let's just say Loren Meredith has set his cap at you, Lillie, and that's all that really matters in the situation."

"Set his cap." Lillie smiled. "I've not heard that in a long while."

"Well, it's true," Hugh affirmed. "Now, moving on, you look quite cold, and I have an old jumper in the box right next to you that I'm taking to St. Mark's jumble sale. Put it on for a bit, and it may chase the chill."

Lillie worked to remove her wet coat. She pulled a large grey jumper from the box and held it high, long sleeves dangling.

"That's a bit tatty." Berdie eyed the worn thing. "It's stretched out, even for Hugh. You'll swim."

Lillie ran her fingers over the worn threads. "Ah, but it's wool."

"Right." Hugh nodded. "Toasty."

Lillie pulled the garment over her wet curls and draped it on her body. She rubbed her hands, once she got them out the extra-long sleeves, up and down her arms. She smiled that delightful smile only Lillie possessed that enchanted all in her presence. *And about time, too*, Berdie thought. Lillie let go a giggle.

"What?" Berdie questioned.

"That must have been a right hoot for the ladies in the Copper Kettle when we bumped, and I lost my umbrella."

"I'm sure we seemed a pair of ninnies." Berdie chortled, and Lillie joined her in a hearty laugh. It was good to have Lillie back to her old self.

"Another fifteen minutes and we'll be in Timsley," Hugh announced with a lilt in his voice that almost sounded like a spring serenade.

6

The interior of the Timsley train station bustled with the crowds of travelers, commuters, and day-trippers. People in a sea of dripping humanity bumped and twisted their way along, most managing as little interaction as possible while on a quest for their destinations.

Berdie and Hugh held hands and rode the crest of the wave while Lillie, behind them, just managed to keep pace.

"Number four," Lillie shouted from behind.

Berdie observed the approaching crowd. She espied tall, handsome Dr. Meredith walking among them, but she was sure the woman with whom he walked wasn't Roz. He pulled a wheeled trolley bag behind him, and the strange woman had her arm wrapped around Dr. Meredith's elbow like ivy around a lamppost. The woman's facial profile wasn't familiar. Berdie strained forward and pushed her glasses tightly against the bridge of her nose.

"There's Meredith, but that's not Roz." Hugh spoke what Berdie was thinking.

Lillie now deposited herself next to Berdie and made the same observation.

The woman and Loren walked with matching strides, laughing and chatting. A bit closer now, Berdie realized indeed it was Roz, but she looked nothing like the Roz they had seen previously. Voluminous auburn hair, not brittle blonde, just touched her firm shoulders. A rather tightly-fitted top and slacks revealed hither-to unrevealed curves and legs that went on forever.

"I say." Hugh's eyes became saucers while Lillie's eyes narrowed into tiny slits.

"Has she returned to her natural hair color?" Berdie asked anybody.

"If she has"—Lillie's tone could give pluck to lemons—"it's the only bit that is natural."

"It looks she's lost a smidgen in just the right places." Berdie craned forward.

"And decidedly added some perky bits in just the right places.

"I say," Hugh repeated.

"Hugh, you can close your mouth now," Berdie prompted her stunned husband.

She watched Loren's eyes dance from her husband to herself, then to Lillie. Surprise registered itself on the doctor's face.

"Lillie, you decided to come," Dr. Meredith blurted upon his arrival. "Rather a surprise."

Roz released the doctor's elbow.

"Yes, well I can see that," Lillie said curtly.

Berdie perceived that Lillie had become frightfully aware that the warmth of the old jumper she wore had wooed her into a forgetfulness of its tatty appearance.

Lillie removed a curl of wet hair that fell across her mascara-washed eyelid. The doctor simply stared at his usually impeccable Lillie. A corner of his mouth turned upward.

Roz cleared her throat.

"Oh sorry," the doctor apologized. "Reverend Elliott, Mrs. Elliott, Lillie, this is Doctor Rosalyn

Harvey."

"That's Doctor Rosalyn Chase, actually," the woman corrected. "I've gone back to my maiden name." She looked at Loren.

"But you didn't say." Dr. Meredith's words stumbled.

"I see," Hugh offered after a moment to fill a rather stark silence.

"No concern really." Roz directed her nonchalant comments to Hugh. Her obviously volume-ized rosy lips pushed the words out. "Gerard and I were only married three minutes, separated longer than we were together, and now I'm free as a bird."

Tweet, tweet, Berdie thought while her husband politely smiled and nodded his head.

Roz softly ran a painted fingernail down her curved neck that came to rest on a long golden necklace and returned Hugh's smile. The former cigarette-stained teeth glowed whiter than a full moon on a cloudless April night.

Lillie's right, Berdie noted. *Are there any bits that haven't been smoothed, inflated, or vacated?*

Berdie leaned closely against her husband's side.

Lillie crossed her arms looking at Loren for some kind of reassurance.

"Well, the best laid plans and all that." Loren offered with a weak smile. "The lab called just a moment ago and bang goes our plan to lunch together." Loren's grasp on the wheeled trolley tightened. "They want Roz and me at the lab as soon as we leave off her gear."

"And where will you be staying, Dr. Chase?" Lillie asked Roz with quiet restraint.

"Some mate's named Colley."

"Dr. Chase is staying at Colley's flat while he's off visiting friends," Loren said rather hastily.

"Colley?" Lillie's restraint was not as quiet towards the doctor. "The Colley McCurry whose flat is next to yours?" Lillie's crossed arms tightened.

"We'll have buckets of work, being next door is perfect." Roz smiled.

"Oh yes?" Lillie gave Dr. Meredith a hard stare.

"Well, you know work demands," Loren explained while Roz, once again, sneaked her hand into the crook of the doctor's arm.

"Lillie…" Loren appealed but was interrupted by Roz.

"We really must get going, Loren."

"Indeed."

"Nice to meet you," Roz offered without any real conviction.

"Yes," Hugh said.

Berdie simply lifted her eyebrows.

"Well then." Loren had an edge of discomfort that betrayed how everyone appeared to be feeling, except Roz, of course.

With a nod of the head, Loren and Roz departed, she still clinging to his arm, he looking back at Lillie to see if he may find a bit of exoneration there. By the look on Lillie's face, none was to be found.

⁂

The downpour of yesterday departed and the train station dilemma now history, Berdie looked forward to the morning walk that would take her to the other end of the village. Berdie observed herself in the pub mirror that hung in the oak paneled hallway by the front door of the vicarage. Her glance was a final check before departing for Kirkwood Green Bed and Breakfast to meet Cherry for tea. Berdie hoped the offer of her apologies concerning the lack of action in the Wilkie Gordon falderal would be met with mercy.

She ran a finger over her lifted eyebrow and reviewed the rest of her day. Hugh was out on church business. After tea with Cherry, she would, meet with Ivy, Lillie, Cara, and Mrs. Braunhoff at the Butz home.

"Designing the children's Easter festivities," was the way Hugh put it when he placed the responsibility of it squarely on Berdie's shoulders. She then, as a good vicar's wife, adeptly passed it on to Ivy Butz. The mother of six was so very good at this sort of thing and despite her many demands as wife and mother, Ivy enjoyed every minute of creating and hosting a fête.

Then, there was dinner this evening at Le Petit Chaumier, the lovely French Restaurant in Timsley. Dr. Meredith invited her and Hugh to accompany him and Lillie to dinner, an attempt Berdie was sure, to bandage the effects of yesterday and the Roz ordeal.

Yes, now dinner at Le Petit Chaumier, that was something quite worthy of eager anticipation.

Berdie approvingly checked her light coral lipstick, a new shade that complimented her increasingly red hair and tortoiseshell glasses. She was decidedly happy with the look when the hallway telephone rang.

"Oh, bother," Berdie fussed and stepped to the ringing apparatus. "Vicarage," she announced with a pluck in her voice.

"Thees ees Senora Elliott?"

"It is," Berdie replied with a note of caution, "with whom am I speaking?"

"Ah, Senora Elliott, I ama Ortensia Orono. I ama the aide to Contessa Santolio."

"Yes, good morning." It took considerable effort to follow the heavily accented words.

"The Contessa, she wishes you for tea tomorrow, three thirty. Yessa, you come?"

"How very kind." Berdie didn't hesitate for a moment. "Please tell the Contessa thank you, *grazie*, and yes, I will come for tea."

"Ah, *bella*."

Berdie could hear the smile in the aide's voice.

"Tomorrow. *Pronto*."

"Oh, indeed, I'll be on time," Berdie assured.

Click.

Berdie looked at the receiver. "Apparently the conversation is over." She placed the receiver in the telephone cradle. "Hum, I wonder why the contessa's inviting me to her lodgings. Nonetheless, an invitation to spend time with the mystery benefactor, I couldn't have planned it better."

Berdie glanced at the hall clock. "Deary me." She took a deep breath and raced out the door for Kirkwood Green Bed and Breakfast.

It was a cheerful walk down the High Street. The fresh-washed air brought a sparkling scent to her nose. Shopkeepers cleaned and cleared their storefronts in the aftermath of the previous days' deluge. The light kiss of sunlight felt warm on the cheek.

Villette Horn, who wiped the exterior of the large Copper Kettle window, even managed a bright smile and a "Good morning."

Jamie Donovan stopped his work lorry dead in the middle of the road to tell Berdie that he had found Snowdrop playing with Fritz near the Gordon's home.

No surprise there.

Berdie decided it must have been the return of the sun lifting its royal head above the occasional clouds that brought a sense of well-being to the village. Not one person asked about the bones.

By the time Berdie reached the front step of Kirkwood Green Bed and Breakfast, she was ready for a hot cuppa.

When she rang the buzzer, she could see the figure of Cherry Lawler through the door's etched glass window.

Cherry advanced towards the door, a lovely smile decorating her pixie face.

Berdie admired the energy and work ethic of both Cherry and her husband, Jeff. It was a sizeable operation, this twelve-room inn. They took it over from Jeff's father just a year ago almost to the day they returned from their honeymoon.

Berdie became aware that someone from behind approached the step where she stood. She turned to see Patricia King. Yes, indeed, she was Aidan Kirkwood's own version of Pat the Postman. Athletically built, and very unlike the character of the children's books, she raced her route with great precision and very little conversation.

"Mrs. Elliott," she greeted, then thrust a stack of mail in Berdie's direction. "Going in? Give that to Cherry please."

Before Berdie could respond, the stack was in her hand, and she watched Pat the Postman hustle off in manic fashion to the next domicile. "You're welcome," she called after the woman.

The large door opened. "Mrs. Elliott, please come in." Cherry greeted her in denim jeans and a short buttoned cardigan, smart yet practical for the type of work a B and B required.

Berdie handed Cherry the clustered mail. "Special delivery," she chortled.

"Thanks." Cherry laughed and held the mail close to her body.

The hostess showed Berdie through the wallpapered hallway into a side room with large glass double doors. It served as a sitting room for guests. It was cozy with upholstered furnishings, an inglenook that stood pertly in a fireplace surround, and a coffee table laid for tea.

"Whatever happened to village postal service where the dear postman gave jovial greetings?" Berdie memorialized.

Cherry nodded. "Patricia can be curt. Certainly not like old Mr. Orson." She paused. "Oh please, sit down." Cherry waved Berdie towards a sofa then did a rapid shuffle of the multiple envelopes.

"Orson?" Berdie leaned back on the sofa.

"Mum and I lived in a tiny village near the sea." Cherry stilled the shuffling. "Orson was the postman. 'Good morning, Mrs. Gordon,' he'd say to my mum, very warmly, and he'd always have a sweetie for me. But then that was years ago." Cherry eyed the top envelope in her hand. "Now that's odd." She squinted.

"What's odd?" Berdie asked with interest.

"This letter's addressed to my grandfather, but it has our street number." Cherry took a closer look. "It's from the continent."

"Really? Wilkie's name and your number, from the continent?"

Cherry handed the letter to Berdie. Indeed, the return address looked to be German.

Berdie read aloud. "Doktor Herman Schultz, twenty-five Morgan Strasse, Heidelberg." Curiosity getting the better of her, Berdie lifted the thin airmail envelope up to the morning sunlight that flooded through the glass doors. She tried to scrutinize its contents.

Cherry spotted the backside of the envelope and emitted a quick gasp.

"What?"

"It's slightly open." Cherry looked at Berdie, chin down and eyebrows raised.

Berdie tried to adjust her 'vicar's wife hat. "This is a personal correspondence," she advised. And then the vicar's wife hat went askew. "Is there a chance he may have intended the letter for you?"

Cherry grasped the envelope from Berdie's hand and gingerly moved her finger along, lifting the flap of it ever so carefully. Then, with great concentration, she pulled out a single tri-fold sheet of office paper and unfurled it.

Berdie made every effort to stay glued to her seat. She tried desperately not to be overly eager.

"Oh, it's a bill," Cherry informed with a bit of disappointment. Then her eyes enlarged. Berdie held back the impulse to grab the paper and read it herself.

"A bill for thirty thousand pounds," Cherry all but shouted.

"Thirty thousand pounds?" Berdie lifted her well-kept brows.

"Hang about." Cherry ran her finger over the paper. "This is a confirmation of payment. It's a receipt. He's paid thirty thousand pounds." Cherry was agog.

Berdie calmly nodded while grasping the arm of

the sofa.

Cherry waved the paper in the air without caution. "Where did my grandfather get thirty thousand pounds?"

I only wish I had the answer to that question Cherry, that and several other questions that surround your grandfather. "Nest egg?"

Without warning, four very rapid rings of the door buzzer made Cherry jump and Berdie stand to her feet.

"Guests," quickly fled Cherry's lips like a child caught in the Easter sweeties. "No clean rooms." She tried to refold the letter, but her haste made it worse.

"I'll get the door."

"Oh, yes, please."

Berdie swooshed into the hallway. "I'll greet the guest, introduce myself, tell them their hostess will be with them shortly. Yes, that should be enough time for her to recover." Berdie opened the door.

When she did, she came up short. There on the step was the churlish man from the coach tour, the man who left without so much as an 'I'm away,' and who had caused Mathew Reese a great deal of consternation. The fellow, bags in hand, spoke the question Berdie thought to ask.

"What are you doing here?" He frowned and looked past Berdie in search of a familiar host. "Church taken to raising funds by bell-hopping luggage?"

"Cherry, your hostess," Berdie nearly scolded, "has her hands full at the moment." She eyed the man's two large leather bags. "And by the looks of it, so do you."

"I need my room."

"The coach tour's moved on."

"I'm well aware of that," the impatient man

barked as he bumped Berdie's shoulder in an attempt to move forward.

"Mr. Smith." Cherry was now behind Berdie. "I thought I recognized the voice. You've returned?"

"I *am* standing here," he retorted dryly. "I need my room."

"Yes, yes, please come in."

Berdie pursed her lips and moved aside. Mr. Smith handed one of his large bags to Cherry. *Well, I never.* Berdie restrained the words from departing her lips. True, petite Cherry was an innkeeper, but really.

Cherry bumped and scooted the heavy bag along the hallway. "Jeff," she called out, summoning her husband, then continued conversing with the returned guest. "It's good to see you back, Mr. Smith."

Berdie was not having it. *Mr. Smith my eye.* "You left so suddenly last you were here, Mr. Smith. Is that John Smith?" Her tone was stilted. "Mathew Reese tried desperately to ring you. I assume he was successful."

"Assume what you like," he spouted and followed Cherry down the hall to reception, a small wooden counter with a key rack behind.

"I'm looking for a seasonal let," the man directed towards Cherry. "I'll need a room until I find a suitable one."

"A seasonal let?" Berdie realized her volume was elevated.

The man tossed a furrowed glance at Berdie. "I'm looking to settle here in Aidan Kirkwood," he announced, "if it's any of your..."

Berdie reared her chin back and crossed her arms.

"If you care to know," Mr. Smith finished.

The door buzzer erupted with its startling blast

once again. Berdie turned to see a family of six wrestling with the door, trying to avoid the second of Mr. Smith's bags.

"Jeff!" Cherry trumpeted a second time.

Berdie leant herself to greet the family and brought them into the hallway.

Rapid steps made themselves known on the stairwell near reception. Jeff Lawler, a winsome lad and captain of the village football team, stood at the foot of the stairs. His well-kept goatee and short spiked brown hair enhanced his pleasant manner.

"Welcome, make yourselves comfortable in the sitting room if you like." He shot the words down the hallway to the lively family. "Hello Mrs. Elliott, Mr. Smith," he added in a rush.

With gusto to spare, he grabbed the large suitcase. "Room three is ready," he informed Cherry and sprang back up the stairs.

Berdie watched as the family helped themselves to the tea sitting on the coffee table in the sitting room.

"Isn't this delightful, Rodney?" the woman asked while pouring a cup.

Cherry leaned over the counter. "Mrs. Elliott, sorry. Can we postpone?"

Berdie could just make out the words over the noise of the rollicking children. She nodded. "Ring me." She found herself shouting above the sound of a crash she recognized as a dropped teacup.

Once outside, Berdie began her trek to the Butz home for the organizational meeting. Her apology to Cherry would have to come later. She strode across the green and onto the road that lead to the Butz home. She hardly noticed those around, her head was spinning so.

"Madness," she mumbled as she went. "Thirty thousand pounds." Did Wilkie truly have a nest egg? No, a retired groundskeeper doesn't have that kind of readies. Mr. Smith, whatever his real name, upping sticks? Just who is Mr. Smith? Why in heaven's name is he coming to live in Aidan Kirkwood? Well, if indeed, any word from his mouth can be trusted. "The whole of it, madness."

Berdie was in a stew when she arrived at the front drive of Ivy and Edsel's home. She looked down at the black tar of the paved drive. "Dark as lies and deception." Berdie frowned.

"Now whose face looks a wet weekend?" Lillie called to Berdie. The slender woman entered the opposite end of the drive with lively steps. "Well, Loren rang. We're getting things sorted. But by your frown I'd guess things didn't go well with Cherry."

Berdie sighed. "Cherry? Yes. Well, no. I mean, I really must meet with her away from her workplace."

Lillie now stood next to Berdie. With resignation, Berdie pulled her shoulders back, lifted her chin, and looked Lillie in the eye. "However, I can tell you one thing that's certainly not going well. Too many questions, questions stacked one upon another and not one decent answer. It's unnatural."

Lillie's eyes became enlivened.

Berdie continued her rabbiting, "There's too many oddities to be ignored. And it's all somehow to do with those disturbing bones."

"Yes," Lillie said enthusiastically. "I love it when you get on your high horse." She lowered her voice. "Will there be any kind of mischief?"

"What a silly question to ask a vicar's wife." Berdie smiled coyly, laying her finger aside her nose.

"I'm in," Lillie piped. She excitedly rubbed her hands together.

"There's just one little thing that could send the horse back to the stables," Berdie cautioned.

"Oh, come now. When have you not been able to bring Hugh round? He knows that your gift of setting things to rights is for the benefit of all."

"It takes something approaching an earthquake before Hugh gives in to my investigating, I mean really investigating. And I fear the very earth rumbles as we speak. Keep watch on the Richter scale." Berdie turned her attention to the opening front door of the Butz home where Lucy Butz paused then bounced along to stand by the small car in the drive.

"Hello," she called out and waved a wooden hockey stick in greeting towards Berdie and Lillie. Her long auburn hair was pulled back into a single plait, and she wore a red sport jersey with matching bottoms that showed off her maturing figure. "I'm number seven." She smiled.

"Hello Lucy," Berdie answered while Lillie sent a ready smile and wave. "I didn't know you played."

"Oh, I don't." She shook her head.

"I see," Berdie said resolutely.

Lillie leaned towards Berdie and whispered. "Is that supposed to make sense?"

"She's a teenage girl." Berdie spoke quietly. "Does anything have to make sense?"

"Hurry, Lila, we're going to be late." Lucy yelled loudly enough to make the curtains twitch across the road.

Lila Butz, one year Lucy's junior, timidly stepped from the doorway. She, too, wore a red sports jersey. It appeared just ever too small for her ample body.

Indeed, it looked as if her shoulders should pop through the fabric at any moment. Her matching shorts, however, were quite large, even room for an extra leg or two.

Lila's "Good Morning Mrs. Elliott, Miss Foxworth," was truly obligatory and barely audible. "I should step into the garden if I were you." She gave a weak smile and nudged her black rim glasses against her brow nearly tripping over her hockey stick.

Lucy grabbed Lila's stick and, along with her own, tossed them through the open window into the backseat of the car. The younger teen entered the car's passenger side.

Heeding Lila's advice, Lillie and Berdie stepped out of the drive into the garden.

"Does Lila not play as well?" Lillie questioned Lucy with an uncertain tone.

"I should say she does not." Lucy laughed and entered the driver's seat.

The car started, it lurched, charged in reverse down the drive catching the edge of the garden then stopped abruptly.

"My boyfriend's sister plays you see," Lucy shouted out the open window. "Two of her teammates are chucking it in, won't play, and the team will forfeit. So Lila and I are hasty replacements, benchers really. We'll make the full complement of the team you see."

"Very community spirited of you," Berdie verbally applauded.

"Not really," Lucy admitted. "I'm doing it for my boyfriend, and Lila's doing it because I've promised to change Dottie's nappies for the next six weeks."

With that, the car accelerated out into the street, paused momentarily, and rocketed forward.

"God's speed," Berdie called after the auto.

"I should think you mean that literally," Lillie quipped.

"Yes, well, after Nick and Clare's adolescence, surprisingly enough I still have kneecaps."

"Kneecaps?"

Berdie grinned. "I mean I nearly wore out the knobby old things praying for my offspring in their growing up years."

"Yes, well, growing up." Lillie sighed. "Lila and Lucy seem to do all right, really. Opposite ends of the stick, but both doing well."

"Indeed," Berdie agreed. "Siblings. Clare was always so intense and Nick so carefree." Something stirred in the back of her mind. "Yes."

Lillie moved towards the front door, Berdie close behind.

"Now Mathew Reese was always the good boy of the village when he was growing up," Lillie continued. "And Dave Exton attended St. Elizabeth's you know, but he only stayed one year. Got on better at the village school."

"Did the Darbyshire girls board for their schooling?"

"Yes. They went to St. Elizabeth's as well." Lillie paused. "Until their sixth form when Robin went to some posh school further afield. Colonel Preswood read her abilities and started grooming her for his protégé. Her first time back to Aidan Kirkwood, she had gone off small village ways altogether. Her brown hair was black, eyes dramatically blue, contacts of course, clothes exclusive."

Berdie knocked on the large door of the Butz home. "But she still made occasional visits to her family?"

"Oh, far more than occasional. She went off village life, not her family. No, she stayed ever so close to the family."

"I have a great curiosity about the Preswoods in general, another situation of more questions than answers."

"Yes, I recall something about elephants," Lillie teased.

The door opened widely and Ivy Butz, cheeks bulging at the ends of her grand smile, greeted with delight. "Hello. Hello."

A pink bow adorned her brown hair. It complemented the bright pink floral dress she wore. "Please come in Mrs. Elliott, Lillie. I'm still waiting for the others to arrive."

The women entered the hallway, and Ivy continued her chatting.

"I just got Dotty to sleep. We've so much business to attend to for the children's fête. I'm considering a decorated egg hunt in the front church garden, you know. Certainly not the back garden."

"Certainly not the back," Berdie reiterated.

"Lots of details to sort and even some knots to untie," Ivy blustered.

"Indeed," Berdie replied. She glanced at Lillie. "Details to sort, knots to untie."

Lillie flashed her impish grin. "I'm ready for the hunt."

7

Berdie loved this time of year, spring in its resplendence. The twilight of evening approached at a much slower pace. The cherished sunlight lingered a bit longer each day as if to enjoy the scent of spring florals. The meeting at Ivy's now far behind her, she stood in Timsley, here at the entrance of Le Petit Chaumier, which only added to the delight of dusky shadows and light breezes.

The immensely popular, prize-winning French restaurant was housed in what was once a stone washed garden cottage. The size of the structure, petit, and the fact it had a thatched roof, invited the romantic vision of a jolly chaumier, humming as he worked, grooming the thatch which kept warmth within and storms without.

Even though they had reservations, Berdie, Lillie, and Loren, joined other expectant diners on the front walk, while Hugh still circled the nearby car park for a coveted spot. The area buzzed with conversation as hungry humanity waited and happily sated patrons departed.

Berdie smelled of rose from her pampering soak she enjoyed earlier. She chose to wear her tailored celery green silk top. The sensuous feel of it against her skin delighted. Her very comfortable straight black skirt, she decided, complimented the top quite well. It struck just the right note between style and ease.

Lillie, on the other hand, looked luxurious in a black sheath with a white organdy shrug that absolutely teased. It exposed her slender arms and curved shoulders, a move Berdie recognized as a counter attack to the oversized tatty jumper of two days ago.

Loren stood close to Lillie. The allure of his smoky dark eyes and graying temples was given a boost by his darkest-of-blue suit.

Berdie took in how really handsome Lillie and Loren were as a couple. However, it appeared to be a tender truce that held them together at the moment, Loren a bit off his game and Lillie hardily entrenched in hers.

"Perhaps we should call out the local constabulary to search for my dear husband." Berdie created a light note to the evening air.

"Ah, yes, speaking of constabulary." Dr. Meredith moved his eyes in a quick sweep of the crowd. He lowered his voice. "We've made some headway on the ID of your garden bones."

"Indeed?" Berdie kept her voice subdued. "Go on then. Don't keep us on tenterhooks."

"It seems the victim, a lad approximately two and a half to three years of age, died about twenty-some years ago."

"You can tell that?" Lillie quizzed.

"Not especially easily, but yes. He was well nourished with no apparent signs of battering."

"But you said there were indications of trauma," Berdie recalled.

"Yes." The doctor once again glanced about the crowd. "The injuries are more consistent with a sudden impact."

"Like an auto accident?"

"Perhaps, but we believe the child may have had a severe fall and from a fairly significant height, died on impact."

"Poor tot," Lillie murmured almost under her breath.

"So, from a tree, a balcony, or a landing, down a stairwell." Berdie reasoned.

"Quite possibly." The pathologist nodded. "Most likely a firm surfaced interior, not out of doors."

"That's a very broad sketch." Berdie was keen to know if there could be something more.

"We've one hopeful detail that could be central for the investigation."

Berdie's ears stood at attention.

"Not much mind you." The doctor looked Berdie in the eye. "This information is given in confidence that it will be used well."

"Indeed." She knew the truth of what he was saying. "In the right hands, not much can become a great deal, Loren."

Dr. Meredith became pensive. "We found a shard of very distinctive glass lodged at the base of the skull. Very rare glass and worth a small fortune when intact. It's opalescent. Produced in Venice during the seventeen hundreds."

"But you just said the death occurred twenty years ago," Lillie interjected. "How does eighteenth century Venetian glass fit with a child that died in the eighties? And in English soil at that."

"Perhaps you should ask Berdie that question," the doctor recommended. He lifted his dark brows.

"Well?" Lillie directed towards Berdie.

"One of the first lines of inquiry: where would you

find antiquated, expensive, Venetian glass in England?"

"A museum, in my thinking." Lillie shrugged.

"Or a collector of that design." The doctor dipped his chin.

"Right. Museum is too public for a clandestine cover up. But now, collectors. Yes. And it's highly unlikely that a worker at the Super Sudsy Launderette would collect costly, rare glass," Berdie twittered with a note of irony.

"So a rich glass collector with a landing," Lillie summed up. "Well, that narrows it down to only one third of the population of England as suspects, I should think."

"Well done, Lillie," Berdie congratulated. "It's taken only two minutes to eliminate two thirds of the populace."

The doctor laughed. "That's certainly glass-half-full thinking."

"The point is, it's a place to start, and our little village is ground zero." Berdie smiled. She had a distant thought that came tumbling forward. "In fact..."

Berdie was interrupted by a rush of laughter. "Imagine seeing you here."

A high-spirited Charles Swindon-Pierce deposited himself next to Berdie. "Hello, all." He grinned, Robin Darbyshire at his side. Both were in trendy dress. "Where's the collar then?"

"If you mean my husband," Berdie worked at being agreeable, "he's due to arrive any moment."

"I see," the man responded.

"Lovely evening, isn't it?" Robin smiled.

Lillie was quick to introduce Dr. Meredith.

Charles tipped his head politely, but Robin seemed completely uninterested.

"Just arriving?" Charles asked. And before any could respond, he went on, "Let me recommend the *Boeuf Fumé au Truffes*, a cut of superb beef, laden with fresh and," he raised an index finger, "they're truly fresh mind you, aromatic shaved truffles. Absolutely a five-star dish."

And a five star price I shouldn't wonder. Berdie made a step back as the animated Charles, so wildly exuberant, just missed giving her a bump. It was very unlike the man she met at Bampkingswith Hall. And his words were also bumping—into one another, that is.

"Come Charles," Robin said warmly. "You're boring them."

"Not at all." Dr. Meredith grinned.

"Ah, my husband approaches." Berdie wanted the couple to notice how handsome and stately the "collar" was.

"Vicar," Mr. Swindon-Pierce acknowledged. "I'm just making recommends you know." The young man swirled into an accolade of the featured dessert. "*Chocolate du la Fleur*," he raved. "Truffles, not the earthen ones," he said shaking his well-groomed head, "no, these are fine chocolates infused with *eau d'orange* blossom. Absolutely brilliant, weren't they Robbie?"

"Charlie," Robin pleaded. "Yes, absolutely brilliant." She giggled. "Now let them go have their dinner." She gave Hugh a tip of the chin, slipped her arm around Charles' elbow, and began a forward motion. "Please excuse us," she offered as a fare-thee-well.

"Robbie never finishes her food." The young man

continued pontificating even when taking steps. "But she ate all her *Chocolate du la Fleur*." He called over his shoulder, "And they're served with as much champagne as you wish."

"Of which I'd say his wishes were fully granted." Hugh had a gracious way of expressing things.

"That certainly explains his affable behavior." Berdie looked after the couple who hailed a taxi.

"Affable and then some." Lillie did not seem remotely amused.

"Thank you for the suggestions," Loren called out to the man as a postscript then turned to Hugh. "He's right, you know. The chef has been offering more truffle dishes, 'earthen ones that is,'" he parodied. "The beef with shaved truffles is a gourmand delight. I had it just last night."

"Just last night?" Lillie tipped her head. "But you didn't say."

The doctor looked like a child who's just gotten caught eating an Easter bun before mealtime. "Didn't I?"

"Dare I ask with whom?" Lillie had a hard edge in her question.

"Lillie," The doctor spoke softly and took her hand, but she appeared unaffected. "Some from work."

"Some from work." Lillie's hard edge became sharp. "Could that some include the free-as-a-bird Roz?"

"Lillie, please. It was a late night reprieve, a bit of a lark, after being at it all day."

"Oh, I can imagine." Lillie thrust the words like bullets.

"Please, let's enjoy our evening." Loren squeezed her hand.

Berdie hooked Hugh's elbow. "I'm parched, love." She stretched the truth. "Perhaps we can go get Pimm's in the lounge." She looked knowingly at Hugh, that discreet We-Should-Leave-Momentarily look.

"Oh, indeed." Hugh nodded. "We can meet you at the dinner table." He cautiously looked to Loren and then Lillie.

A barely audible vibrating bzzz of a mobile phone cut into the conversation. It may as well have been the ear-piercing spring call of courting grouse.

Berdie's shoulders went taut.

Hugh raised his left eyebrow.

Lillie churned and Loren took a deep inhale.

Hugh stuck his hand into his trouser pocket feeling for his mobile phone.

"Not mine," he said with relief. Berdie then realized that Hugh's respite was probably Loren's demise.

"No." Lillie squeezed the single word out of her tightened lips.

Loren took another deep breath then pulled the mobile from his inside pocket.

"Meredith," he answered.

Lillie pulled her hand from his grasp so abruptly it made her dark curls dance.

Dr. Meredith's jaw tightened. "Now?"

Lillie lifted her chin and crossed her arms.

Berdie, Hugh in tow, took a step towards the restaurant door, but Lillie caught Berdie's arm. "Stay," Lillie mouthed without speaking.

Dr. Meredith spoke into the mobile. "Did you try to get Harry, Roz?"

"Even worse." Lillie's eyes narrowed. "Did she know we were having dinner together, here, this evening?" Lillie's volume was not polite.

Loren raised his palm, indicating a need for Lillie to quiet. He muted his voice, but every word was clearly overheard, "Give me forty minutes."

Judging by Lillie's stiff posture, Berdie had the sense the worst was yet to come. Mind you, the doctor clearly had his duty, but was Roz really his duty? Still, Berdie felt compelled to reason with her friend.

"Lillie, try not to overreact," Berdie said discreetly. Her comment was met with not even an ounce of acknowledgement.

"Yes, all right, OK," the pathologist sounded frayed. "Thirty minutes, then." Loren snapped the mobile back into his pocket. "Lillie…"

"Thirty minutes." Lillie had a face like thunder, and her voice matched it. "You have the nerve to offer me, us, thirty minutes of your precious time."

Several people in the crowd had stopped chatting and were now staring at what was unfolding.

"Well, let me tell you how many precious moments I have to give you this evening." Lillie blazed. "None."

She turned on her heel and began a rapid push down the walk. With great drama, she lifted her hand and moved to the road's edge. "Taxi," she bellowed, her face gone scarlet.

"Lillie, it's the demands of my job," Loren appealed.

"Of your job. Demands of a designing woman you mean."

By now, all eyes were on the lovely Lillie turned raging storm. She stood in the street flaying her arms. "Taxi," she shouted again.

"Can't you do something?" the perplexed and

desperate Loren asked Hugh.

Hugh balked. "Sorry mate, it's between you and her." He said it with some sympathy.

Loren looked to Berdie.

"I take Hugh's part."

A taxi screeched to a halt, and Lillie clamored inside. Like a startled April hare, the vehicle hastily retreated down the road.

Loren put his hands on his head and drew them to the back of his neck. He released a heavy sigh.

Murmurs swelled through the awaiting diners. A young woman who had observed the entire episode approached Loren.

"Swine," she breathed and huffed off.

Loren looked startled. He became stunningly aware of the crowd who gazed at him then turned away. His bewildered eyes fell upon Hugh and Berdie.

"Well," was all he could muster.

"Yes, well," Hugh restated.

"I'm so sorry. Perhaps I should push off." The doctor's voice sounded like a Sunday balloon that's lost all its air. "Roz is waiting for me at the lab."

"Yes," Hugh agreed. "No need to hang about on our account."

"Loren, if I may." Berdie heard the swirling words inside exit her mouth. "I should be very careful. Your work, and loyalty duly noted, is one thing. But, an attractive female who certainly gives off the sense that she's willing to, well frankly, put it about a bit, is quite another matter."

"Berdie!" Hugh scolded. Face flushed, he turned his full attention to Loren. "When you feel up to it, ring me. We can meet for coffee."

Loren smiled weakly. "Right." He nodded. "I

should think I'll need that."

Berdie could see Loren work at standing tall. She had never known him to lose his moorings as he apparently had now, at least momentarily.

"Cheers, then." He nodded again.

"Cheers," Berdie and Hugh said simultaneously.

Loren pulled car keys from his suit pocket and began a lonely trek to the car park.

"God go with you," Hugh offered.

And with us all, Berdie thought. "Hugh, did we have such fuss and speculations when we were going out?"

"You don't remember?"

"Oh, dear." Berdie was circumspect. Then a distant memory of Hugh's first days in the military popped into her present psyche. Ah, yes, Hugh's dutiful and gorgeous assistant. "Lieutenant Julia Goodwin."

"Right in one."

"Yes, well we managed our way through that one, didn't we?"

"Quite well, as I recall."

He glanced about, looking past the voyeuristic crowd. He inhaled the freshness of the spring dusk. Berdie could see by Hugh's expression that he was taking in a new opportunity to find goodness and all it had to offer. "You know, I believe I fancy a good sausage and mash." He smiled his enigmatic smile that never ceased to win Berdie's heart.

"I've never been fond of truffles, really." Berdie partook in the general sentiment. "The earthen ones that is. Umm, but I do love the chocolate ones."

She and Hugh enjoyed an easy laugh. He put his arm around her shoulder.

"What say we grab a quiet snug at the Pork and Barrel? And a three layer double chocolate cake for afters."

"I've always thought the Pork and Barrel a fine eating establishment," Berdie quipped.

"To the off then."

Arm in arm, Berdie and Hugh made their way out of the crowd towards the bottom of the road.

"Did I say?" Berdie asked. "I'm invited to tea with the contessa tomorrow."

"Indeed. I was invited as well, but I have a meeting with Reverend Wainwright in Mistcome Green." Hugh didn't look very disappointed. "You must tell me all about our mystery benefactor."

A large pig, carved into a wooden half-barrel sign, came into view. It confirmed the presence of the Pork and Barrel.

Berdie and Hugh walked with an easy rhythm, anticipating their comely but appreciated evening meal. Actually, Berdie coveted this time alone with her life partner, and now it was just the two of them in the April dusk. Berdie squeezed Hugh's arm.

"I love spring evenings," she breathed.

Hugh placed a light kiss on Berdie's cheek. "And it is a fine evening."

❧❧

A steady drizzle of rain wetted the windscreen of Berdie's car as she turned into the short drive of Bampkingswith Lodge, the temporary home of Contessa Santolio. The thoroughly wet two-story house was modest compared to its great cousin that sat at the top of the road. Still, the lodge looked a fit guardian, keeping watch over the entry to the spreading grounds of the Preswood estate.

Lillie was standing at the bottom of the front garden walk, umbrella in hand, just where she said she would be waiting for Berdie to arrive. "Good," Berdie said aloud.

After the telephone conversation she had with Lillie this morning, she wasn't at all sure her friend would be keen to socialize. Following last evening's events, Lillie confessed she had gone straight home, burrowed under multiple quilts where she swilled mugs of Horlicks, watched a Jane Austen DVD, and refused to answer calls. Even today, she was still reeling. Though apologetic for the dramatic departure, her simply put, "I don't want to talk about him, or her, or any of it," squelched any conversation Berdie had hoped to have on the matter.

"Berdie." Lillie gave Berdie a hug watching carefully that umbrellas did not collide.

"Better spirits, then?" Berdie asked wryly.

Lillie became enlivened. "You know I've decided this could be a great deal of fun, discovering who this contessa is, what she's about."

"Indeed." Berdie noticed the ravishing not-seen-before scarf that graced Lillie's neck. "That's new, and it suits you."

"He sent it." Lillie sniffed as if unaffected. "A parcel from White Window Box Gifts and Garden Shop, and three dozen red roses arrived this afternoon." Lillie lifted her chin. "Typical. Flowers and gifts are supposed to put everything right. A reconciliation it is not, but it is lovely. She ran her fingers across the scarf. "And the roses do fragrance my home remarkably."

"It's a step in a forward direction," Berdie quickly pointed out with an eye to getting on. "Now, onward to our discovery then."

They walked to the entrance where Berdie rang the door chime. Almost instantly, a young woman was at the doorway.

"Please come," she invited warmly. She stopped momentarily and drew close. "If you excuse," the woman whispered. "The Contessa invites six people to tea. You are the only ones who come." Her demonstrative brown eyes pleaded. "Contessa Santolio ees a good woman."

Berdie sensed the tender heart of a caring person, modest and loyal. "Yes." She nodded.

The woman stood aside so Berdie and Lillie could enter the quaint hall laid with earth-colored natural floor tiles. The walls were painted a handsome russet shade graced with paintings of the hunt. And the furnishings were fit for a country home.

The greeter took Berdie and Lillie's umbrellas. She deposited the wet implements in an equine-shaped ceramic stand designed for that purpose.

The greeter's coal black hair was pulled back in a French roll. She wore a bright yellow sundress that, Berdie decided, quite matched the sunny attitude of this woman. Her intense olive tone skin contrasted beautifully.

"The contessa ees een the drawing room," she announced with a sense of decorum.

With gracious movement, she guided Berdie and Lillie the few steps needed to enter the room where the contessa stood near an antique sideboard.

"Mrs. Elliott, Meess Foxworth, thees ees Contessa Carlotta Francesca Santolio."

Berdie wasn't sure if she should curtsy or applaud after that royal introduction. Instead, she simply smiled. "Thank you for inviting us to tea, Contessa."

"Yes," Lillie added.

"I'm so glad you could come," The contessa spoke with only the slightest of Italian accents.

Her fashionable dark hair just touched the shoulders of her silk print dress that was bright with the colors of a Mediterranean village. The rose of her cheeks plus shimmering lips brought drama to the light tan skin that appeared casually kissed by the sun. "And you've met my assistant, Ortensia."

The yellow clad aide offered a swift tip of the head.

"Please, sit down." The contessa waved her hand towards the leather couch where Berdie and Lillie seated themselves.

"*Ortensia, porti gli antipasti per favore,*" the contessa gently directed.

Ortensia left the room.

Elegantly, Contessa Carlotta positioned herself in the leather chair opposite the couch.

Though the meeting was formal, Berdie didn't have an overwhelming sense of pretense from the woman. In fact, the aristocrat seemed fairly grounded. But a nagging uneasiness also attended the meeting.

"It's gracious of you, Contessa, to invite us to tea. Are you enjoying Aidan Kirkwood?" Berdie asked politely.

"It is a respite." The contessa turned her face to a nearby window that overlooked the garden road. Even in grey light the contessa's striking eyes shone lightest of liquid green. This was not unusual for an Italian, especially if their roots were Northern Italy.

"Italy is lovely as well." Berdie worked at establishing some kind of conversation.

The contessa turned her face back to her guests. "My husband and I lived in Milan." The lovely woman paused. "Count Santolio died eighteen months ago. He was a wonderful man." Her voice held a solemn note.

"Oh, I'm sure he was. I am sorry," Berdie consoled, "I wasn't aware."

"No. Nor I," Lillie added. "So, have you been on a tour then?"

"Tour?"

"What I mean is," Lillie's verbal pace slowed some, "when a friend of mine lost her husband, she went abroad, just after, to ease her grief."

"If you are asking why I am in Aidan Kirkwood, no, I am not touring."

Lillie rubbed her hand on the arm of the couch. "I see."

The contessa arose and stood by the window. She clasped her hands together. "Just after my husband received word of his critical health diagnosis, we came to England. It was for business, but we prolonged our stay. It was a holiday, a momentary reprieve from his demanding work. We spent a quiet day in your village: unattended, peaceful. It was a gift."

Ortensia entered the room with a tray of chocolate truffles. The contessa nodded. The aide offered the silver tray of delights, along with gold-colored linen napkins, to Berdie and Lillie.

"Thank you," they said almost in unison.

When Ortensia offered the tray to the hostess, she waved it away.

Berdie bit into the truffle and nearly swooned. The rich chocolate was liquid silk that clung to the tongue and slid down the throat, after which an edge of orange sweetly tingled in the mouth.

"These truffles are very good," Lillie gushed.

The contessa returned to her seat. She smiled. "I'm happy you like them. It is a special order from a French restaurant in Timsley."

"I see." Lillie showed somewhat less enthusiasm.

"*Chocolate du la Fleur*," Berdie remembered from Charles Swindon-Pierce carrying on. "No wonder Robin ate every bit."

"I'll send some home with you." The host spoke to Ortensia in Italian and the aide left the room. The contessa appeared delighted that her guests were enjoying themselves.

"Very generous, thank you." Berdie wiped a smudge of chocolate from her lip. She laid the napkin in her lap. "Contessa, I'm pleased that Aidan Kirkwood is a pleasant memory for you. How did you come to be a patron for our church garden, if I may ask?"

The door chime sounded. Oh, bother, who could that be? Berdie wondered. She caught a flash of yellow sundress through the sitting room door. Loyal Ortensia was about her duties.

"Ah, the church garden. Yes, a question I expected from the vicar's wife. It is very simple," the host began.

Berdie could hear the familiar voice of Pat the Postman, curt and efficient, making an attempt to discuss something with Ortensia in the hall. A bang of the door announced Patricia's departure.

Ortensia entered the sitting room holding a small parcel.

Carlotta Santolio gave a hard stare to her aide. "Yes, Ortensia."

"Thees come for you," she stumbled in English. *"Importante, molto importante."*

Berdie could just see the large red words *open immediately* stamped on the box.

"Excuse me." The host redirected her gaze. "Yes, open it, Ortensia. *Aperto.*"

Adeptly, Ortensia worked her fingers to open the parcel. She unsecured the top and removed a piece of white tissue.

All three women now watched every nuance of the aide for a clue concerning what she was discovering.

Ortensia furrowed her brow. She brought the box closer to her face. Her eyes became slits then widened with intensity. Attended by a horrified gasp, Ortensia threw the box to the floor. A string of Italian words even Berdie could recognize as expletives gushed from the woman's lips.

Startled, Lillie dropped her half-eaten truffle on her lap.

"Ortensia?" The Contessa abruptly stood.

That's when Berdie saw it, there in the box, an eerie dark object against the white tissue.

In a flash, spindly appendages began to awaken and move. Berdie blinked, working to comprehend what she was watching.

The creature erected itself on its coarse legs and instituted a spine-chilling sway, as if presenting itself in utter domination. The dance of death. The great, terrifying spider, in one electric movement, leaped from the box and fastened itself onto Ortensia's leg.

The woman shrieked. She shook her leg with such intensity Berdie thought it would dislocate. But the creature couldn't be dislodged.

The contessa recoiled in horror. "Holy Author of Peace," she entreated.

Lillie repositioned herself to stand on the couch, alternating fretful yelps with gasps of repulsion.

Instinctively, Berdie stood and gathered herself. She vowed the creature would not prevail. Umbrella! She determinedly dashed into the hallway and pulled her umbrella from the stand with such force, the ceramic rack fell to the floor shattering into a hundred pieces.

Berdie approached the aide with haste. "Watch out Ortensia," Berdie screamed above the bedlam. "Dear Lord," she invoked the Almighty. Putting all her weight into it, Berdie used the pointed end of the umbrella, and in one precise stab, sent the ghastly spider tumbling onto the floor where it lay stunned. The blood-red mark on Ortensia's leg was decidedly visible.

Ortensia screamed, tears plummeted down her face, and profuse perspiration was already raising the flag that something horrific sent it's shockwaves through the servant's body. She escaped into the hallway.

"Lillie, get your mobile, go to the kitchen, and call nine, nine, nine," Berdie commanded while she warily inched her way towards the still spider. "Get a jar, a bowl and bring it promptly."

Lillie leapt off the couch and moved like a frightened gazelle.

"Contessa, carefully, get Ortensia to lay down on the couch, now!"

Berdie was close enough to the arachnid now to see it beginning to rouse. "Stand clear," she yelled. She knew the blow must be ferocious. Berdie gripped the umbrella, engaged every muscle, every ounce of stamina within her and sprang the implement forcefully upon the creature. Once, twice, and on the third strike, the umbrella busted apart. Berdie judiciously lifted the debunked umbrella to find the corpse of the offender. She released a long, heavy sigh then turned her attention to Carlotta Santolio and her aide.

The contessa had just settled the wailing Ortensia on the couch.

"Contessa," Berdie prompted, "please do your best to calm her. The spider's dead."

The royal put her hand on the shoulder of her loyal helper and spoke Italian words in a soothing tone. And though Ortensia's panic began to appease, her tears were sincere. In between sobs, Ortensia verbalized something to the contessa.

"She's complaining of pain," the contessa reported. "Her foot is trembling."

Berdie observed the red spot that now sat atop a growing red mound. "Poison, deadly poison." Berdie quietly swallowed the words.

Lillie reentered the room holding a large empty bowl. Berdie grabbed it and placed it over the dead perpetrator. "You made the call?"

"Yes, and I called Dr. Honeywell, too."

"Good going." Berdie moved closer to her friend and whispered. "Lillie, I want you to think Girl Guides. Remember the emergency aid training? How do we treat a poisonous bite?"

"Poison!" Lillie gulped. "Yes, poisonous bite. Clean the wound with soap and water. Um." She squeezed her eyes shut. "Place a cool cloth on the bite." Her eyes popped open again. "Elevate and apply a tourniquet above the lesion."

"A tourniquet, what can we use as a tourniquet?" Berdie eyed Lillie's new scarf.

"Of course." Lillie responded in an instant. She untied the beautiful fabric that hung about her neck. "This should do for now."

Berdie spun on her heel. "Contessa, please fetch a clean towel and soap from the bath." She spun back around. "Lillie…" Before the words left Berdie's mouth, she realized Lillie was already at Ortensia's side, tying the scarf on the woman's leg.

The contessa moved next to Berdie. Her eyes welled with liquid. "Please," she pleaded. Her voice was weak. "Ortensia is not just my aide. She is my only true friend."

Berdie took the woman's hand. "We're doing everything we can. Pray, Contessa, pray with all your heart."

The noble shook her head. "Yes." She sniffed, a tear slipping down her cheek.

"Now, get that towel and soap."

The woman tipped her head in response to Berdie's command and set to on her assignment.

The roar of an approaching vehicle announced the arrival of Dr. Honeywell.

Berdie suddenly found herself in need of fresh air. She moved to the front door, trying to avoid the shards across the floor, and mustered just enough strength to open it. The coolness of the life-giving rain invited her to release the great weight of the moment. "Great God of mercy," she breathed, "please spare Ortensia."

8

"Here, my dear lady." Hugh handed Berdie a rosy polka-dot teacup full of steaming Tips with a splash of milk and one sugar, just the way she liked it.

The master bedroom of Oak Leaf Cottage felt a haven as Berdie nestled into her Queen Anne chair.

"Oh, thanks, love." She sighed and took a sip of the hot liquid. She felt the warmth of it renew her sense of well-being.

Constable Albert Goodnight's lengthy attempt to inspect the lodge following the spider incident was done with great inaccuracy. His questioning of Berdie and Lillie was far too brief and didn't include anything truly key to the investigative process. It frustrated Berdie profoundly.

Still, here she sat, safe as houses and sipping tea with her husband. And for that, she was truly grateful. She let the aroma of it tickle her nose as she took another relished sip of hot brew.

"I'm not quite sure if I should applaud your courage or chide your foolhardy bravado." Hugh's voice was gentle yet firm. "But, by all accounts, your response may have saved lives." He paused then smiled. "Well done my amazing wife." He placed a sweet peck on her forehead.

Berdie couldn't hide her appreciation for Hugh's support. A broad smile played across her lips.

"How is Ortensia? Have you heard?" Berdie knew

the woman was rushed to hospital with Carlotta Santolio at her side.

"Still critical I'm afraid. The doctor said she'd probably be dead if not for your quick action."

"By God's grace and Lillie's rapid treatment. I just did in the perp." Berdie grinned.

Hugh sat on the couch near the chair and leaned forward, elbows on his knees, and clasped his hands together. His left eyebrow elevated, which alerted Berdie to the fact that conversation to come could be a bit touchy.

"Tell me honestly, Berdie, what do you think about the whole contessa-spider affair?"

Berdie looked her husband straight in the eye. "I think someone wants the contessa gone. There's not an ounce of doubt in my mind. That venomous creature was intended for her, not her assistant."

Hugh shook his head. "Do you think it was meant just to scare, or to actually kill?"

Berdie shrugged. "A person lies perilously ill in hospital."

Hugh went on. "I know the incident's only hours old, but have you thought about whom may…?"

Berdie interrupted and was resolute. "Who might want Mrs. Santolio out of the way? As you say, early days yet." Berdie took a deep inhale. "I know her husband died not long ago, I should think she's come into money."

"Ah, family who stand to inherit? Greed at its worst," Hugh reasoned.

"Possibly." Berdie took another deliberate sip of tea.

Hugh tipped his head. "You don't sound convinced."

Berdie knew what she was about to say had most probably already danced through her husband's mind and it needed to be out there.

"The postmark on the package was London, not Italy where family should reside. Six guests were invited to tea, only Lillie and I accepted. Now, what does that tell you?"

"I was one of the six. People are busy."

"Oh come, Hugh. Apart from you, there's been a wind of ill-will towards her since the woman arrived. People have expressed dismay, even outrage. She did, after all, uncover the bones. Who's to say? Could the person who buried them there have been at the sod turning?

Hugh leaned back in the chair and folded his arms. "OK, Miss Marple, who in Aidan Kirkwood wants to do in the contessa?"

"Now, Hugh." Berdie put her cup down. "I'm an investigator not a prophetic seer. You know I can't answer that question right now, but there are possibilities about. They would be, at this point, speculation."

"I don't want speculation, I want truth."

"As do I," Berdie added and blew ever so slightly across the teacup, eyes resolutely on Hugh.

He sounded as if his military intelligence background was raising its head. Still, it was certainly party to his responsibilities as vicar of this parish to get to the bottom of things.

Berdie struck while the iron was hot. "Now, if I were given your permission to pursue a proper investigation, be it in an attitude of stealth, I should hope I could jolly well give you the answer." Berdie felt a slight flutter of anticipation.

"I knew that's what you would say." Hugh was pensive. He stood, went to the fireplace, grabbed the poker, and placed it in the empty hearth. "There's a stipulation," he announced.

Berdie finished his sentence. "I shan't let it interfere with my church duties, and I shall be extremely careful. We've been here before, Hugh."

"Yes, but there's more. I don't want you to carry out your own work so much as to aid Goodnight's investigation."

Berdie's flutter turned into a furious spin. "What?" Her voice was intense and full of fire.

"Tomorrow, you go to Goodnight and offer your services. If he says no, it's off."

"Hugh, the only aid Goodnight wants from me is to clean his rugs."

"If he says no, it's off," Hugh reiterated and banged the poker in the hearth.

Berdie's spin now became desperately close to despair. Hugh's demand could put an end to even subtle investigating on her part. What were the chances Goodnight would allow her to do more than fetch his brew?

∂∞∾

All through the next morning's walk to Goodnight's home, Berdie hardly noticed the people about. Nor did she relish the aroma of freshly brewed coffee along with an almost-taste of morning sausages emanating from the Upland Arms. She didn't even gaze at the overcast sky that allowed only occasional peeks of sunlight. Her energies were spent on considering all the ploys she could marshal to get

Goodnight to accept her, and her gift to sniff out the truth, into his proceedings. Nothing seemed plausible.

When she arrived at the constable's row home, she stood before it with little hope. "Well, Lord, I'm here," was the only offering she made, and that in a disheartened voice.

Harriet Goodnight answered the door holding an overflowing laundry basket. She smelled of fresh bacon and offered little greeting.

"He's got someone with him, but I reckon you can join the party," she squalled.

Once inside the home, Mrs. Goodnight's rapid knock on the door of the front bedroom that served as the constable's office was followed by the bang of the door flung open against the inside wall. It was topped off with Harriet's shrill, "There's another one come."

"Harriet," the constable shouted from behind his desk, "if I've told you once, I've told you a hundred times."

Berdie was thus launched into Albert Goodnight's morning.

The policeman swamped the desk so that it looked he might not be able to arise except with great difficulty. The chintz curtains on the window behind him reminded that this was hardly a proper police station, and a half eaten toast with strawberry jam sat within his arms' reach. Still, his too-small uniform gave him a certain sense of crude authority.

The man seated in a dilapidated chair opposite Goodnight's desk turned to espy the newcomer.

"Well, blow me over. Berdie Elliott, is that you?"

"Chief Inspector Kent." Berdie beamed. "What an unexpected pleasure."

Goodnight furrowed his thick brows. "You know

the vicar's wife?" he grumbled.

Chief Inspector Jasper Kent paid the constable no mind. He stood and offered his chair to Berdie. Clad in his worn brown overcoat, she wondered if he even bothered to remove it when bathing. In all the years they had been part of the same professional circle, she'd never seen him without it.

"Last I saw you was that traveler's case in Mistcome Green."

"And the perp was brought to justice," Berdie added and sat in the chair.

Albert Goodnight observed the conversation. An ugly sneer stole across his face. He stabbed his finger in the inspector's direction. "You religious then?"

"I understand you had a spot of bother, a rammed car I believe." The Chief Inspector tipped his head and continued his conversation with Berdie, still ignoring the constable.

"Now when has something like an attempted bump off ever made me less keen to follow the scent?"

Kent grinned. "That's my Berdie. Nothing stands in the way of bringing the bad guys to justice."

Goodnight ran a finger through his bushy mustache, and then cleared his throat, loudly. "We done with the love fest?"

Berdie and the Scotland Yard inspector turned their eyes to the constable.

"Good fortune this." Jasper Kent put his hand on the back of Berdie's chair. "You've got a deft hand in your court, Albert. No gutter press here. Real integrity, investigative prowess. Indeed, you've got a real asset." He nodded in Berdie's direction.

"I've got what?" The constable spit the words out like so much over-ripe cheese. "Inspector Kent and me were about our business," he protested in Berdie's direction.

"Oh, yes, indeed," the inspector agreed. "Yes, Berdie, the constable and I were just discussing the cold case, the church bones." Inspector Kent leaned his head close to Berdie. "We don't cater to cold cases, but this one"—he discreetly nodded in Goodnight's direction—"raised such a fuss."

"What you going on about?" Goodnight strained forward, tapping his finger on the desktop.

The inspector stood tall. "I'm telling Mrs. Elliott that we've sent a forensic anthropologist to assist you in the bones case."

Goodnight crossed his arms. "Any of her business?"

Berdie smiled at Goodnight. "Oh yes, Dr. Roz Chase. Yes I've met her. Quite capable. She'll be invaluable no doubt."

Goodnight ran his tongue across his top teeth making a kind of sizzle sound in the process, face going pink. "Indeed."

Berdie turned to Kent and went on. "The church bones, Inspector, is that why you're here?"

"In part. I'm actually looking into the contessa Santolio affair. Very odd. We had a similar situation in London a few years back. Wandering Brazilian spider, deadly as they come, arrives by post, bang goes the unfortunate gift-opener. Never solved. Albert tells me you were there with the contessa when she got her big surprise."

Goodnight verbally pounced like a fox on a hare. "If there's trouble about, this one"—he jabbed his finger towards Berdie—"comes part and parcel with it."

"Doesn't she though?" Jasper Kent nodded. "Yes, that's why I insist she be a part of the investigation."

Goodnight gazed in stunned silence.

"As you've requested, top brass have been called in. Still, it's your patch Goodnight, your investigation. But consultation with Mrs. Elliott is a must. She's not police, but she's a bloodhound in tracking down the truth."

Berdie feared the bulging veins on Goodnight's neck might bust.

The constable picked up the nearby toast and jam. He scrunched it so tightly in his hand that his fist went white. Strawberry jam oozed through his fingers. He pushed away from the desk and stood with such force, the chair he sat in knocked against the window behind. "Is that all?" he asked Chief Inspector Jasper Kent.

"I believe so, Albert."

Constable Goodnight nodded towards the door. "Don't let me keep you."

"Yes, well, I appreciate your time. Indeed, must push on," Jasper said.

"Yes," Berdie added. "Thank you, Albert."

With that, Berdie and the Scotland Yard inspector exited Goodnight's room and dashed from his humble dwelling.

"Inspector Kent," Berdie called after the departing investigator.

The gentleman opened the door of an awaiting car, a driver in attendance.

"Thank you, you're a miracle answer to prayer, you know."

Jasper Kent smiled. "Tell my wife that. And Berdie, come to the big smoke. Ring up Billy Beaton in records if you want to know about that London spider case. Nothing official, mind you."

Berdie laid her finger aside her nose. "Nothing official," she repeated.

The inspector winked. He entered the car, closed the door, and took off like a London cabby.

"The big smoke," Berdie repeated. "Nothing like London in the spring. The scent of oily streets and diesel fumes mixes quite delightfully with investigating foul play." Berdie felt a great excitement run through her body. "Billy Beaton will be getting a call within the hour."

☙❧

"I feel like a spy." Lillie tittled like an over-excited school girl.

"Nothing really spy about it," Berdie corrected. "It's simply an alfresco repast to meet a friend I called yesterday. We'll be better informed for solving crime, all above board."

Glancing about Trafalgar Square, Berdie was glad the morning train ride was behind her and Lillie. The Square was its usual afternoon self. The area was encumbered with gawking tourists holding brochures, adoring Nelson's column, and dipping fingers in the huge fountains. They were joined by local residents relishing an out of doors lunch from busy city offices, and a few disenfranchised youth who were sprinkled about the crowd as well. Cars, lorries, buses, both single and double-deckers, whizzed about on the streets surrounding the massive pedestrian area.

"What time is he supposed to be here?" Lillie asked Berdie, glancing at her watch.

"Half past one, as I've told you ten times already,

Lillie. It's gone only five minutes past, he'll arrive soon."

Lillie shifted her seated weight and scrunched her nose. "This bench is hard on the bum, you know."

"More of a problem for you than I." Berdie half grinned. "One of the few times that possessing a natural rear cushion is a plus. Stand if you wish."

She glanced about while Lillie stood. "I told him we'd be near the tritons at the fountain's edge."

"There's two fountains." Lillie pointed out the obvious.

"True, but very near each other, and it's not been a problem in the past."

"How often have you done this?" Lillie sounded extremely curious.

"Ah, I see him," Berdie chirped. Lillie seated herself quickly. "Just there, about two o'clock." Berdie indicated by the nod of her head.

Lillie craned her neck.

Berdie described the fellow. "Medium height, average build, sandy brown close cut hair, glasses, dark green sport coat."

"Looks as if he's the cat that just ate the budgie?" Lillie asked, eyes focused.

"You've spotted him then." Berdie discreetly lifted her chin and the gentleman made his way to seat himself at her side.

"Berdie, dear," he greeted in a muted voice. "It seems donkey's years."

"Hello, Billy." Berdie bounced the words.

"I understand you have a new vocation." Billy grinned. "A shepherdess of the church."

Berdie nodded. "And you, Billy Beaton, are still gatekeeper for reams of villainous information stored in the depths of the department."

"Don't let her new vocation fool you." Lillie entered the conversation. "She's still in the hunt."

"Billy, this is my colleague, Lillie Foxworth."

Billy scanned Lillie's face.

"As discreet as the length of day in July," Berdie assured.

Billie grinned and nodded towards Lillie. He placed a Sainsbury's carrier bag he had toted close to himself. "I spoke to Kent after you rang me."

Berdie opened the cooler bag she had carried with her. She retrieved a cling wrapped sandwich and handed it to Billy.

"You remembered." Billy sounded cheerful.

How could she forget? If Billy was a can, sliced ham sandwiches were the tin opener. "Sliced ham. Your very favorite."

The clerk unwrapped the sandwich as he spoke. "Right to it then. Brazilian Wandering Spiders."

"And their victims," Berdie added.

"Are they really from Brazil?" Lillie interjected.

"Jungle forests, north Brazil, south Venezuela." Billy took a bite of the sliced ham. "Umm." He closed his eyes as if to savor the contents of his palette without distraction and began to chew. His glasses moved up and down with the chewing motion while his thin eyebrows held high. "Smoked, dressed with salad cream, bits of celery," he said as if diagnosing a wine's bouquet.

"Right," Berdie quipped.

His eyes popped open, once again re-entering the business he was about. "This spider wanders you see, no webs, holes, just wanders the moist dark forest floor and pounces its prey. Creatures as big as mice mind you, paralyzes them, and dinners on." Billy took another large bite of sandwich.

Lillie looked a bit wan as she blinked.

"Lethal." Berdie gave Billy a paper napkin.

"Not always with humans." He used the napkin to wipe his mouth. "Don't like humans really, but if disturbed or agitated, well, fight not flight." Billy continued to chew.

"Could these spiders just have been a scare tactic?"

"I can think of less lethal creatures that could accomplish fright. No, deadly is deadly."

"Illegal to purchase in this country, I should think."

"Probably gotten through a pets black market." Billy nodded and wiped his hand on the napkin.

"Pets?" Lillie squirmed.

"Probably?" Berdie forged ahead.

"All right. Yes, we had a trail, but it dried up. Economy's down you know. Less market for the exotica sorts." The clerk swallowed and took another bite. "One black marketer goes down, another pops up." He shrugged.

"And the victim in the London case?" Berdie mentally took notes. "What can you tell me?"

"Female, lived in council housing, picked up bits and bobs of work, single. Apparently, no real enemies. Even fewer friends." Billy wadded the sandwich cling wrap into a ball. "What an epitaph."

"So no suspects?"

"Not really. Checked out a former employer with whom she had an apparent dust up. He was clean. No real motive. Not much of a pursuit after that. Finally decided it was a random prank or the wrong address."

"I don't believe that for a minute. Random prank." Berdie pursed her lips. "A pressure ridden law enforcement agency with bigger fish to fry, more like."

"Can't disagree with you there." Billy nodded.

Lillie frowned. "Is that just?"

Billy drew back his shoulders and looked Lillie right in the eye. "Who said anything about just? It is what it is."

Berdie's jaw grew taught, but she worked at remaining calm. "This woman, she has a name?"

"In the paperwork." Billy wiped his lips with the napkin.

"Well, she may have been a faceless victim to some, but she was still a someone in God's economy. She deserves better."

Billy chortled. "You're going to go after this like a dog to a bone, and you're going to gnaw it to a nib, aren't you?"

"Does Monday follow Sunday?"

Billy shook his head and gave a long sigh. "You always had more scruples than ten put together." He pushed the Sainsbury's carrier bag discreetly to Berdie. Several papers were just visible inside. "Nothing that isn't public record, really."

Berdie handed the cooler bag of sandwiches to Billy. "I'd eat the lot within twenty four hours."

Billy nodded and took the bag. "I always enjoy doing business with you, Berdie." He stood and nodded to Lillie. "Must push off."

Berdie caught Billy's hand. "Thanks, Billy. This information could be incredibly important." She released her grasp. "God's speed."

"Cheers," he answered and then added, "now go preserve justice." With that, he joined the throng that moved along and blended in like a moment of time to the hour.

Lillie looked after him. "A rather odd fellow."

"Um, good chap really. He loves his sliced ham." She was already fingering through the papers in the bag. "Her name was Wanda Pitts. Don your walking shoes, Lillie. We're going to do a visit."

"Visit whom?" Lillie puzzled.

"One Joby Weston, neighbor to the deceased. He reported her missing. Yes, well, we'll visit if he still lives at the same address and if he's willing to speak to two complete strangers."

"Doesn't sound promising." Lillie arose discreetly rubbing her posterior.

"And the Red Sea didn't seem promising to the Israelites at first glance either, Lillie. But they walked across on dry land."

"OK, Moses," Lillie quipped while Berdie stood. "But, I do not want to wander in the wilderness for forty years or past tea for that matter."

Getting to the council estate where Wanda Pitts had once lived, among others with housing assistance needs, was as simple as a ride on the Underground. The subterranean transit system was quick and efficient. But once there, it required a great deal of wandering through concrete hallways, not desert sands. All of it done to locate the residence of the singular source of information concerning Wanda Pitts, Joby Weston.

Finding that the lift in the tower block where Joby reportedly lived was out of order, Berdie and Lillie climbed nine flights of littered stairs that smelled of mixed spices, stale brew, and sweaty socks. It left Berdie panting and Lillie trying to catch her breath.

Two youths passed by, clad in island gear with colorful knitted caps. Berdie called after them, giving in to tired feet. "Excuse me, gentlemen." She smiled.

The two turned to look behind them as if trying to spy the gentlemen. Then they looked at each other. "Yeah," one of them offered while the other one chuckled.

"We want," Berdie took a big gulp of air, "number eighty-seven." She let out a slow exhale.

Lillie clutched her handbag to her chest.

"You law?" The young man lifted his chin.

"With the church, actually," Berdie returned without waver.

The young man raised his eyebrows, as if quite surprised and grinned. "Yeah? Keep going, bottom of the hall." He turned and continued on, his friend laughing rather loudly.

"Was that wise?" Lillie huffed.

"We know where we're going now, don't we?" Berdie began a move down the hallway.

"This is a bit rough," Lillie observed when they reached the dilapidated door of number eighty-seven.

"Keep your voice down, Lillie," Berdie whispered. "The walls are paper thin. As you've observed, everything about is a bit rough."

Berdie knocked on the door with several rapid thumps. The metal number seven of the eighty-seven attached to the door dropped off with a clink and spun across the hallway. Lillie went to retrieve it just as the door cracked open.

Two questioning eyes could be seen peering through the crack, a frown barely visible. Music of a faraway culture sounded in the background. There was a stretch of silence between Berdie and the stranger then Berdie spoke.

"I'm Berdie and I was hoping Mr. Weston was in."

"No," came the quick reply and the person started to close the door. Berdie caught the handle.

"Does Mr. Joby Weston live here?"

As Berdie asked the question, Lillie, who had retrieved the errant number, tried to hand it to the occupant through the small opening. "This fell off..."

"No," was followed by the crash of the closed door and the offered metal number clamoring to the floor.

"Your door." Lillie finished and wiped her hand on her skirt. She turned to Berdie. "My, that was fruitful."

"Thank you for that observation, Lillie." Berdie was already knocking on the door once again. "Please don't be frightened."

From behind the closed door came a voracious, "Go. I call police."

"Now that's a switch," Berdie noted with a twinge of irony. "All right, Lillie, let's begin our descent then." Berdie sighed. "I can't help but think there's something here though."

"I can tell you what I wish was here. I could do with some tea and bread, nicely toasted, with jam."

When Berdie and Lillie arrived in the car park by the tower block, a very loud wail assaulted their ears.

A small child sat on the ground as if on strike. Despite the mother's best urging, the tot refused to arise. The fact that the attending young woman's arms carried not only another younger child but two market bags of goods didn't help either. As she attempted to bend over and lift the wailer, her market bag slipped to the ground sending food stuffs sprawling across the pavement. A look of desperation played itself across the face of the dark skinned woman. When she set the smaller child down to gather the items, the wee one stood on wobbly little legs. He looked to be just past a year old. A couple sways, and the tyke had his sea legs. The bundle of energy grinned and commenced a wobbly dash across the car park.

"Ezra," sprung from the mother's lips. "No, no Ezra."

The other child still wailing, Berdie could stand by no longer. "We may not have gotten what we came here for, but we can certainly help that poor woman."

"Bang goes the tea and toast," Lillie mumbled.

"May we be of help?" Berdie called out.

The woman was a bit hesitant, but an auto turned into the car park. "Oh, please."

As the mother scooted after Ezra, Lillie gathered the food and placed it in the bag.

Berdie knelt down by the wailing wonder. "Bye baby bunting, daddy's gone a hunting," Berdie began to sing.

"We're trying to calm the child, not frighten him," Lillie poked.

The tot appeared to be somewhat startled. He stopped crying and stared hard at Berdie with his large eyes then went into a whimper.

When the young woman returned with the captive Ezra, the seated child finally stood and clung to his mother's leg.

"Come now, my son," she said to the previous wailer who looked to be near four years, "you're my big helper."

The woman gazed at Berdie. Her stunning coco colored skin tone, attractive almond eyes, and slender body gave the woman an unmistakable beauty that was only enhanced by her silky voice. "Thank you."

Lillie held the woman's market bag, once again full.

"Can we help you to your door?" Berdie offered. "You do have your hands full."

The woman looked into Berdie's face as if searching for assurances of good intentions.

"We had hoped to visit someone," Berdie explained. "We're from Saint Aidan of the Wood Church." Berdie could see a touch of relief in the lovely eyes.

"I have nothing to give," the woman said humbly.

"Oh, my no, no, we're not collecting. As I say, we came to visit someone but they weren't in. I'm Berdie. This is Lillie."

The woman smiled. "I'm Coral, and these are my sons."

"And such handsome young men," Berdie said with a grin.

The older boy now smiled a smile that could light up the entire housing complex.

"I'll carry your market bag if you like," Lillie offered.

"I can take the second bag." Berdie was instinctively aware of a protective mother's desire to keep her children close at hand, especially with two, albeit nice, strangers. Coral passed her second rotund market bag to Berdie.

"My flat is in this block, over there, on the ground floor." Coral pointed.

"Oh, jolly good, jolly good," Lillie exclaimed with a great deal of exuberance then sighed.

Coral looked inquisitively at Berdie.

"The lifts aren't working."

"Many times this is a problem." Coral took her oldest boy by the hand, still holding little Ezra on her hip, and began a forward motion, "This way," she nodded. "Who is it you come to visit? Perhaps I can help?"

"We're hoping to locate Joby Weston," Berdie said.

Coral's forward motion ceased. "Joby Weston?"

"You know him then?" Berdie could tell by the lovely face gone sour that it was a loaded question.

"Know him?" Coral's jaw tightened. "He is, was, my husband."

"Was, really?" Lillie repeated with a definite surprise in her voice.

"One morning I find the note on the kitchen table, 'Going back to Jamaica. Will come for you.' That was almost two years ago, and Ezra was his parting gift." Coral knitted her thin brows. "We never hear from him again. I don't know where he is, and I can't pay any of his bills."

"We're not bill collectors. We only hoped that Joby, your husband, could tell us about Wanda Pitts," Berdie assured.

"She's dead," Coral said baldly.

"Yes, we're aware, but we hoped to learn more about her for the sake of one in our parish." Berdie looked at Lillie who nodded.

Coral grabbed an apple from the market bag Berdie held and handed it to her oldest. "Here Jo Jo, go play by the door."

The child scampered off and took a bite of his red treat.

"My husband tells me to stay away from Mrs. Pitts in the flat next to us. This is when we live in eighty-seven. The only times he sees her is to move her from our doorway where she sometimes lay full of hard drink. My Joby puts her in her flat. He tells me 'she is on the dark road.'"

"On the dark road?" Berdie mined and listened intently.

"Something dark troubled her. 'Earth now cares for my little evergreen.' She would cry and scream it over and over. 'My sweet evergreen, they will do best for my little evergreen.'"

"What evergreen?" Lillie queried. "Certainly not a tree?"

Coral quieted her voice and leaned closer to Lillie. "My husband asks her this one time when she has a clear eye. 'I don't know the person.' That's what she says."

"Person," Berdie breathed.

"Do not go by that woman, Joby warned." Coral shivered. "Then one day, she tells my husband she's going to be rich, and she will leave this horrible place to live in her own house with a fancy car and good riddance to him and everyone. Ten days later she is dead."

"And did Joby tell this to the police?" Berdie asked.

"Oh no, Joby doesn't like police. He doesn't tell police anything. Only he smells a bad odor from her flat and calls them. Joby tells them nothing. After that we move."

Ezra squirmed in Coral's arms and reached his arms downward. Coral started moving towards the flat once again. "I must go."

Berdie and Lillie stayed in step with her, carrying the bags.

"Yes, of course." Berdie toted the bag and sat it at

the door's edge when they reached the flat. "You've been most helpful, Coral."

The woman nodded.

"That dark road your husband spoke of, well what you've told us today will bring light to that road, the light of truth that will chase the dark away."

"I am glad." Coral smiled.

"God go with you," Berdie blessed. And Coral, Ezra, and Jo Jo entered the flat.

Lillie shook her head. "The seas have parted."

Berdie grinned. "Oh yes, didn't they though. We're on to something, Lillie. We were meant to get that information. Oh, yes, we're on to something big."

And with that, the women began their trek back to the Underground station and a train ride home to solve a mystery.

9

Berdie stared hard at the floral arrangement she was creating, or rather attempting to create.

She pushed the long sleeves of her new knit jumper up her arms. She purchased it just this morning during a busy day of helping with St. Mark's jumble sale in Timsley. The jumper was a warm fashionable peachy color, and it suited her.

She hadn't any space today to muse on yesterday's London outing and all the information it brought to light. And now she was stuck in on this job that took every ounce of her concentration. She stabbed another hydrangea in the vase.

Hugh had laid out all the necessary gear, including the fresh cut flowers, on a table just outside the sacristy. With some detail he gave Berdie the report that Mrs. Potter, the usual designer, had unexpectedly left town to live with her niece in Lewes due to poor health, and could Berdie please do the floral arrangements for tomorrow's Sunday service.

While Mr. Castle rehearsed "Lift Up Your Hearts" on the organ, Berdie tipped her head to observe the vase as if that may make the arrangement somehow look better. It didn't. She pulled the just placed floral out of the vase and sighed.

The sound of the opened church door, along with the unmistakable stride of Lillie Foxworth clattering on the stone floor, incited a sense of relief in Berdie.

"Coo-ee," Lillie called out as she crossed the nave to Berdie.

"Oh, Lillie, you do have a creative touch. What an absolute godsend that you've arrived just at this moment." Berdie beamed.

Lillie eyed the floral arrangement with a tip of her head. "Isn't it just," Lillie confirmed, and handed a copy of the Kirkwood Times to Berdie who grabbed it gladly. "Have you seen this?"

Berdie read it. Special Edition was in bold letters across the top and the headline read 'Do You Know This Face?' Just below it, taking up almost the entire page, was the drawing of a young child's face and the caption, 'Forensic Anthropologist Creates Likeness of Church Garden Child.'

"Church garden child." Berdie shook her head. "Poor Hugh."

"And, apart from the hope that Dr. Roz Chase has completed her work and will soon move on, look at this." Lillie pointed to the chin of the drawn face. "This child has their parent's chin I'd say, clearly."

Berdie pulled down her glasses and studied the picture.

"Look," Lillie said pointedly and covered the upper part of the head with her hand leaving just the chin revealed.

"Oh I see, well spotted."

Lillie removed her hand. "Who's a clever girl then?" She had a note of pompous pleasure in the fact that she had detected an apparent clue.

Two more sets of steps clip-clopped on the stone floor. Berdie observed the indomitable Bridget McDermott and tender Maggie Fairchild. The two shared the chairmanship of the church garden committee. Each gripped newspapers in their hands and wore less-than-happy visages as they made way towards Berdie and Lillie.

"Mrs. Elliott," Bridget's ample voice echoed across the hallowed stone walls. "Have you seen the special edition this afternoon?"

Berdie held the paper up to signal an affirmative.

"They're calling him the church garden child," Maggie Fairchild stated in a hurt voice.

"But that's not the worse part." Bridget was now almost in a full gallop. "There's more."

The women now stood, like fortified pillars, at Berdie's side.

Bridget held the paper so the illuminating front page could be easily seen by Berdie. "Look at the child's nose. Inherited from mother no doubt. Now, look at it." The woman put her index finger on a nostril. "Whose is it?"

"Shameful," Maggie added, "one of our own."

Berdie studied the nose and shook her head. She saw nothing truly familiar there.

Bridget leaned forward and lowered her voice. "If that isn't the nose of that slightly unhinged Mary Gordon."

"Mary Gordon?" Berdie looked closely.

Suddenly the organ music stopped. Mr. Castle's voice sounded from behind the great organ pipes that nearly dwarfed him. "Look at the forehead," he said with a certain command. "I'm not naming names mind you. But do look at the forehead."

Berdie put on her vicar's wife voice. "Let's not be hasty."

"What?" Mr. Castle called.

They had long marveled at the uncanny way he

could hear conversations while playing the organ but had difficulty making out words when it was silent.

"I said, let's all of us calm down and not be hasty," Berdie yelled back.

Like a hare springing from its burrow, Hugh appeared from the sacristy. "What's this that needs calming?"

Berdie held up the newspaper.

"Oh yes, that," he said with a less-than-pleased tone.

Mr. Castle again commenced his organ practice.

Bridget McDermott shook her newspaper, her voice commanding. "Reverend Elliott, you must get right down to that silly newspaper and let young Mr. Exton know that this just won't do. Church garden child, really."

"I understand your sentiments, Mrs. McDermott," Hugh acknowledged. "But, I should think that the editor is only using a term the police have created to identify the case. That being said, I'm afraid negotiating with newspaper editors is more my wife's expertise."

Berdie gave Hugh the eye message, a slight, well-focused squint, which said "thanks for dropping me right in it."

"I'll speak to Mr. Exton, but as Hugh said…" Berdie shook her head as a means to finish her sentence.

Mrs. McDermott held the paper up, just as she had for Berdie, so Hugh could see it clearly. "Now, tell me vicar, whose child is this? Look at the unmistakable nose. Someone has not been forthcoming. You know that nose I'm sure."

"My dear Mrs. McDermott," Hugh's voice was

without waver, "speculation without proper knowledge, such as the police would garner, is a dangerous business. Nose aside, we wouldn't want to make false accusation and hurt someone's standing, would we."

"Indeed," Lillie added with a quick glance Berdie's way.

Berdie wanted to make sure Bridget was keenly clear on what Hugh was saying. "And when those who are investigating the case identify the child and his parents, you can be glad in the knowledge that you were quietly correct, or grateful that you didn't publicly make a fool of yourself."

Hugh cleared his throat and gave Berdie a wee nudge on her back.

Bridget pulled the paper down and folded it. "Well, be that as it may, we all have eyes."

"For which we're grateful," Hugh agreed. "And by God's grace, a genuine sense of discretion." He raised his eyebrow and turned to Maggie. "Do you agree, Mrs. Fairchild?"

"Well, yes, Reverend Elliott." Maggie Fairchild responded with a certain sense of understanding.

"And wouldn't you agree?" Berdie targeted the intrepid Bridget McDermott.

Berdie felt Hugh's finger nearly bore a hole on her back.

Mrs. McDermott pulled the folded paper close to the bodice of her dark blue dress and straightened her back. "Well, I suppose," she uttered with a certain reticence and a half scowl.

"Good." Hugh nodded. "Now, is there anything else I can do for you?"

"Thank you, Reverend. I believe you've addressed

what we came here for." Maggie Fairchild smiled, took Bridget's elbow, and the women exited quickly.

"Well said, Vicar," Mr. Castle called from behind the organ, playing the hymn's fourth stanza.

"Thank you," Hugh acknowledged loudly then directed his whisper voice to Berdie. "I appreciate your support, love, but a woman like Bridget McDermott can be inflamed by your verbal delivery."

Lillie smiled.

"Well, Hugh, with a woman like Bridget McDermott, any conversation that isn't frank and full on won't be heard." Berdie widened her eyes so that her eyebrows lifted above her tortoiseshell glasses. Her verbal delivery now became buttery. "Besides, if anyone in this congregation should order you about"— she lifted her chin and grinned—"it should be me."

"Oh, yes?" Hugh chuckled.

"Speaking of order." Lillie cast her eye toward the disarray of what was supposed to be a vase of arranged flowers.

"Oh." Hugh's tone had a note of dismay as he observed.

Berdie pursed her lips.

"I thought you enjoyed organizing flowers, love."

Berdie straightened. "It ranks right up there with a hot stick in the eye. Well, I mean, to assemble a posy for the breakfast table is fine, but a multi-flower formal church arrangement. I should ask Lillie to do it if I were you."

Lillie was quick to respond. "You know who's jolly good with florals?"

"Cara Donovan," Berdie answered.

"Who is home attending poor Katy who has a tummy ache," Hugh inserted.

"Rosalie Darbyshire," Lillie finished.

"Is she?" Hugh was keen.

"She only attended the Judith Blacklock Flower School."

"I'll fetch her." Berdie offered without hesitation. "She's one to give it a go on a moment's notice."

Hugh ogled the vase. "Ring her up."

Berdie was on her mobile as she walked through the church door, beckoning Lillie to come as well.

Rosalie not only assured Berdie that she would be happy to do the flower arrangement but she could also do it straight way if she could get a ride. Berdie was more than happy to oblige.

"Any headway on the Pitts investigation?" Lillie asked once the car was on the way to Bampkingswith Hall.

"Ruminations, no headway really."

"Have you heard about poor Patricia King?"

"My, Lillie, aren't you the hotbed of information today. Have you been to the Copper Kettle?"

"Actually, I saw Mr. Raheem this morning, and he had just spoken with Patricia's sister," Lillie rattled on without taking a breath. "Patricia feels so badly about all that's happened she's considering leaving the mail service."

"Truly?"

"Very distressed that she didn't take better note of the parcel she delivered that held that dreadful spider."

"She's so terribly efficient; I can imagine it should be difficult for her. I would hate to see her quit."

"Yes."

"Not one to linger, but she delivers the mail jolly well on time."

Lillie glanced out the car window then returned her gaze to Berdie. "Why is it we're fetching Rosalie? She has her own car."

"Colonel Preswood has taken it to the garage for fresh lubrication. But this is perfect. I needed an excuse to go back inside Swithy for a bit of a look-see."

"To see what?" Lillie twinkled, "Something's waiting for discovery, isn't it?"

"Not so much discovery as scrutiny."

Lillie grinned and tapped the paper she still carried. "Chin-wag is it?"

"Among others," Berdie confided and picked up speed.

The gentleman in black answered the door at Swithy Hall and directed Berdie to gather Miss Darbyshire, who was expecting her, from the upstairs bedroom where she readied herself.

"Second door left," he directed. "I apologize for being so informal and not bringing Miss Darbyshire down." He balanced a tray in one hand and held fairy liquid in the other. "The house cleaner has been out ill most the week, and I'm meeting myself coming back from the going."

Berdie and Lillie assured him it was no problem and ascended the large stairway.

"At least it's not nine floors," Berdie commented when they reached the first landing.

Lillie sniffed the scent of a large spring bouquet on a table nearby. "Nor does it smell like yesterday's take away."

It was then that they realized the first floor hall extended to the right and left. There were entrances to the various rooms on both sides of the hallway.

"Second door left." Berdie glanced down the hall

on her left, then to the right. "Go left and then the left side of the hall, second door?"

Lillie observed the situation slightly puzzled. "I should say we turn left and then, clearly, we have two choices."

Berdie thought to question the gentleman, but when she peeked down the stairway, he had disappeared.

"Turn left, second door on the left," was Berdie's decision. She and Lillie moved down the hall and paused in front of the door they expected to be Rosalie's room.

"Hello." Berdie made her presence known. She knocked and the unlatched door opened.

"Is she there?" Lillie asked.

"I think we'd all be quite taken back if she were." Berdie stepped aside to let Lillie peer into a cavernous bathroom.

"Quite," Lillie agreed glancing about.

She and Berdie stepped into the luxurious space where they took in the two large windows dressed in floral fabric that allowed the sun to reflect off the freestanding roll top Victorian bath. A marble splash back sat elegantly between the ample sink and a framed mirror that ran nearly to the ceiling. A small crystalline pink chandelier clung to the ceiling like a cherry atop a cake.

All this was home to a full-wall wardrobe, brocade slipper chair and matching chaise. A small end table held a petite lamp and several stacked books. And under it all, lay a gracious parquet floor that was clad with a pastel woven rug in the seating area. Even the rubbish bin had a gold edge. And it was this that caught Berdie's eye.

"Far too pretty to hold rubbish."

"Of all the lovely things and you're interested in the rubbish," Lillie scolded while running her hand over the bath.

Berdie spied two pieces of glossy paper inside the gold-edged receptacle. She picked them out of the basket. "Well, what have we here?"

"Oh, really, Berdie."

"Look." Berdie placed the two pieces side by side in her palm and showed them to Lillie.

"It's a photo."

"It's a torn photo," Berdie corrected.

Lillie's eyes sparked. "We've seen this before."

Berdie nodded. "The twins, just after discovering a mud puddle, being served a bit of refreshment. Remember the pink satin photo book?"

"Why would someone tear it?"

"Why, indeed." Berdie held the pieced picture closer and pulled her glasses down her nose. "Yes, indeed."

Lillie pointed to one of the large windows. "Look there, isn't that Mr. Raheem walking away from the back garden?"

Berdie observed momentarily. "So it is."

"Found the guest bathroom then?" Rosalie Darbyshire's voice made Berdie and Lillie start.

"We're thinking of living in." Lillie nervously chuckled.

"Yes." Rosalie nodded. "A bit ostentatious."

Berdie pushed her glasses back to their appropriate place. "We got a bit lost."

"My room is just cross the hall." She pointed.

"Ah," Berdie nodded. "Turn left and second door on the right."

"Are we ready to go then?" Rosalie caught sight of the ripped photo in Berdie's hand. "What's this?"

Berdie reluctantly held it out to her.

Rosalie's face went scarlet. She grabbed the damaged treasure. "What are you doing with this?" Her green eyes bored into Berdie's face. "What's this all about?" She frowned. "You didn't…"

Lillie balked. "I should say not."

"We discovered it here in the rubbish, just as you see it," Berdie said with unwavering resolve.

"Who would destroy it? It's so very precious."

"Apparently there's someone who doesn't agree," Berdie stated matter-of-factly.

Rosalie's first flush of anger turned into perplexity, and she eased herself into the slipper chair. "Aunt Flora never liked the picture, but to destroy it, no. Robin was embarrassed by it, but then all our early snaps embarrass her." Rosalie stared at ragged edges that ravaged her favorite photo.

"Your uncle?" Lillie asked.

"I doubt very much if he's even aware the snap exists. Besides, no one in the family uses this room."

"Have you had guests recently?" Berdie glanced through the window to the now empty back garden. Rosalie lifted her chin and paused.

"Charles, really, I mean overnight, but that was a few days back. Contessa Santolio made a momentary stop." The young woman shook her head. "That's grasping at straws."

"Straws are often worth the grasping." Berdie had a hint of play in her voice.

"Grasp away. It won't mend my photo." Rosalie stood and sighed, still poring over the snap, aligning it to fit together.

"Perhaps there's some professional photo repair service," Lillie offered.

"Yes, perhaps," Rosalie said wistfully.

"The important thing, it has quite inadvertently been rescued and is back in the hands of the person who treasures it most." Berdie touched Rosalie's hand. "Where it belongs."

Rosalie Preswood smiled timidly. "Yes, well."

"Perhaps I can find a service to mend it, as Lillie suggested."

"That's a very kind offer." Rosalie appeared to waver. "Do be very careful, won't you?" The young woman relinquished the torn snap.

"I'll handle it like hidden treasure," Berdie assured as she accepted it. "We'll have it repaired in no time."

"I need to get my jumper." Rosalie pointed towards her room. "I'll meet you downstairs in the hall, and we can get on with the tasks at hand."

"There's a dear," Lillie breathed.

Rosalie entered her room while Berdie and Lillie made their descent.

Lillie, it seemed, could hardly contain herself. "Who do you think did it and why?" she tittered in a low level.

"I don't know," Berdie whispered, "but I'm going to find out." She paused on a stair and put the torn pieces in her bag. "Now, let's say a person who doesn't want this snap around retrieved it, tore it perhaps hastily, and then stashed it in the guest bathroom rubbish. It's a somewhat nondescript spot anyone at any time could use. Yes, I should think it gets cleaned daily, the rubbish would be removed." Berdie perked. "But, the gentleman said the cleaning lady has been out ill this week."

Lillie inhaled. "He did. Yes, he did."

"Still, what's the motive"? Berdie leaned closely towards Lillie. "I haven't worked it all out yet, but a detail I noticed along with something Rosalie said, has given me an idea on that front."

"Mrs. Elliott," The man in black's strong voice broke way into the conversation. "Did you find Miss Darbyshire?"

"Yes," Berdie answered, "Thank you." She and Lillie continued their descent just as Flora Presswood entered the large entrance hall.

"Bradford, once again those silly men who are to raze that dilapidated greenhouse have not kept their appointment, no doubt satisfying their thirst at a nearby pub."

"Yes, madam."

"Oh, and Bradford, there's a delivery in the kitchen. Could you see to it?"

"Yes, madam." Bradford hadn't finished the words when he had already departed.

Berdie and Lillie were at the bottom of the staircase.

"Mrs. Elliott, Miss Foxworth, I didn't realize you were here." Mrs. Presswood spoke with a hint of displeasure.

"It was rather sudden, I'm afraid. We're here to gather Rosalie, she'll be down presently," Berdie explained.

"She's going to arrange the flowers at church," Lillie added with a disarming smile.

"I see." Flora lifted her distinctive chin. "She didn't say."

Lillie gave Berdie a slight nudge. "Chin," she whispered.

Berdie, in return, gave Lillie a discreet nod while Flora Preswood came near to them.

A moment's silence played itself into an opportunity.

"These are quite fetching." Berdie pointed to a lighted shelf in the nearby cabinet that she had noticed when she was previously here for dinner. The shelf was home to two opulent pieces of stemware.

"You're taken by them?" Flora drew near the pieces. "They are splendid. It's the iridescence you know, Venetian."

Berdie nodded.

"Colonel Presswood's great-grandfather purchased them in Italy. They're eighteenth century, I believe."

Lillie's eyebrows elevated and her jaw dropped.

"I should love to see them more closely." Berdie knew it was slightly rude, but she had to try it on.

"Oh, no." Flora Presswood lost her smile. "This is a locking cabinet, and Randal has the key." She admired the stemware. "There was a time when we displayed them on the Venetian table you know." She pointed to the shapely end table near the bottom of the stairwell. "They're irreplaceable, sadly."

"Sadly?" Berdie asked in an innocent manner.

"It was originally a set of three, but a piece was stolen. Horrible."

"Dreadful," Berdie commiserated. "So you never found the thief?"

"Oh, we know who took it. Well, my sister Rose was aware and informed the colonel and me. A young maid, actually quite trainable." She shook her head. "One can never tell. Of course she insisted she was innocent. Sadly, I had to dismiss her." Flora lifted her nose and sniffed.

Berdie caught a glimpse of Lillie from the corner of her eye. The choirmaster, still agog, eyed the top of the stairs. She went pale.

"Your sister must have been astute," Berdie plied.

"Yes, she and the girls just arrived here at Bampkingswith Hall from overseas, trying to find safe haven, I shouldn't wonder."

"And the twin's father? He wasn't with them?" Berdie continued to peel back the layers.

"The colonel wouldn't allow him in the house." She scowled. "But you see, my husband was on special assignment at the time. As he often was. No, Rose noted, and told me later, that the domestic was dusting the display on the table one evening and in the morning, the glass was missing. While the cats away as they say. It was quite obvious who did it."

"With your grand sense of order Mrs. Preswood, you didn't notice it missing?"

Mrs. Presswood looked at the floor. "I," she ran her hand across the bodice of her dress, "I was visiting friends in London." She paused and observed Lillie. "Are you all right, Miss Foxworth?"

"What?" Lillie looked at Flora and blinked.

"You're quite pale."

"Lillie's feeling a bit queasy," Berdie offered on behalf of her friend.

"Not flu, I hope."

"No," Berdie answered while Lillie, again, just blinked.

"So you didn't press charges against the domestic. What did you say her name was?"

"I didn't actually." Mrs. Preswood put a finger on her chin. "Grainger, I believe. Yes, Lolly Grainger. And no, we didn't press charges. Too messy, bad for the colonel's business."

"Ready to go?" was accompanied by Rosalie's rapid footstep.

"I should deposit Miss Foxworth at her home right away," Mrs. Preswood advised.

"Yes, please," Lillie spurted and caught her breath.

Berdie took Lillie by the elbow and led her in the direction of the outside exit.

"Let me get that for you." Bradford re-entered the room and stepped lively to the door.

He carried an enormous basket of fruit. Lemons, limes, grapefruit, and oranges of all varieties were wrapped in rosy pink transparent wrap. A large yellow bow was tied to the handle. "A gift for the Misses Darbyshire."

"Whatever for?" Mrs. Presswood eyed the basket with a certain distain. "Really. Who from, Bradford?"

"It doesn't say, madam."

"Rubbish bin," Rosalie instructed the gentleman. "Lovely but intolerable."

"Yes, Miss Darbyshire." Bradford spoke without any hesitation, and opened the door for the departure.

Rosalie gave her aunt a peck on the cheek. "I shouldn't wait for me."

"Thank you, Mrs. Preswood." Berdie continued aiding Lillie who just nodded.

It seemed but a snap of the finger that Lillie was safely deposited in her home with the promise of getting together to talk after church tomorrow. Then a minute's drive until Berdie and Rosalie reached the church.

Berdie marveled at how gracefully Rosalie was able to create the elegant floral arrangements.

However, it did take a great deal of time.

When Rosalie was finished, it was nearly four thirty and time for tea. So, Berdie invited Rosalie to join her and Hugh at the vicarage for Panzanella with toasted almonds, courtesy of Mrs. Raheem who created and sold the custom mix at the produce store. Berdie added an olive cheese loaf, and a sticky toffee pudding to round the meal. It was the least she could do in gratitude for Rosalie's availability.

It was approaching dusk when Hugh dismissed himself to go back to the church following the meal. It was even later when Berdie and Rosalie were on the road back to Swithy Hall.

As they turned into the drive past the lighted lodge, Rosalie told Berdie she understood Ortensia, still hospitalized, to be improving after the awful spider ordeal.

"Yes, well, by God's grace." Berdie was appreciative and relieved.

"You know, after living in South America, my mother was terrified of spiders, even the little tiny ones. She and Little Miss Muffet." Rosalie laughed.

"I've wondered, Rosalie, how is it that you came, once again, to live in England?"

"It depends on who you ask. According to mummy," Rosalie smiled, "she always said that she wanted Robin and me to live on 'the isle that rules the waves,' as the song says. Now, Aunt Flora's version is quite different." Rosalie half smiled. "She says that our father got tangled up in some oil scheme gone bad that put the whole family in jeopardy, and we fled to England, to the safety and security of Bampkingswith Hall." The young woman sighed. "Whatever the reason, my father eventually abandoned us. Rosalie sounded matter-of-fact. "I dare say Aunt Flora and Uncle Randal have been our refuge, for which I'm grateful."

"Yes, wonderfully generous, and a well-provided-for home to grow up in, I should think." Berdie perked as she thought of her pledge to Rosalie. "And I'll have your precious photo repaired and to you as quickly as possible."

Berdie brought the car to a halt in the drive right near the front door.

"Well, thank you for the tea and the ride, Mrs. Elliott."

"And thank you for rescuing the day. I'm sure if the congregation ever saw my sad floral attempts, they would echo my sentiment."

Rosalie gave a hearty chuckle and a quick wave.

Once the young woman was inside, Berdie sped down the Swithy Hall drive.

Passing by the lodge, she noticed the lights were now off. "I must talk to our contessa," Berdie noted, turning on to the main road. "But first, I need to get some rather stray ducks in a very straight row. Then we'll see to Carlotta Santolio."

By the time Berdie almost finished her quick ride back to the vicarage, she remembered that her house key lay on the hall table at the locked vicarage. "No bother," she said to the dark sky. "I'll stop at church to get Hugh's." She knew he had work to do.

When Berdie arrived at church and stepped inside, two low lights near the door softly lit the stones of the central aisle up to the altar where two more lights gave a gentle holy glow to the entire church. Berdie loved gathering with the community to worship, but the night silence of this sacred place also fed her soul.

She saw the light under the sacristy door. It became apparent Hugh was not alone. She could hear muffled voices; Hugh of course, the other certainly male, but not distinct.

She decided to give her husband and his guest a few moments more before she disrupted their meeting.

She sat near the sacristy in a shadowed pew when the sacristy door flew open. Light from the small room flooded the sanctuary floor, making it almost white. Preston Graystone burst from the sacristy, his angular features creating distinct edges in the play of light. His rapid footsteps rattled on the stone floor until he reached the church door where he exited.

He mustn't have seen me, Berdie realized.

Hugh stepped out into the sanctuary, and something caught Berdie by surprise. Hugh wore his stole. The long length of fabric that graced his neck was given him by Nick and Clare as a 'congratulations, Dad' gift upon Hugh's ordination. If his collar was his badge of office, his stole was his mantle of service.

"Service," Berdie muttered to herself. She took a deep breath. "An act of confession, surely." Like a bolt, her mind put the scrambled thought into a frame; Preston Graystone, secluded evening, an official act of the church in which his words would be under protection. He was after all a solicitor, words outside the scrutiny of the law.

Hugh removed the stole and sighed. His busy Lenten schedule was quite demanding, and he wore the duty of it in his brow. Still, he stood tall. This lighting accentuated the silver of his hair. His blue eyes dazzled. Berdie's pulse gave a flutter. She decided to tuck away Preston Graystone in a corner of her memory to be conjured up at a later moment.

"Hugh," she spoke with a touch of cream.

He slightly jumped. "Oh, love, you gave me a start."

"Forgot my key." Berdie stepped to her husband and put her arm around his waist. She stared into those ravishing blue eyes and leaned close. "Come home with me, Hugh Elliott," she whispered.

Hugh's face took on the glow of a spring afternoon. "My beautiful wife, I've been waiting for an invitation like that all day." He gave her a warm kiss.

In less than three minutes, Berdie and the man she loved most in the world made their way home, leaving humankind with all its contention behind them and relished a few stolen moments of time together.

Having settled in for bed, Berdie was roused from her sleep by an annoying sound. It was the vicarage telephone, giving out its distress signal in the darkness. She opened one eye to see Hugh in deep sleep.

"Really." Berdie sighed and leant her body cross her husband to lift the receiver and bring it to her ear. "Vicarage," she said with a crackled voice.

"I need you to meet me on Monday," a garbled voice commanded.

Berdie mentally shook her head. "Do you need the reverend?"

"I want you," the voice boomed.

Berdie began to wake. "Who is this? Do you have any idea of the time?"

"Will you meet me or not?"

"What do you want?" Berdie tried to sound commanding.

"No, I have something for you. Monday, six AM, behind the Pork and Barrel in Timsley."

"Six AM, Pork and Barrel?" Berdie had both eyes

opened now. "Who is this?"

Click was followed by a definite bzzz.

"Well, I certainly hope you sleep well now because I certainly won't." Berdie's words spewed into an empty line. She plunked the receiver back in the cradle and nudged Hugh. Still, he slumbered on peacefully.

She lay down, head spinning. She pressed herself to push the upheaval out of her mind and yield to her need for sleep. She must be fit for a robust day of active worship and service, which were only hours away.

10

The alarm clock was akin to a sledgehammer that assailed Berdie's brain. It seemed she had just fallen back to sleep.

The odd conversation on the phone allowed her only intermittent sleep, not being awake enough to really put things well together and yet not able to truly put them out of her mind.

Besides the call, the Venetian glass played itself into the scramble of facts that paraded through her mind all night. Lolly Grainger, the name was not recognizable, yet there was something certainly familiar. Coral Weston, Wanda Pitts, Wilkie Gordon, ripped photo: from London to Aidan Kirkwood, all had their own space in which they fitted that would complete a puzzle.

She muddled through her morning routine, while Hugh set eagerly about his preparation and was off to church far before her.

When she finally arrived at the church door, Hugh and the young acolytes bedecked in their albs and holding steady the candle lighter, were gathered there to begin the procession down the central aisle.

"Ah, you made it." Hugh looked relieved.

Berdie took a deep breath and nodded.

"Vicar," Jeff Lawler approached Hugh. He wore a hoody over his football jersey along with his game shorts. Jamie Donovan, in the same attire, attended Jeff.

"Wanted to give you fair warning. We'll be sneaking out a bit early."

"We play Mistcome Green for the Pelé Cup this afternoon, I'm sure you're aware." Jamie smiled.

"Indeed." Hugh grinned. "Wouldn't miss. Although I'll be a touch late. It really wouldn't do for the vicar to sneak out early."

"No." Jeff returned the grin, and Jamie chuckled.

"Our village is the proper place for that cup. Bring it home, lads." Hugh had a grand note of cheer in his words.

"We'll do our best," Jeff promised.

"It's ours," Jamie said with great pluck.

Jeff and Jamie sauntered to a seat just as the first notes of "Lift Up Your Hearts" resonated from the organ. Berdie, by Hugh's nod, flew in after the young men, just steps before the acolytes and Hugh.

She found a spot near the back of the church. Though she worked to keep alert, the rest of the congregants were abuzz. More to do with the upcoming football game, Berdie thought, than the opportunity of sitting on a hard pew. There was an eagerness that hung in the air amongst the throng, the sense of a community that had negotiated a difficult week and now sought out great encouragement to take them into the next.

Edsel Butz read the New Testament reading for the day from St. Matthew chapter seven verse three. His booming voice rang clear. "Why do you look at the speck of sawdust in your brother's eye," his barrel chest heaved as he gave the rest of the verse full throttle, "and pay no attention to the plank in your own eye?"

Berdie wondered if all the village hadn't heard his

reading. She noticed several people sat a little straighter in their pew after.

Hugh's sermon was a bit gentler than Edsel's boom, but he was firm. Berdie heard Hugh say that one must take care of their own soul business, not making charges concerning someone else's, when his voice seemed to become muffled and distant.

The next thing Berdie heard was Mr. Castle setting to on the organ for the closing hymn of the service. She jerked her chin up and noticed the young woman next to her smiled widely, then whispered to her mother who eyed Berdie furtively. In fact, most the row where Berdie sat wore smiles, although a few had frowns.

It was then Berdie became aware that she had taken a wee siesta at her husband's expense. Oh, no, she thought. I can just imagine what they'll be saying at the Copper Kettle.

Berdie managed a quick look-about, trying to appear absolutely astute. It was clear that Jeff and Jamie were not the only congregants to sneak out early.

As a matter of fact, Hugh, who stood at the door when the service was ended, sent off a less populated crowd than had arrived that morning.

Berdie went directly home. The first thing she did when she got home was to enter the kitchen, put on her kitchen pinny, and make a strong pot of tea. Lillie joined her, Hugh following. Berdie poured a cuppa for all three of them.

Lillie blew on the hot liquid. "Did you think your congregation was being spirited away today, Hugh?"

"In truth, I appreciate that they showed at all." He spooned sugar in his brew. "Priorities: they seem to have the stick by the right end."

"Yes." Berdie rubbed a tired eye.

"So, give me your thoughts on today's sermon, Berdie." Hugh grasped his cup and lifted it to his lips.

Berdie pulled some sliced ham from the refrigerator, the smell of it delighting the nose.

"Quite good," Berdie said with a hint of hesitation.

"Really?" Hugh's eyebrow arched upward.

"Oh." Berdie paused. "You saw me then?"

Hugh simply tipped his head.

"Didn't we all?" Lillie tittled.

Berdie pursed her lips. "I'm sorry, Hugh, really. It's just that call last night, at all hours, you know."

Hugh briefly shook his head in the negative.

"What call?" Lillie snatched a bit of ham she quickly popped in her mouth.

"Dead of night," Berdie began. "A call, some fellow says he wants to have a clandestine meeting, very cloak and dagger."

Hugh placed four pieces of bread out on the counter.

"What man?" Lillie said abruptly.

Berdie handed the mustard jar to Lillie with a knife. She pointed to the bread. "If you would please."

"What man?" Lillie repeated and dipped the knife into the seasoned mustard jar.

"I was awakened from a sound sleep. The conversation was clipped, something sounded familiar, but." Berdie separated the ham slices. "He wants to meet behind the Pork and Barrel, can you imagine?" Berdie placed several thin slices of ham on the dressed bread.

"Be careful, love," Hugh cautioned. He cut a tomato into slices on a bread board.

Berdie stopped short. "He said he had something to give me."

"How many people know you're investigating things?" Lillie asked cautiously just as she put the last swathe of mustard on the top bread slices.

"Who doesn't know might be a more appropriate question," Hugh injected. "This is a small village."

"Was it Wilkie Gordon?" Lillie rammed the words together rapidly.

"Wilkie Gordon?" Hugh stopped slicing.

Berdie placed ham on the remaining dressed bread. "Something's going on with Wilkie, yes. But it wasn't he who called."

Hugh put the knife down. "Why is Wilkie even in this conversation?"

Berdie glanced at Lillie then proceeded. "Hugh, I know it's difficult for you to think of Wilkie Gordon poorly. However, too many things are out of sort with him since the garden fête. Something's off."

"Wilkie Gordon, hurt a child? Preposterous," Hugh proclaimed. "That is what you're suggesting?"

"I'm simply saying something's off." Berdie lowered her voice. "At this point."

Lillie looked down and took a quick swallow of tea.

Hugh shook his head. "No." He plunged the knife through the tomato cutting a particularly thick piece.

Lillie pointed her spreading knife towards Berdie, eyes big. "It was Colonel Preswood who called."

"Preswood." Berdie cocked her head.

Hugh chuckled. "Oh, ladies, you do reach." He placed a tomato slice atop the ham. "Preswood."

"Well, they've got Venetian glass in their home, just the kind that was imbedded in that poor child," Lillie bleated.

"What?" Hugh stopped dressing the sandwich.

"And there's Flora Preswood's chin, as well."

"Go back to the glass bit," Hugh directed.

Berdie chimed in. "There was a piece of eighteenth century Venetian glass stolen from the Preswood's home, and from what I could gather, about the time of the child's death."

"Really?" He placed the last tomato slice. "Now that could be something. You must get Goodnight to look into that."

Berdie began to top the tomatoes with lettuce.

"Right? Goodnight? You are giving him aid and all?" Hugh checked with an eye to Berdie.

Berdie glanced at Lillie. "I should think so."

Berdie opened the cooler bag while Lillie placed the top slices to complete the sandwiches. "Now, a little cling wrap and you're off to cheer on the home team."

"That John Smith, vanishing from the tour, suddenly returning, it could be him." Lillie continued the guessing game.

"Where are my Scotch eggs?" Hugh opened the cupboard door, surveyed, and reached into the crowded space. "Now if anyone is suspect, I should think he would be." He brought the shrink-wrapped goods to the counter. "Slightly erratic, wouldn't you say?"

"Would say." Berdie wrapped the last sandwich with cling film. She placed the sandwiches in the cool bag.

Hugh poured hot tea into the large awaiting flask while Berdie put the Scotch eggs in the cool bag aside the sandwiches then popped in a couple of apples.

"Mathew Reese tried to ring the fellow when he first departed the tour you know," Hugh rattled. "He rang up the number Mr. Smith gave as a home telephone, but Mathew got a pet store in Norwich. Can you imagine?"

Lillie and Berdie came to a dead stop. Berdie inhaled. "What pet store?"

"What?" Hugh stopped pouring the tea when he saw the interest generated by his comment.

Berdie walked her index and third finger, with a scurrying motion up her arm. "Possible black market."

"Oh yes, well spotted." Hugh nodded. "Hadn't thought of that." He continued to fill the flask. "You'll have to ask Mathew about that."

"Or John Smith himself." Berdie closed the cool bag. "When we find the spider-tender, we settle the bones account."

Hugh fastened the cup atop the flask. "You think the two are connected, and it's that simple?"

"Did I say simple? But yes, I think the two are connected."

"How? Just how does an attempt on the life of a beautiful and gracious well-to-do Italian noble relate to an English child's death in the eighties?"

"Ah, well, that's the bit I have yet to work out." Berdie wiped her hands across the yellow gingham kitchen pinny she wore.

"I should say that's a very large bit."

She handed him the fastened cold bag. "I will work it out, you know."

Hugh placed a kiss on Berdie's cheek. "Presumably."

"Have fun at the game." Lillie smiled. "You certainly won't starve. You've enough there to feed three people."

"Two actually." Hugh walked to the kitchen door.

"Who's that?" Lillie was bright.

Hugh looked at Berdie, than Lillie. "I'm meeting Loren," he clipped and left the kitchen.

Lillie's visage took a turn. "Oh," she said somberly. "No Dr. Chase to accompany then? Your husband had better hope Loren left his mobile at home. That's the only guarantee they'll see the game out."

"Are you still putting Loren off?" Berdie's displeasure showed itself in her slight frown.

"He stopped ringing me up."

"And who's to blame for that?"

Lillie took a taste of tea. Berdie could see moisture gathering in the corner of Lillie's downcast eyes. "I'm not sure I haven't lost him for good." Lillie sniffed and took a deep breath. She shook her head appearing to make an attempt to dismiss the world around her. "Can we not talk about this?"

"What would be best, Lillie, is to stop dallying about and ring up Loren to talk exactly about this. You're practically sending Loren into Roz's awaiting arms," Berdie barked.

"Oh, Berdie, you think I don't know that?" Lillie barked back. "I don't know where to begin."

"No I s'pose not." Berdie suddenly became aware of how peckish she had become, the lack of sound sleep taking a toll. She took a slow drink of tea. "I'm all-in Lillie. What say we meet at the church an hour before evensong tonight? We can sort through all this bother then, together. Yeah?"

Lillie shook her dark curls in an affirmative nod, the corner of her eye still glistening.

Berdie pulled a fresh tissue from her pinny pocket and handed it to Lillie who dabbed at an escaped tear.

"I've let him steal my heart you know."

"Yes, lovey, I know."

Lillie took Berdie's hand and squeezed it. "And you get some good kip this afternoon." She smiled bravely. "And sweet dreams with it."

Berdie nodded and returned the affectionate squeeze. "An hour before Evensong, then, fresh as an Easter daisy."

Within a moment, her best friend in the entire world departed for home while she made her way to the ample bed in the master bedroom.

When Berdie arose, she was much more refreshed. After some hot soup, tea, and a fresh plum, she was ready to be among the living once again. In fact, she had promised Hugh to help with some simple data entry on the computer at church and decided to go over a bit early to work on it. She would make quick work of it and be ready to spend undistracted time with Lillie.

When she entered the sacristy, she left the door half open so she could hear Lillie enter. The data entry was a snap, and Berdie was happy she could help Hugh. So much of her time recently was spent investigating.

Just a little over half the work completed, Berdie heard the church door open. She glanced at the time on the computer.

"She's rather early."

Berdie closed the file and took a deep inhale. She must be in the appropriate state of mind to let go of an unfinished task to take up another. She exhaled slowly. Yes, ready, indeed.

She arose and entered the lowly lit sanctuary where sunlight from the windows began to cast afternoon shadows across the peaceful edifice.

"Oh." Berdie could not suppress her surprise. It wasn't Lillie at all. *Of all people*, Berdie thought. *Ready for Lillie, yes, but ready for this?*

"Is your husband in?"

"No, no he's out at the moment."

Dr. Roz Chase shifted her weight.

And if I have my way, my husband will be out as long as you are present. Berdie found herself having to work at courtesy.

The grey business suit the doctor wore paled her some and was a bit too big. Berdie decided the cut of it did not show off the woman's new features very well. Her dark hair was pulled back in a severe bun at the back of her head making her face contours somewhat harsh. And not a gold necklace in sight.

Roz fumbled an unlit cigarette in her fingers then jammed it in the pocket of her suit coat.

"At the game, then?"

"Yes."

"Loren didn't tell me with whom he was going."

"No. I see."

She's checking to see if Loren went with Hugh as opposed to Lillie. Well, thank heavens he did. Berdie's lips went tight. She just wanted Roz to go far away and quickly, but Dr. Chase didn't seem eager to depart.

The woman shifted her weight again. "She doesn't deserve him you know."

Berdie blinked. "Sorry?"

The woman stepped closer to Berdie. She looked at the stone church floor then reared her face up so that her bronze-colored eyes pierced hard into Berdie's face. Facial enhancing aside, the hardness of a life that daily mingles with the worst part of humanity's doings could not be erased from the doctor's visage.

"I tried it on with him you know," Roz said coarsely. "And I could sense him beginning to yield. Does that shock you?"

Berdie didn't flinch. "Loren's a handsome man, and I dare say you're a needy woman."

With those words, Dr. Chase took hold of a pew. It was as if her strength couldn't hold her, as if the truth of Berdie's words had just punched her in the stomach and rendered her weak. She sat down, head low.

There was a part of Berdie that wanted to let Roz sink in her apparent weakness. Berdie flashed back to the railway station with Roz running her manicured fingernail down her lovely neck and smiling at Hugh.

Remove the plank from your own eye. Edsel's New Testament reading sounded in Berdie's head. It was then the plank in Berdie's own eye hit her over the head. *Bonk.* Ah, jealousy was indeed an ugly thing. Perfect proportions and a redesigned face were too easily cast-off because of simple envy.

Now, the better part of Berdie, the redeemed Berdie, could see before her the real woman. Right proportions or not, Roz was very much at a loss. Berdie purposed to turn away from that insipid green that had blinded her so easily.

She seated herself on the pew directly in front of the visitor and turned to look into Dr. Chase's face.

Roz lifted her head. "But he didn't." She paused. "Yield, that is."

"Oh, he yielded, Roz," Berdie said smoothly. "It just wasn't to your charms; it was to a still, small voice inside."

Roz's eyes grew moist, but she raised her chin as if impervious to any sense of vulnerability. "He mumbled something about how attractive I was, how cherished I was as his dear friend, and that he loved someone else."

Berdie nodded. "Roz, if I may, why the romantic pursuit of someone you've known as a friend?"

Dr. Chase swallowed and inhaled deeply. "Gerard became tired of eating dinner alone, you know. It comes part and parcel with my career. He left." She tilted her head. "But now, Loren and I share the same vocation, and along with a little personal redesigning"—she ran a hand across her new waistline—"I thought; now there's a promise."

Berdie couched her words with a certain comforting tone. "Roz, as difficult as it is right now, Loren did what he knew to be right and actually spared you a great deal of deep heartache. That proves he's fond of you."

Roz crossed her arms. "Really?"

"You're a bright woman. You know there's always a certain element of risk when you maneuver yourself into someone's life, in this case Loren's."

Roz took another deep inhale. "Yes."

Berdie leaned closer. "We can't make them fall in love with us, no matter how attractive, can we?"

Dr. Chase's drooping shoulders straightened a bit. A stern jaw was all she offered. Then she lifted her well-shaped brows as if tossing off the entire conversation. "Anyway, I've been called in on an active investigation in London."

"Are you finished here?"

"If you mean is my work done, no, it isn't. The only reason this case had my services was because I made it a certain priority and now it's not." The woman gave a pasted half-grin. "I've been told you have excellent investigative skills, you take up the work." Dr. Chase stood. She turned her body and took rapid steps to the church entrance.

"But I'm not a pathologist," Berdie called after the departing woman.

Roz opened the door then paused. She turned to run her eyes across the quiet nave. "I can't remember the last time I was in a church. Something almost reassuring about it." Dr. Roz Chase disappeared behind the closed door.

"Dr. Chase," Berdie appealed. All she heard were her own words bouncing across the stone walls.

"Lillie." Berdie realized there was a good possibility the two women might meet in the going and coming. "Oh my, where's my whistle and zebra shirt?"

Berdie returned her body to sitting position on the pew. "Maybe that wouldn't be such a bad thing if they met."

True, Roz's visit had caught Berdie by surprise, but overall, something positive came of it. She had discovered the plank in her eye, and Roz, hopefully, was a step closer to finding her way. Yes. She decided if she heard something like spatting cats and saw bits of hair flying by the church window, then she would search it out. Otherwise, let it be.

To continue her data entry work, that was her task at hand. She moved to the sacristy, but when she had only worked five more minutes, the sound of the opening church door reached her ears.

"Lillie. Lord may she be of good humor." Berdie turned on her heel to see once again it wasn't her dear friend. It was Hugh. And Loren accompanied him.

"We won," Hugh announced to Berdie and, it seemed, to anyone within a mile.

"Did we?" Berdie grinned.

"Jeff and Jamie both played brilliantly, didn't they Loren?"

"Brilliantly indeed," Loren had a zip in his words. "I must say that Jamie Donovan is a topnotch striker."

"And Jeff's quick." Hugh was animated as he swayed his body side to side. "Jolly good fun."

Just as the last word escaped Hugh's lips, Berdie observed the church door opening yet again. This time, indeed, it was Lillie.

She wore a creamy colored washed-silk cardigan, fully buttoned with little pearls. A slim pink skirt hugged her slender waist and fell just below her knee. Her dark short curls fell enchantingly around her face. Lillie, in a careful poise, stepped quietly into the space.

Loren straightened; he pulled a shock of dangling hair into place, but it fell loosely across one brow.

And the exuberant Hugh lost his tongue. The vicar turned a somewhat bewildered gaze at Berdie.

"Am I interrupting something?" Lillie asked with a wistful voice. Her apologetic glance towards Loren said far more than her words.

"No, Lillie, no," Berdie fumbled. "We were just discussing the football game." Berdie waved her hand towards the sacristy. "It's just that I'm working in the sacristy and…"

"Right," Hugh's voice broke in. "She wants to hear all the details but…"

"He needs to speak to me while I work, must get on, you see."

"Really?" Lillie crossed her arms.

Loren looked at the stone floor with a half grin.

"In the sacristy." Berdie bobbed her thumb toward the room.

"Oh, yes." Hugh moved towards Berdie. "Yes. Quite the game."

Berdie scooted into the cozy room, and Hugh was soon next to her.

"Shut the door Berdie."

Berdie eased it almost shut.

"Poor fellow. I don't think Loren was prepared for this," Hugh said. "We were to have a discussion here concerning just what to do about his situation with Lillie."

"Lillie and I had planned to talk as well."

Though Hugh stood near his desk, Berdie found it hard to leave the door. The close-by office lamp that now declared itself across the darkening nave was easily extinguished by Berdie. She nearly closed the door, but wide enough to peek through the open space.

She could just see Loren and Lillie, ensconced by the low shadows of the afternoon window light. They both stood rather at loss for words.

"Berdie," Hugh whispered. "Why did you turn the light off?" He motioned her to the desk.

"Well, what if they have a horrible row? What if some unsuspecting soul should walk in?"

"Oh my. I hadn't thought of that." He joined Berdie at the door but didn't avail himself of the opening through which to observe the unsuspecting couple.

Berdie could see Lillie move closer to Loren. She just barely made out the words that Lillie formed.

"Loren, I've been foolish."

The doctor stared at Lillie as if beholding, for the first time, an exquisite work of art, examining all its fine detail and brilliant color. "What do you know? I was about to say exactly the same to you."

Lillie took a very deep breath. "I'm afraid I let my own insecurities take the better part of me." Lillie's voice had a bit of waver, as if on the very edge of tears.

Loren moved next to Lillie. His broad, masculine hand reached out to lightly touch her slender fingers. "Lillie," he breathed.

The penitent woman twined her responsive fingers into his, and their touch became a gentle grasp. "I've missed you desperately, Loren."

"What's going on?" Hugh questioned Berdie.

"Shhh."

She could see the doctor move his hand to Lillie's waist. He drew her closely to himself.

"I was so blind, Lillie, you were right about Roz. Please believe me, I would never hurt you."

Lillie nodded.

Loren drew Lillie into a gentle embrace. She placed her arms around his lean waist and laid her head on Loren's broad shoulder.

"I never knew I could miss someone as much as I've missed you." Loren was just barely audible. He put his finger under Lillie's chin and tipped it towards him. He bent forward to touch his lips to hers.

Plunk. The door quietly closed, Hugh's broad hand upon it.

Berdie pulled back. "Hugh," she scolded.

"Hardly a row, is it love? And none of our business at that."

"Oh yes?" Berdie turned to face her stalwart husband. "And who was it that said, 'what's going on'?"

"What's going on?"

"Yes, when I was looking, and you asked what's going on'?"

Hugh straightened. "That was when there was a question of a possible row."

"It was to satisfy your curiosity."

"Concern, Berdie, not curiosity." Hugh used his military voice.

A light rapping sound came at the door then quickly opened.

Lillie stood at the entrance, Loren next to her. Both wore quiet smiles. Lillie leaned close to Berdie. "You can open the door again."

Berdie felt slightly silly, and Hugh positively squirmed.

"We're going for a walk." Loren gently grasped Lillie's elbow.

"Oh, that's well and good." Berdie smiled and Hugh nodded. "Yes, well." Berdie pointed to the computer. "I'll get on with my work."

"And by the way," Loren added, "you can turn the light back on as well."

Berdie felt the heat rise on her face. "What a fine suggestion."

"We'll be back by Evensong," Lillie chirped.

"We'll see you then." Hugh turned the lamp back to a lighted state.

"Mind how you go." Berdie obliged but didn't shut the door.

The couple left, hand in hand.

"They've more discussion ahead of them, but on the whole, that seems to have worked itself out then." Hugh was now bright.

"Yes." Berdie, too, brightened. "It's always encouraging when love gone wrong gets set right."

She sat herself before the computer. "And, I can only hope that the unraveling of current crimes should go as smoothly. The mystery man of Pork and Barrel awaits at dawn."

"Mind how you go," Hugh cautioned and gave her a sweet peck on the cheek.

11

Berdie turned on the left turn indicator of the car, the blinking brightness sending patches of light across the Timsley predawn darkness.

"I can't believe you dragged me out at this hour," Lillie grumbled. "Loren didn't get me home 'til quite late." Lillie wore a dreamy expression. "A lovely dinner in Timsley." She paused. "A late lovely dinner. And here I am, back again." She tipped the beaker of hot tea to her lips. The coolness of the morning played with the steam that curled off the receptacle.

Berdie could almost sniff the approximation of bacon in the pan as they neared the Pork and Barrel, even though the place didn't open until ten AM.

"I'm glad you and Loren are getting on again. And good news on my front, Lillie. I think I have worked out who Mr. Cloak-and-Dagger may be."

"Oh yes?" Lillie yawned.

"Do you remember what Hugh said to me yesterday when we were talking about the mystery man?"

"What, all of it?"

Berdie deepened her voice. "Be careful, love."

"He would say." Lillie rubbed a tired eye.

"Actually, it's what he didn't say."

Berdie was confident as she approached the entry of the Pork and Barrel car park.

Lillie took another large gulp from the beaker

around which her hands warmed. "So am I considering what he said or what he didn't say?"

Berdie set her jaw and went on without as much as a twitter in answer to Lillie. "I need to go with you, Berdie. That's what he usually says if he thinks I'm risking danger. Or he raises any number of things in a kind of protest."

Lillie blinked. "Yes."

Berdie steered the car into the car park. "But he didn't say any of those things and you know what that means?"

Lillie furrowed her brow. "I love being your Watson, Berdie, but I don't fancy it at five thirty in the morning."

"It's nearly six." Berdie nodded toward the car's clock.

She directed the vehicle to the back area behind the building. A couple skips of rubbish made their odiferous presence known. Berdie brought the car to an abrupt halt.

"Be quiet and stay low in the seat, Lillie," Berdie commanded. "He may do a runner if aware of another person about." She turned the engine off and opened her car door.

"What if there's mischief?" Lillie queried in a hoarse whisper.

"Not this time." Berdie answered with a very solid confidence.

Her feet no sooner hit the ground and one quick flash of car lights hailed from a dark nook in between two out buildings. Berdie straightened and took self-assured steps towards the dark space.

As she approached, she could just make out a black late model Mercedes. Immediately, she smiled.

Her hunch as to who the informant may be was indeed correct. It all came together.

"It's OK. There are no malicious sorts about," Berdie announced. "Show yourself."

In a long black coat, a neck scarf wrapped round his chin and a black hat pulled low, Preston Graystone emerged from his vehicle.

The corners of Berdie's mouth turned slightly upward at seeing the village solicitor now in the roll of a stealth informant.

"How very cavalier of you." Graystone spit out the words.

"Yes, good morning Mr. Graystone," Berdie greeted with no care to volume.

"Shh." The man looked to the left and right. "You needn't address me."

He came closer to Berdie where she was able to make out a nervous gravity written in his eyes.

"I'm doing this by the urging of your husband and to protect my legal station."

"Indeed. But if you don't mind me asking, why tell me and not the proper law?"

"Because Albert Goodnight has about as much discretion as flies on pigs." Preston Graystone flared. "Your husband assured me most ardently that you would keep a confidence."

"I would indeed."

"Strictest of confidence, mind you." Graystone shook a skinny finger towards Berdie. "Any of this gets out, and I'll deny it."

"Of course you will."

The man glanced side to side once more. "There was this man you see." Graystone's voice had a distinct edge. "Bumped into him by accident in the woods near the Preswood estate, some distance from the families' summer house"—he cleared his throat—"and near the church wood. It was about the time they think that child was allegedly disposed of those many years ago."

"Twenty years ago. You still have a memory of it?"

"It was the tragic night my wife first went into hospital in London."

"You were here and your wife in London," Berdie reiterated with a questioning tone.

"Isn't that what I just said?" Graystone gathered his brow and spoke impatiently. "I'll not soon forget that night. It was the beginning of her ordeal to which she eventually succumbed."

"You remember the evening, obviously," Berdie said tenderly, and moved on in her investigative posture. "Are you saying you may know who the perpetrator of the crime is?"

"I am not," Graystone nearly shouted and threw his hand into the air. "Blimey woman, let me speak without interruption." Graystone stuck his angular chin out. "I'm giving you three minutes and no questions."

Berdie raised a reassuring palm towards Graystone and used a soft voice hoping to calm the fellow. "Go on then." She realized she'd have to phrase her questions in an affirmative manner.

"Couldn't make out the man's face very well, but he wore a woodsman's hat, much like the kind Wilkie Gordon wears. And he had a spade in tow. It smelled of fresh earth."

Berdie spoke cautiously. "His face was camouflaged then."

"No, no," Graystone protested. "Not camouflaged,

it was dark, desperately dark, as it would be at three AM."

"In the wood, not far from the Preswood summer house, at three in the morning. That's slightly odd."

"Now see here." The solicitor narrowed his eyes. "Odd does not enter into it. I will not give details." He swallowed. "I assure you there were no indiscretions and under no circumstances will I divulge or cast dispersions on the good character..." Graystone dropped his head in silence.

"Flora Preswood," Berdie finished.

The man straightened. He raised his eyes only quickly to Berdie and resumed looking at the ground. "Of course not," came quietly from his mouth without any real conviction. It was all Berdie really needed to be aware of.

"No, Mr. Graystone, no indiscretions." Berdie was suddenly appreciative of Hugh as parish confessor. "No real description of the fellow then."

"Average height, seemed cautious, furtive, unknown, and yet somehow familiar."

A work lorry pulled close to the front of the Pork and Barrel. Graystone ducked back against his car.

"No indiscretions mind you. I've never had this conversation with you," he clipped, fervor returning to his voice.

Berdie sealed the clandestine dialogue with a question. "What conversation?" She smiled. "And thank you, Preston."

Like a rabbit to its burrow, Preston Graystone hid away in his car, motioning Berdie to leave the area.

Obliging the anxious solicitor, Berdie returned to her car where Lillie had, indeed, stayed low. So low, as a matter of fact, Berdie had to nudge her awake in order to seat herself properly in the driver's seat.

By the time Berdie eased the car onto the road, Lillie was upright and just cognizant.

"You're all right, then?" Lillie blinked.

"And what would you've done if I wasn't? Snored loud enough to alert the police?"

"You weren't out all hours last night." Lillie stretched her arms above her head. "Anyway, who was it?"

"Not to tell, dear girl."

"Berdie!" Lillie sounded somewhat put out. "Really, all this way at this time of day, or dark, or whatever it is, and you won't tell me who it was?"

"Can't really. No, matter of honor and you know how I am about that. But I can tell you this, Lillie dear. You snooze, you lose."

"Thus endeth the lesson?" Lillie itched behind her ear and emitted a low giggle. "Yes, well, not exactly a feather bed, these seats."

"I should say." Both women laughed heartily.

"What say we breakfast at the Upland Arms?" Berdie still had the scent of rashers in her nose.

"Oh, yes, please. I believe I'm awake enough to jolly well do that."

"I thought as much." Berdie chuckled. And the return trip to Aidan Kirkwood was underway.

The Upland Arms' wee car park was full when Berdie and Lillie arrived.

"Is it everyone's day out?" Lillie glanced about at all the vehicles.

No sooner had the words left her mouth than Jamie Donovan exited the building, carrier bag in hand. His muscular build fitted the Butz and Sons Electric work uniform well. His gracious white smile contrasted with his black hair as he waved a greeting to Berdie and Lillie.

Berdie put down the car window and stuck her head out. "Well done I hear, Jamie. Brilliant was the word Hugh used to describe your football play."

"It was a team effort," he called back. "But thank you." He pointed to his work lorry. "This space has your name on it, Mrs. Elliott."

Berdie gave Jamie a thumbs up, and he moved to his vehicle.

She heard the approach of an engine, quickly realizing Mr. Raheem had just pulled in behind her in his green grocer delivery vehicle. She supposed he had a produce delivery for Dudley Horn. Mr. Raheem bounced from his auto and greeted Berdie at her window.

"Good Morning, Mrs. Elliott, Miss Foxworth. You're about it early." Mr. Raheem spoke in his slight Punjabi accent and wore his voluminous grin.

"Yes, we've joined the masses at the Upland Arms. And I should think you're feeding them."

"I bring the produce. Mr. Horn feeds them." He wiped his hands on his white work pinny. "When Reverend Elliott began morning Lenten Matins at church, the business here, it booms." He had a lilt in his voice. "All praises to God."

Lillie leaned towards the window of conversation. "We saw you at Bampkingswith Hall the other day."

"Oh yes, I have so many deliveries there." Mr. Raheem announced it proudly.

"Really?" Berdie pried.

Mr. Raheem lifted his brows. "Of the fruit baskets, glazed clementines, even a fresh carafe of Sangria my wife prepares. And all gifts from the most generous visitor to our town."

"A generous visitor. That would be Mrs. Hall's aunt." Berdie pried even further.

"Oh, I'm sure Mrs. Hall's aunt may be generous. But no, Mr. John Smith is the generous person I speak of. A generous giver of gifts to the Preswood family."

"Generous, indeed," Berdie verbalized keeping her surprise disguised.

By that time, Jamie had pulled his vehicle out of the parking space and eased past Berdie's vehicle, nodding to the empty spot.

"Nice to chat, Mrs. Elliott." Mr. Raheem tipped his head to her.

"Thank you, Mr. Raheem. God go with you." Berdie pulled the car into the now-empty space.

"Fancy that," Lillie quipped. "John Smith sending gifts to the Preswoods."

"Yes. Generous is not a word that springs to mind when thinking of the incalculable Mr. John Smith. What is he up to?"

"Oh my word." Lillie gasped and pointed discreetly towards the door of the Upland Arms. "It's him. It is. It's him."

The average height, average build, and salt and pepper hair of "the generous giver of gifts" seemed momentarily larger than life as he exited the establishment. The pensive glare from beneath his silver glasses brightened when he saw Mr. Raheem. They began what appeared to be a very cordial conversation.

"Out of the car Lillie, quickly. I want to speak to our Mr. Smith."

"This could be worth the early rising." Lillie slipped out.

Mr. Raheem entered the pub. Mr. Smith took steps across the car park.

"Mr. Smith," Berdie called.

The man continued walking.

"Mr. John Smith," Berdie called again.

The fellow glanced at Berdie and took two more steps before stopping short. "Yes, sorry, good morning." He greeted almost pleasantly.

"May I have a word with you, please?

"I am in rather a rush. Could it wait?"

"Only a moment of your time." Berdie came closer to the man who switched his carrier bag to the other hand.

It was then Berdie noticed that the man's neck was covered with tiny red bumps. She couldn't help but stare. Surely not measles.

Mr. Smith apparently could feel her ogle.

"Some fool put lemon in my tea this morning at that B and B. Allergic," he pronounced. "Now what is it you want?"

Berdie stood firm and took a deep breath. "Mr. Smith, are you aware that when Mathew Reese tried to ring you at the number you gave as your home phone, he got a pet store in Norwich?"

The man frowned. "What matter is it to you?"

"I have to ask. Are you particularly fond of Venezuelan spiders?"

"Spiders?" He pulled his head back. "Why should I have an interest in those wretched little creatures?"

Berdie lifted her chin.

The man's eyes flashed and his cheeks flushed. "Just what are you implying, vicar's wife?" He narrowed his eyes. "You're accusing me of planting that dreadful spider at Swithy Lodge."

"I'm not accusing you of anything, Mr. Smith," Berdie said firmly. "But you must admit your behavior has been anything but reliable. A bogus telephone number and the Mr. Smith identity is hardly masterful. Tell me why I shouldn't consider you a possible malevolent?"

The man raised his chin and stuck his chest out. "I should not be named in the same breath as that vehement spider, because I haven't anything to do with the dreadful episode. I shouldn't wish that woman any harm," he snapped. "And why does a self-appointed busybody stick her nose into my personal business? As plainly as I can put it, clear off."

"You must realize, Mr. Smith, that the truth will eventually be known."

The gentleman shifted the carrier bag back to the other hand. His eyes bored into Berdie's face. "The revelation of truth is of great concern to more than just yourself you know."

The man, as if in military posture, turned his back to Berdie and walked away, taking long, strong, confident strides.

Lillie came near Berdie. "That was rather direct."

Berdie shook her head. "What an odd fellow. I really think he's telling the truth about the spider bit. But he's hiding something, sure as dafs bloom in spring. And it's something core to this whole messy business." She shook her head. "I'm sure I've seen him before."

"What did he mean when he said you weren't the only one who wanted the truth?"

"What did he mean indeed?" Berdie shook her head, again. "What a morning: a man who offers information to clean his soul and one who denies information to keep his mask firmly in place."

Two couples and a group of five walked cross the car park and entered the Upland Arms.

"What say we get our breakfast take-away." Lillie eyed another person who approached the door. "I don't fancy waiting weeks for a seat."

"And especially when the vicarage has so many comfortable empty ones."

Twenty minutes later, Berdie and Lillie were munching on fried eggs, sausage, bacon, beans, tomatoes, mushrooms, and a fried bread: the full English breakfast, in the quiet comfort of the vicarage kitchen. And accompanying the meal, they had a fresh pot of steaming hot PG Tips tea. The kitchen was near silence as the two tucked in.

"Wonderful sausage." Berdie finally spoke.

"Eggs cooked to perfection." Lillie wiped her lips with the napkin and took a swallow of tea. "Did I tell you? I've invited Loren to my music festival in St. Erts." Lillie took a bite of tomato. "Aunt Margaret's country house in St. Ives is just a jaunt away. She said she'd love to meet Loren and has invited us to stay with her during the festival."

Berdie nodded her head, chewing a piece of sausage.

"He's going to try to get the time off work."

Berdie widened her eyes and swallowed. "What did you say?"

Lillie scooped some beans. "Loren's going to try to get the weekend off."

"No, before that."

"Aunt Margaret has offered to host Loren and me when I attend the music festival in St. Erts."

"Saint Erts," Berdie exclaimed.

Lillie took a sip of tea. "Yes, that's right, St Erts."

Berdie put her fork down and sat straight back in her chair. "Lillie, you're brilliant."

"So my mother was right all along, then." Lillie smiled and munched.

"We need to go over to the church." Berdie hopped from her chair.

Lillie swallowed. "Excuse me, I'm eating breakfast."

"Yes, well, bring it with you if you like. I need to get on the computer." Berdie was already at the kitchen door. "Stay here if it suits you."

By the time Berdie reached the vicarage hallway, Lillie was right behind, plate and cup in hand, her fried bread clenched in her lips.

When they arrived at the church, Berdie buzzed into the sacristy. She moved some papers aside on the desk to make room for Lillie and her food.

Berdie moved to the computer, opposite Lillie, at the desk. Lillie continued her breakfast while Berdie sat in the large desk chair and danced her fingers on the computer keyboard.

"Are you going to tell me just what we're doing?" Lillie asked in between bites of egg.

"You, dear, are finishing your breakfast. I am searching for answers." Berdie concentrated on the monitor. "Do you remember what lovely Coral at council housing in London told us? There was something her husband, Joby, heard Wanda Pitts say repeatedly when full of the drink."

"My head hurts?"

"Very droll, Lillie. Now think. In fact, think trees."

"Oh yes," Lilly mumbled. "What was that? Beech, Willow."

"Evergreen," Berdie corrected. "'Earth cares for my Evergreen'. Remember? 'They will do what's best.' It struck me odd at the time, and I've puzzled over it since."

Lillie nodded and took a sip of now lukewarm tea.

"What if Wanda Pitts was not saying earth, but Erts?"

Lillie squinted. "Erts will do what's best?"

"Look." Berdie pointed to the monitor. "St. Erts Church, the village of St. Erts, The Benevolent Society of St. Erts." Berdie touched the computer screen. "St Erts Children's Home, St. Erts Shelter for the Needy of London. We're on to something here."

With gusto, Berdie reached across the desk to get the phone. "I've got to ring up Billy Beaton." In the process, her elbow bumped Lillie's hand that held her teacup. Brown liquid went air born, sloshed from the receptacle, and splashed all cross Hugh's desk, soiling several papers.

"Lillie." Berdie wiped drops from the computer screen as well. "What have you done?"

"What have *I* done?"

Both women were on their feet. Lillie used her napkin to soak up the errant fluid while Berdie grabbed tissues from a nearby box and began a hectic blotting of the papers.

Berdie examined the damp papers closely. "Oh no," she all but shouted.

"What?"

"It's christening certificates." Berdie groaned as she pulled down her glasses and inspected the certificates. "These are copies. Yes, I believe so."

"Not so bad then." Lillie's voice was slightly buoyant while she continued the cleanup.

"Charles Montague Swindon-Pierce," Berdie read. "St. Marks in Earl Court." Berdie perked. "Oh, these are the copies Hugh requested for the marriage procedures." Berdie placed another certificate on top of Charles' paper and dabbed it lightly. "Yes, this is Robin's. Roberta Daniela Darbyshire." She squinted and ran her finger across the moist area.

"Where was she christened?" Lillie asked still mopping.

"Here, of course. England. Remember? The moment they touched English soil Flora Preswood said."

"There's another one." Lillie pointed to a third sheet of paper.

"Quite right." Berdie put the paper on top of the others and dabbed it lightly. "Rosalie Diana Darbyshire."

"Why would Hugh have Rosalie's christening record?"

"I don't know. Perhaps Hugh requested it." She pushed her glasses back up her nose and ran her finger across Rosalie's document.

Lillie stopped cleaning and scanned the length of the desk. "What's Hugh going to say?"

"Hugh." Berdie pursed her lips and looked at Lillie. "Yes, well, we'll find out when you tell him."

"When I tell him? He's your husband."

Berdie laid all three certificates in a row next to one another. "So that makes me the messenger for all messes?" She blew on them.

"That's not what I implied."

"It was your tea."

"It was your elbow."

The door opened and Hugh quickly stepped into

the fray. "What are you two jabbering about?"

Both women went silent. Then Berdie said "Um" at the exact same moment Lillie said, "Well."

Hugh frowned. "I see." He crossed his arms. "Put it to me, then."

Berdie half smiled and waved her hand across the wet certificates. Lillie grabbed the plate and cup from where it sat.

Hugh moved to the desk. His left eyebrow arched when he saw the christening certificates.

"These things happen." Lillie tried to hide the empty cup behind her back.

"I don't want to know," he said as he picked up a certificate, took it in, and nodded. "Tea I'd say, right cross the lot."

Berdie clasped her hands together. "Truly sorry, Hugh."

"Yes," Lillie added.

"Fine." Hugh ran a finger over the wet print that read Charles Montague Swindon-Pierce. "No sense crying over spilt milk, or tea, as it were." He looked at Berdie then Lillie. "You were in here for..."

"Computer." Berdie pointed.

Hugh nodded.

"As you're here, I believe a conversation with you is in order,"—Berdie said with a slight lilt—"concerning the cloak and dagger I met at the Pork and Barrel."

Hugh straightened. "Absolutely nothing to talk about concerning that, nothing at all. Am I making myself clear?"

"Abundantly." Berdie winced.

"I'm expecting Mr. Webb any moment. He's offering a five hundred pound reward for the person who brings to rights the perpetrator of Contessa Santolio's spider attack. He wants to post it on the church web page." Hugh waved a certificate in the air, as if a flag, to dry it. "Off you go then." He waved his hand towards the door.

"Look closely at those, Hugh." Berdie's voice was restrained.

"I intend to," Hugh clipped. "Now don't let me keep you."

Berdie and Lillie, rather like sheep, left the room.

"That was a bit dismissive." Berdie looked to her friend.

"Well, can you blame him, really?" Lillie brought the cup out of hiding.

"I s'pose not."

Walking while chatting with Lillie, the few yards to the vicarage, Berdie spotted Cherry Lawler on the other side of the road. The young woman walked swiftly in the direction opposite.

"Cherry." Berdie called and waved. "Good morning."

Cherry hesitated. She turned her pixie face towards Berdie and Lillie, but it wasn't dressed with its usual warm smile. In fact, a nod of the head is all she offered, then turned quickly, and continued on her way.

"We must speak." Berdie elevated her voice.

"Must we?" Cherry shouted. The woman kept her pace and turned down the High Street.

"Dismissal number two, I should say." Lillie watched the departing figure. "She's attending to something urgent?"

Berdie sighed. "Could be. I owe her my apology for all the Wilkie Gordon business."

"You still haven't done that?" Lillie looked surprised. "No wonder she's not keen on spending time with you."

"Every time I've gotten a moment to give a proper apology, something interrupts."

Berdie could see Cherry nearly jog. "Or maybe there's more to it. She didn't even offer to ring me later."

"Come to think of it, that's not like her at all. Even in a rush, she gives a greeting."

Berdie stopped and tipped her head. "Large amount of pounds," she mused. "And she's aware, that I'm aware, but her grandfather's not aware of what we're aware of." Berdie widened her eyes. "But what if Wilkie has become aware and given her information she doesn't want to make aware to me?"

Lillie scrunched her nose. "And I'm aware that you're not making any sense."

"Oh, perfect sense, Lillie." Berdie shook her head. "I believe Cherry Lawler's avoiding me." Berdie tapped her finger on her chin. "Not for long, I dare say." She smiled. "In fact, I believe I shall coincidently be at the Copper Kettle tomorrow when Cherry fetches her tea buns for the B and B. Fancy a cuppa, my dear?"

"Does Monday follow Sunday?" Lillie winked.

12

Berdie, almost finished with her morning chores, continued to consider how to nab dear Cherry. Catch her unawares, that would be the best approach. Apologize and then with careful reassurances, find out if that was the only reason Cherry was dodging her.

Berdie's musings were interrupted when she heard the sound of youthful voices emanating from nearby. She peaked across the diminutive table and chairs she was cleaning to the small kitchen window, just beyond, that faced the back garden.

A dark haired young man who was already developing a distinctive barrel chest, much like his father's, was in plain sight. Indeed, twelve-year-old Milton Butz was hanging about the now dismantled crime scene with two other lads. They were dressed in blue trousers, and blue sweatshirts, with white shirts underneath, which Berdie recognized instantly as the village school uniform.

"What are they doing?" Berdie said aloud.

With quick steps, she opened the back door and decided to approach the young men rather than call to them. Better able to see what they were up to, she reasoned.

As she made her way to the area, the trio scrambled to retrieve books and notepads that littered the ground.

"Mrs. Elliott," Milton greeted when she arrived.

"Hello Milton."

The two others stood quite still, holding their school goods.

"Lovely day." Berdie smiled.

"Yes," said one of the boys whom she didn't recognize at all.

The other boy, she realized, was the grandson of the indomitable Mrs. McDermott. Yes, his wiry mop of red hair and matching freckles made him quite recognizable. What was his name?

"This is where they found that little boy," the young McDermott blurted pointing to the freshly restored dirt.

"Kevin." Milton Butz frowned.

"I see Kevin takes after his grandmother." Berdie nodded. "Yes, Kevin, sadly it is."

"Well, if some no-good grabbed my little brother, I'd knock him in the head." He shook his fist while wrinkling his freckled nose.

"Yes, I believe you would, Kevin."

"Me, too," Milton added, "if someone tried to hurt Duncan."

Twelve-year-old boys think themselves nearly invincible, Berdie thought. The boy's bravado reminded her of her Nick when he was their age.

"I'm sure your little brothers would appreciate your care for them. But, tell me boys"—she slightly dipped her chin— "why, exactly, are you here?"

"Oh." Milton spoke with vim. "This is Bobby." He pointed to the blond-haired, blue-eyed lad Berdie hadn't recognized. "He's new."

"A blow-in," Kevin confirmed in a less than cordial way. "We said we'd show him where they found the body."

The young man in question shook his head affirmatively.

"Where they found a skeleton," Berdie corrected. "Welcome to Aidan Kirkwood, Bobby." Berdie knew a redirection of the conversation was in order.

"Thanks." He smiled.

"I'm Mrs. Elliott. My husband's the vicar here."

"Oh." Bobby's face turned lightly pink. "We don't go to church much."

"You really must come to a Sunday service." Berdie's tone was welcoming. "We've great youth activities." She looked at Milton. "It's nice of you to show your new friend round the village. But aren't you supposed to be in school?"

"We are in school," Kevin grunted.

"Science outing." Milton nodded toward the wood. "We're identifying wildflowers."

"Oh?" Berdie looked at the flora nearby. "What have you boys identified then?"

Kevin pointed to a plant right by the overturned earth. "That's a Lenten rose. Except the bloom's gone now."

"It has a purple one, bloom that is." Milton announced it with a certain amount of pride.

"It's an evergreen." Bobby leant his voice to the newly gained flora knowledge being espoused. "I think."

Milton shook his head fervidly. "Yeah, it is."

"Evergreen," Berdie repeated.

A loud voice boomed from within the woods.

"It's Dud Head," Kevin alerted.

Bobby, Milton, and Kevin took to scribbling madly on their notepads.

A portly man, bald as a baby's bottom and

sporting a well-trimmed beard, appeared. Encircled by several students with notepads and pens, he espied Berdie and the three boys.

"They haven't been into mischief, have they?" he called cheerfully to Berdie.

"Look, Mr. Dudham"—Kevin spoke before Berdie could respond—"a Lenten rose." He pointed to the plant.

The man and his entourage came and looked at the plant. "Well done, Kevin." Mr. Dudham smiled.

He tipped his shiny head towards Berdie. "Hello, Mrs. Elliott."

"Hello, Mr. Dudham."

"Science outing," he explained.

"The boys said." She smiled.

The teacher turned his attention to the immediate foliage near the Lenten Rose. "Ah," he directed his pen towards a plant. "Milton Butz, can you identify this plant?"

Milton studied the plant. "It's a wild geranium."

"True, and what is it called?" Mr. Dudham looked at Bobby. "I should think you'll remember the common name of this one."

The youngster took a deep breath. He bit his lip. Then a large grin appeared. "Oh, right, It's Herb Robert."

"*Geranium robertianum*, one in the same," Mr. Dudham spoke and pens scribbled.

"In medieval times, it was used for healing wounds and curing diarrhea." Kevin added emphasis on diarrhea with a great deal of gusto.

Most the girls wrinkled their noses except Martha Butz, Milton's twin, who just knit her brow and looked as if she were far too mature to react to such business.

"Splendid." The teacher beamed then looked at Berdie. "They listened after all," he said quietly to her. "With this age group, one never knows for sure."

Berdie chuckled in agreement.

"All right, students, let's move along." Mr. Dudham looked at his watch. We're approaching eleven o'clock."

"Eleven." Berdie widened her eyes. "I must go."

"And you three." Mr. Dudham pointed to the trio of lads. "Stay with the group."

Reminiscent of bees swarming a hive, the science class and their teacher moved back into the woods. This time Milton, Kevin, and Bobby were buzzing alongside.

And Berdie buzzed herself into the vicarage and on her way to the Copper Kettle. "Evergreen," she said quietly as she went. "Curative wild herbs."

She was late for elevensies at the Copper Kettle where people mobbed the entrance. The Cow-Mobile was parked in front of Mr. Raheem's produce store, just cross from the Kettle, and it seemed all of Aidan Kirkwood was there.

"Oh, right, it's Tuesday," Berdie remembered aloud.

Every Tuesday Mr. Cathcart was about his butcher business in cooperation with Mr. Raheem. The enterprising team invested in an old ice cream van and did it over to become a mobile butcher shop. Mr. Cathcart provided the straight-from-his-farm cuts of beef, and other fresh meats, while Mr. Raheem provided the perfect spot for smashing amounts of sales: right in front of his produce store. There was always a crowd about the High Street on Tuesdays from ten to six, and the rest of the shopkeepers benefited greatly as well. People were everywhere, and Lillie was among them.

"Where have you been?" Lillie seemed anxious.

"And very good morning to you, as well," Berdie offered while catching her breath.

"It's just that Cherry came. I tried to start a conversation, but it was so crowded, I'm afraid it was to no avail."

"Really?" Berdie harbored disappointment.

"You might be able to catch her up if you go rapidly." Lillie pointed to a figure scooting quickly into the distance.

"Wait here," Berdie instructed and shot off down the road like a hungry fox after a spring chicken.

Cherry was just one door away from the entrance to the B and B when Berdie caught her up. Breathing heavily, she called to her. "Hello Cher-ry."

The young woman, laden with boxes of buns, turned towards Berdie. Cherry's pixie face registered surprise and concern. "Mrs. Elliott, perhaps you should sit down."

"I've been," Berdie took a deep breath, "trying to," she held her hand to her racing heart, "catch you up."

Cherry's surprise turned to pity.

"Quiet place to talk, please." Berdie's words were dappled with pants.

"I need to put these," Cherry nodded towards the boxes, "in the kitchen." She then lifted her chin as a pointer to the bench near the edge of the green, directly across from the B and B. "I'll be there momentarily."

Berdie crossed the road and sat on the wooden bench. She took in a deep inhale of the warm spring air. It was then she realized her approach to Cherry had taken care of itself. Desperation, to the point of breathlessness, evoked a tender response.

Berdie began to relax, her breathing settling into an ordinary rhythm.

Bird trills called across the small green as if to sing to the spring daffodil displays that dressed all four corners of the square. Just large enough for a standard football game with nets at both ends, and a handful of fans for both teams, it suited Aidan Kirkwood quite well. It played host to village cricket, which would be starting soon. And, of course, there was the annual flower show which drew crowds from all round. Gracious homes, Cherry and Jeff's B and B, a few small shops, and the parish church hall sat opposite the green on the four sides of the road that edged the grassy expanse.

Three cars and a work lorry ambled their way on the cobblestone street at the moment. The fresh aroma of spring grass drying in the morning sun settled Berdie into a sense of well-being. All in all, Berdie nearly always found the village green pleasant.

"Yes, this will do quite well," Berdie said to the sky.

No more than the words left Berdie's mouth that Cherry's petite figure came out the B and B's door and crossed the road. The young woman's sky blue tee shirt, dark twill trousers, and clogs, somehow, appeared quite fashionable. Her short blonde hair that framed her elfin face, the pink cheeks and sparkling eyes, looked fresh as a spring daisy. Still, her twinkle wasn't as vibrant as usual. Her steps were not blithe.

She sat beside Berdie on the edge of the bench with a certain amount of hesitancy. "I have only a few moments."

"Cherry, I need…" Berdie started her apology.

"I know I've been rude," Cherry interrupted.

"Well—" was all that Berdie got out before Cherry interjected.

"It's just that since I confronted my grandfather, I didn't know exactly if I should say." Cherry folded her hands. "And yet, of course, you probably figured it out by now." She unfolded her hands and rubbed them across her trousers. "And I know that you're aware that my grandfather is, at heart, a good person."

"What?" Berdie found herself leaving off her own apology and listening to what Cherry was trying to say. "Yes, your grandfather is a good man." Berdie leaned closer.

"Well." Cherry swallowed hard. "It's really not my place to say. I mean I couldn't betray my grandfather's trust."

"Has this got anything to do with the thirty thousand pound payment voucher we discovered in your mail?" Berdie asked instinctively.

"Could do." Cherry's shoulders sagged like a wilted flower.

"And does it have anything to do with the fact that the jolly mailman of your childhood greeted your mother as Mrs. Gordon?"

"I knew you'd see through." Cherry became animated. "I tried to tell grandpa that." She put her hands to her cheeks. "Oh, this is getting so messy." Cherry's eyes took on a sense of panic. "Grandpa has been so foolish. And ever since the drawing of that poor child appeared in the paper, people have been saying some awful things about Grandma." Cherry shook her head as if to lose the troubling thoughts. "I know Gran has been unwell, but she's already been through so much, far more than I could ever endure."

"Cherry." Berdie took the young girls hand. "I believe you can endure more than you realize." Remembering the nose allegations put forth by Mrs. McDermott at the appearance of the "garden child" newspaper drawing, Berdie went on. "You must remember that lies and destructive speculation never lead to good. Now, say good-bye to verbal rubbish."

"Oh, Mrs. Elliott, I love Jeff." Cherry's chin trembled. "And I love my home, my work in it. But sometimes I can't bear this village."

"I understand what you're saying." Berdie spoke in comforting tones. "But we must never let the small-mindedness of the few color our world as a whole. In time, the truth has a way of setting things right."

"Setting things right." Cherry sighed. "What will happen to Grandpa? You must speak to my grandfather. He can do such silly things, but he does love deeply." She looked down. "Forgive me. I've been avoiding you, and it's not right." Her tone softened as she raised her eyes back to Berdie. "Please, I'm afraid there's no more I can tell you. You really must go see my grandfather."

A cheerful voice from the opened door of the B and B shouted cross the road to the green. "Telephone, Cherry," Jeff called.

"I've really got to get back." Cherry stood quickly. "You do understand, don't you, Mrs. Elliott?"

Berdie nodded her head, and Cherry scrambled across the road.

"I understand your loyalty and love to your grandfather, dear one," Berdie spoke aloud although there was no one left to hear. "But what a place he's put you in." She shook her head. "And I hope to soon completely understand what foolishness and trouble

Wilkie Gordon has gotten himself into."

Berdie rolled her eyes to the sky and sighed. "And I still haven't made my apology."

As Berdie made her trek back to the Copper Kettle, she determined that she must speak to Wilkie Gordon as soon as possible. She began hatching her great plan. Like a newborn chick from an eggshell, it came to life. She was certain the bottom of Wilkie Gordon's goings-on would be known in the next twenty-four hours—sooner, in fact.

When Berdie arrived back at the Copper Kettle, Lillie still stood outside amongst the throng.

"Come with me. We've work to do," Berdie said enthusiastically.

"Did you catch Cherry?" Lillie asked as the two weaved their way out of the crowd.

"I did." Berdie clipped. "Now, if you please, Lillie. Were you out with Loren last night, and are you seeing him tonight?"

"Yes to first, no, to the second."

"Good. Now, I would like you to go to the Cow-Mobile and ask Mr. Cathcart if he's any oxtail. Purchase it, and I should take a nice nap this afternoon."

"What are you going on about?" Lillie paused. "You're up to something."

"We're up to something, my dear." Berdie placed a finger aside her nose. "Be at the vicarage, tonight, midnight. Bring the oxtail, and wear black, not the dinner wear sort. I'll explain it all then."

"Splendid." Lillie beamed.

"Oh," Berdie added coyly, "don't ring the doorbell."

✵

Berdie, who had gathered goods in a market bag, was reading in the library when Lillie arrived promptly at midnight, oxtail in hand.

Having sent Hugh up to bed with a hot milky drink an hour earlier, Berdie was sure he would be sleeping soundly.

Berdie illuminated Lillie to her plan and made a flask of hot tea, after which they made their way to the edge of the wood near the empty crime scene.

"Now we must be very quiet." Berdie cautioned Lillie as they stepped carefully into the shelter of a large bush at the perimeter of the wooded area. There was a small space between the bush and a massive oak tree. "We could be waiting a bit, so I've made accommodation."

There, leaning against the oak, were two folding garden chairs.

"Outdoor furniture." Lillie applauded.

"Shh." Berdie placed a finger to her lips. "I brought them out before Hugh came in for dinner. If we're doing a stakeout at our age, may as well be somewhat comfortable."

Lillie unfolded the chairs and set them closely together to fit the space behind the bush.

"Did you get some kip this afternoon?" Berdie asked her Watson.

"Not really. I had three voice lessons back-to-back."

"The tea's extra strong." The two settled into the chairs. "That will help."

She pulled two torches out of a large market bag and an April edition of *Country Homes and Interiors*.

"Turn on your torch and you can read this for a bit. Berdie handed the silver light tool and magazine to her friend."

Lillie grinned. "This is more a midnight picnic than a stakeout. My nose tells me there's one of your tasty meat pies about." Lillie nearly cooed. "A midnight snack?"

"No," Berdie pronounced promptly, "a secret weapon. Remember, Lillie, we are on stakeout, albeit casual. Wilkie Gordon is hardly an axe murderer, but still, we need to be vigilant."

"Some tea then."

Berdie handed her the large flask and a paper cup.

Berdie was ninety-nine percent sure that this approach to Wilkie Gordon held no great danger or she would never have asked for Lillie's help. Nonetheless, it was a bit of an adventure and Berdie enjoyed it.

An hour and a quarter passed, the half-moon had a moisture ridden lunar corona. The clouds were hiding most of the starry host, and the smell of wet tickled Berdie's nose. "Please hold back the rain," she whispered to He who hears all.

Lillie was in and out of dreamland, but Berdie was alert. She sat up straight and turned her shoulders side to side to relieve a cramp that made way up her back.

Then she heard it. Finally. The clink of metal identity tags danced, just what Berdie had been waiting for. She roused Lillie.

"Get out the oxtail," she informed quietly.

Struggling to become alert, Lillie followed the command.

A not-distant torchlight made itself known. Berdie silently pulled the still warm meat pie half out of the bag and unwrapped it. She broke a piece off then sat it on the ground by the bush. She placed the rest at her feet.

The enticing odor of the fresh baked pie began working its magic. The jingling sound came closer, right next the bush then paused.

"Get ready, Lillie."

Berdie could now just make out the figure of Wilkie Gordon, woodsman hat atop his bald head, white beard in full prominence. He stood near the upturned earth that declared the former grave of a helpless child. Then Berdie espied it. He held a small spade in his hand.

Lillie took a deep inhale as the sight of Wilkie became apparent to her.

Berdie placed her index finger upon her own lips as a signal. Lillie nodded.

Wilkie was mumbling something, but Berdie couldn't make out what he said.

And then it happened. Creeping around the bush, the fish took the bait. First, his wiggly nose, then his wee front feet and Fritz found the temptation that teased his senses. He stopped and ogled Berdie for a moment and then the pie.

"Good boy, Fritz," Berdie whispered. "Good boy. Eat up."

The dachshund cautiously touched his nose to the pie then suddenly took an immense bite. He chewed with absolute delight until all gone.

"Fritz, look." Berdie pointed to the pie at her feet. "More for the good lad."

Fritz stepped lively to the meat pie near her feet.

"And look what Lillie has for you."

Lillie pulled out the oxtail, and placed it on her lap. She sweet-talked the wee creature to her. "Fritz, look."

Crumbs of crust clung to the edges of Fritz's mouth as he investigated the enticement of another treat.

Lillie patted her knee. "Hear, boy, up."

"Fritz," Wilkie called in a low voice.

The little red sausage stopped momentarily.

"Fritz, come." Wilkie was just slightly higher in volume.

Then, with gusto, the disobedient canine put his front paws on Lillie's knees and sniffed. In a rapid flash, the dog leaped into Lillie's lap.

"Good boy," Lillie cooed. She stroked his coat then lightly held him as he chewed upon the bone of the oxtail.

"Fritz, where are you boy?" Wilkie stepped towards the bush. "Fritz?" The aged man now stood only a couple yards from the sheltering bush.

"OK, Lillie," Berdie whispered. "It's on."

"Hello."

Wilkie jumped and lifted his torch towards the bush.

The slurps and slops of Fritz devouring his goodie was as audible as Constable Goodnight consuming fish and chips at the Upland Arms.

Wilkie bent down, gripping his spade tightly and in a stealth manner crept to the bush. At the very moment he came round the vegetation, Berdie turned on her torch, stood, and dazzled him.

"Going walkies are we, Mr. Gordon?"

Wilkie jerked back, eyes large, mouth agape, arm up trying to shelter himself from the sudden light.

Berdie shined her torch on Fritz who stopped eating momentarily, eyed his master, then continued his feast.

"Why, yes, on a walk." Wilkie replied with shallow breath.

"Mr. Gordon." Berdie's voice was now militant as she turned the torch back to the elder. "As the old clergyman once said, don't play puppies with an old dog."

Wilkie's shock turned to resignation.

"Well?" Berdie said with clear determination. "Do you want to tell me the truth or shall I call Constable Goodnight?" Berdie held up her mobile phone.

Wilkie slumped to one knee. He dropped the spade and put his head in his hands. "I'm so sorry," came in a quivered voice.

The penitent man kneeling on the hard earth before her moved Berdie immediately into action.

"Mr. Gordon, please." Berdie scooted the garden chair to the weakened fellow. "Sit here."

Wilkie struggled to his feet and placed himself into the chair, drooping like a wet umbrella at the end of a drenching storm.

Lillie urged Fritz from her lap and the dog, oxtail bone still in his mouth, sprung to Wilkie's feet where he continued his nosh.

Berdie opened the flask of tea and poured some of the still warm brew into a paper cup she pulled from her large bag. She handed it to Mr. Gordon whose face was flushed. He gestured a thank you with a tip of his head and took a swallow.

"Where do I start?" He breathed heavily and stared into the night sky.

"You can begin by telling me what you're doing with that spade," Berdie said calmly.

"That's the whole matter of it, you see." He looked

at Lillie.

"Well." Lillie brushed her lap with her hands. "I can wait inside if you wish to speak to Mrs. Elliott alone."

"No, stay," Wilkie bid. "No secrets now and, truth be told, a relief."

Berdie leaned against the spreading oak that sheltered their little gathering.

Wilkie took a single deep breath. "I have the spade because my little partner," he bent down and stroked Fritz, "and I are on our way out to gather white gold, or black as it may be."

"What? There's ore about?" Lillie blurted impulsively.

Berdie gave her a quick glance and a slight negative shake of the head. Then Berdie put all her powers to play. Thirty thousand pounds paid in full. She eyed Fritz, the spade, and what appeared to be a small carrier bag shoved in the pocket of Wilkie's coat.

"I know we're not in France, and it's not the high season, but could this white and black gold have anything to do at all with Le Petit Chaumier?" Berdie waited for a reply.

"And others. Cherry said nothing gets by you, Mrs. Elliott." Wilkie shook his head.

Lillie knitted her brow. "Le Petit Chaumier?"

"Truffles, black market truffles," Berdie informed Lillie. "And not the chocolate ones."

"Truffles," Lillie repeated.

Berdie folded her arms as she continued to lean against the tree. "It has to be an area completely undisturbed and not for a short while." She tapped a finger against her arm. "Private land I should say, untouched wooded area, oak."

Wilkie removed his hat and fingered the brim, slowly turning it round. "The back woods of the Preswood estate," he confessed. "I made the discovery quite by accident, when I was groundskeeper."

"Did you inform Preswood?"

"Randal Preswood doesn't give a toss about his land, what it needs, or what it possesses."

"*Beouf au Truffes,*" Lillie interjected just coming up to speed. "You're the supplier?"

Berdie remembered Preston Graystone's description of the man he saw in the wood twenty years past. He wore a woodsman's hat, like Wilkie Gordon's.

"How long has this been going on?" Berdie looked at Wilkie intently.

"Just gone one year now."

"Give it to us straight, Mr. Gordon," Berdie ordered. "How long?"

"That is straight." He balked. "I made the discovery years ago, but there was no need."

"Ah." Berdie nodded. She believed the old fellow.

"Need?" Lillie asked what Berdie was considering.

"Yes." Berdie answered for Wilkie just realizing what he meant herself. "Not until your Mary became desperately ill."

"They," Wilkie spit the word out, "said there was no more could be done for her." Anger colored his words. "The quacks told her to go home and die." He squeezed the hat and shook it. "I had to do something, I couldn't let that happen. Do you see?"

Lillie leaned forward in her chair. She placed a hand on Wilkie's knee.

Berdie squatted next to him. "So you got treatment for Mary in Germany. Treatment not allowed here.

Treatment that costs a king's ransom."

Wilkie nodded.

"All paid for with white gold," Lillie reiterated.

"And she's gotten better." Wilkie whimpered. "She finished the course, and she's so much better."

Berdie became suddenly aware of a gentle pitter patter of droplets on the earth.

"And the garden falderal." Berdie's gift of sorting and aligning was ablaze. "You were afraid the water feature would bring more people in, the thin edge of the wedge, and your precious gold would eventually be trampled or discovered."

"Yes, well, and then there was the other." Wilkie hung his head.

Just then a crackle sounded. Fritz jerked his head up from his disappearing bone. He sniffed the air, jumped to attention, and began to bark.

"What's going on here?" Hugh stood in the midst of the odd little huddle wearing his evening robe while his wet weather wellies adorned his feet and a black umbrella sheltered his head. His left eyebrow elevated. "Wilkie? Lillie? Berdie!"

Berdie swallowed. "Shall we all retire to the kitchen for a cup of tea?" she suggested calmly, as if it was four in the afternoon on a balmy day.

"Right." Hugh growled. "I should say one or two things need explaining, wouldn't you, Berdie?"

It was quite obvious. Hugh was not amused.

13

The warmth of the fire Hugh tended in the library gave a warm glow that eased and gave comfort to everyone seated; Wilkie on the large Chesterfield sofa, Berdie and Lillie in the leather chairs. Fritz, still at his bone, sat quietly gnawing at Wilkie's feet.

Lillie's eyes looked heavy. The chill of the spring night now warded off, Berdie found that she, as well, was being courted by the sandman despite the warming tea and the energy it offered.

"I should think, after we finish our tea, all can go home and get some sleep." Hugh was not inattentive. "Most conversations stand best in the fair light of day."

"If you please, Vicar," Wilkie asked politely. "I would like to clear one more matter for your wife. And the truth of it, for me as well. I'll be done with the thing as quickly as the teacup's empty."

"Of course, Mr. Gordon, as long as you're not under duress." Hugh answered with an eye on Berdie.

Berdie returned the ogle.

"No, no." Wilkie sighed. He took a slurp of tea and began his soul baring. "I'm going to be needing some guidance, Vicar. But we can talk about that, as you say, in the light of day. What I'm addressing now is the truth of our son, George."

Berdie became instantly alert. "The baby picture on the dresser no doubt," she said under her breath. She wanted to get every word that Wilkie spoke on this matter.

"There are rumors about the village connecting my Mary and the unearthed bones. There's not a bit of truth to them, and I won't have her name drug through the mud." Wilkie's white beard contrasted starkly with his now pink face.

"Idle gossip." Hugh crossed his arms. "Wicked stuff."

"Our George was born perfectly healthy. It was my Mary who was ill." Wilkie looked down at little Fritz and stroked him. "The long and short of it, my dear wife couldn't cope when the boy came." He ran a finger across the bottom of his nose. "She wasn't herself, had no interest in the wee one, barely able to tend her own self. She became dark, almost lost." He stopped petting Fritz and raised his head, moisture in his eyes.

"Sounds like postnatal depression." Berdie had seen it before.

The old gentleman, in the light of the fire, wore his years of lies all cross his face. "It scared me. Her, too, when she had sense about her."

"Did you talk to your doctor?" Lillie asked the reasonable question.

"We were afraid they'd take George from us. All the things you'd hear on the news. You see, with me working, trying to keep life and limb together, well, I couldn't do it all."

Hugh sat down on the Chesterfield next to Wilkie.

"We gave our George into the care of Mary's brother and his family, just 'til Mary could recover." Wilkie's voice cracked and he took a sip of tea.

It was clear to Berdie, as she was sure it was clear to Hugh and Lillie, this was a scabbed wound bleeding to heal, and dreadfully difficult for Mr. Gordon. She took a try at completing what Wilkie was trying to say. "But it took longer than you thought for Mary to get her sea legs back.

Wilkie nodded. "And by that time, George had become attached to the people he recognized as his parents, his siblings."

Lillie leaned towards Wilkie. "So you put it about that George developed critical needs and was placed in a special care institution."

"I had to protect Mary's delicate state."

"It squelched the painful gossip and explained Mary's sadness." Lillie's eyes held understanding.

Wilkie sighed again. "Mary's brother moved to the Orkney's. George grew up a fine boy, but he didn't want anything of Mary or me. Didn't understand, didn't want to understand. As a young man he met Cherry's mother, married, lived happily I'm told, until he died at sea three years after Cherry was born." Wilkie cleared his throat. "We loved our boy," he whispered.

"You had the courage to love him the best you knew," Hugh comforted.

Lillie nodded then lifted her brow as if something had alighted in her grey matter. "So it was bitter sweet, then, when Cherry arrived in the village. Where and from whom did she come?"

"I invented the story of a previous clandestine marriage, a thin veneer. More lies. Anything to keep the past at bay." Wilkie blinked. "And Cherry agreed to keep the secret." He looked into the fire. "But the scent of fabrication wafted throughout the village. In the end, did living all those years with protective lies really help Mary? And Cherry as well, one secret, than another."

"Whatever has gone before," Berdie was fixed, "part of your George lives on in Cherry. And that's a blessing."

Wilkie laid his eyes upon Berdie, a fresh glimmer about them. "Not a day goes by that we don't thank God for her and that she pledged herself to find us. She's taken us to her heart, and we adore her. Then along the way she found her Jeff, a good lad." Wilkie took another gulp of tea.

"They're a fine couple." Hugh's tone was reassuring.

"But this business that the young child buried in the church garden is somehow tied to my Mary is a burning lie." Wilkie's lip trembled. "I knew the moment those upturned bones were a child it would put my Mary in a state, just as she was gathering strength. Wicked accusations. It's not on. I won't have it."

Hugh stood again, military straight, dignified despite his dressing gown. "Wilkie, you needn't worry yourself anymore on that account." He looked at Berdie. "My wife, with her God-given gift, will root out the truth of the matter, and I dare say soon. That will quiet the groundless accusations, and in a hurry."

Berdie smiled and nearly swooned in the loving public affirmation and trust her husband displayed for her and her abilities.

"Spot on," Lillie pronounced.

"Now, may I suggest we call it a night, or a morning as the case may be, and I'll drive you home Wilkie." Hugh assisted Wilkie to his feet.

Lillie cleared her throat.

"And you as well, Watson." Hugh grinned. He

turned his attention on Berdie. "We'll talk over breakfast. Now get some sleep, love."

When everyone, including the little four-legged truffle hunter, was escorted to the door and on their way, Berdie sat quietly to take her last sip of tea in the library.

"Wilkie's guilt actually clears him from the bones issue," she said aloud. "Stolen glass, broken shards, Flora, that chin, photo, Mr. Smith, certificates, fruit baskets; so many roads lead to Swithy Hall. But then there's Wanda Pitts, St. Erts, Evergreen. How do they tie in? What's my next step?" She ran her finger on the rim of the teacup. "Call Billy Beaton, yes, follow-up, then pay another visit to the contessa." Berdie put her drained cup on the end table near her. "Yes, my dear Contessa, it could be a very bumpy ride."

સ્જ

So far this morning, Berdie had enjoyed her nice morning lie-in plus a refreshment of scriptural meditation and prayer in her favorite Queen Anne chair. She also asked Hugh to call the contessa and ask if Berdie may visit her this morning, which he did willingly. That was the pleasant part.

The lion's share of her time was taken up with an arduous defense to Hugh at breakfast about her approach to Wilkie Gordon.

And Hugh quite adamantly reminded Berdie that she was to work in tandem with Albert Goodnight. He insisted she visit the constable immediately and even rung up the lawman, who was eating breakfast at the Upland Arms. He informed that Berdie was coming straight way. Then he cautioned Berdie to keep Mr.

Gordon out of the conversation entirely, for now, with Goodnight.

All this she had taken in with a certain amount of acquiescence. But now, standing at the entrance of the Upland Arms, she thought it more pleasure to visit a dentist with a toothache.

"Lord, I need your patience." She breathed and pushed open the heavy wooden door to the Upland Arms.

Immediately, the tantalizing whiff of bacon made entry to her olfactory parts. It mixed with the distant hint of last evening's brews and the soot of the open fireplace, which sported a spatter of flame. Imagining the taste of Dudley's farm fresh eggs on her tongue, she instantly regretted she'd breakfasted already.

Berdie glanced about in search of Goodnight. The white lime-washed walls of the place, made the oak ceiling beams appear even duskier than the myriads of smoke-ridden years had turned them. The walls were littered with pictures: home football teams, and the just-won invitational cup, darts champions, prize ribbons, and the list of current winners from quiz night.

People were seated at snugs and tables, standing to wait for take-away, while others chatted in corners.

Then she spotted the blue uniform of the constable seated near a tap, grinding his breakfast with rapid pace, speaking to Dudley Horn. Confidence in her stride, she made her way to the policeman.

"Good morning, Constable Goodnight." Berdie's voice was clear and strong.

"Ah, the vicar's wife," he said with little pleasure.

"I believe a consult is in order." Berdie presented with a hard-pressed smile.

"Oh, of course." Goodnight winked towards Dudley Horn, and then stuck another fork full of baked beans in his mouth. "Been stickin' your nose in the latest gossip, then?"

Berdie worked at remaining even tempered.

Dudley Horn grinned. "May I get you something, Mrs. Elliott?"

Berdie shook her head. "The constable and I need to speak." Mr. Horn, still grinning, stepped to another customer.

"You do know," Berdie said matter-of-factly, "that the Preswoods own eighteenth century Venetian glass, the same as found in the garden child's skull."

Albert Goodnight stopped chewing, slapped his fork down, took Berdie by the elbow, and began ushering her in the direction of the pub's toilets.

"What are you doing?" Berdie protested.

A few strides and they arrived at the tiny hall that held the Ladies' and the Gents'.

"Fewer ears to hear, eyes to pry, and I won't have the Preswoods brought into ill repute." Goodnight shook his finger and scowled. "You know as well as I that they had a piece of that stuff stolen and enough said."

Berdie wasn't going to argue. She knew it would only stir up. Besides, she was attempting to breathe through her mouth as the odiferous quarters brutally assaulted the nose.

A large man with tiny eyes entered the hallway.

"Pete." Goodnight nodded towards the man who bumped Berdie's arm as he returned the nod and entered the Gents'.

"Since your high-flyer inspector got his gob in, if you must know," Goodnight whispered in an irritated manner, "I'm poised to make an arrest."

"Who?" Berdie could barely get the word out.

The constable moved his eyes from side to side. "Patricia King." He grunted pompously under his breath.

Berdie blinked and shook her head. Poor Patricia, who already had to deal with her own feelings of remorse, was cleared by Jasper Kent an hour after he interrogated her.

"Surely not," Berdie steamed.

"She had every opportunity."

"What's her motive?"

"What?"

"Why would she want the contessa gone?"

"A foreigner, pushin' her nose in, actin' high and mighty in our village, bringin' nothin' but trouble?" He sneered. "Why *wouldn't* she want the woman gone more like?"

Berdie put her index finger under her nose. The hall smelled as badly as Goodnight's reasoning. Both were beyond her staying power.

"I shouldn't touch Patricia King." Berdie eked the words out her lips.

"That's it then?" Goodnight ran his tongue over his upper teeth. "Good, my eggs are getting cold."

Berdie swallowed the words she would have loved to yell at the man as he waddled back to his plate. Instead, with great haste, she turned and marched out the pub.

She had bigger fish to fry. She was next calling on the contessa.

Little does the contessa know that my bag holds what could be the tiebreaker in the war of telling the absolute truth. Berdie pressed her finger to the door chime of Swithy Lodge.

When opened, the gracious contessa smiled. "Hello, Mrs. Elliott," she said in her light Italian accent. "Please, come in."

Berdie entered the hall admiring the contessa's lovely aqua blue blouse and matching trousers that made the woman's kiss-of-tan skin sizzle. Her dark hair was pulled to the back of her neck where it was secured with a jeweled clip.

"Thank you for seeing me on a moment's notice." Berdie offered a kind smile.

Contessa Santolio waved her hand towards the kitchen. "If you don't mind, I'm in the middle of preparing Ortensia something to eat."

Once in the large country kitchen, the contessa donned a plain white pinny that hung on the back of a chair. She offered a cup of cappuccino which Berdie declined. "A bit stiff for me."

"I'm not the best at making it," the contessa admitted. "Ortensia is superb. One thing I'll delight in when she's once again able to perform her duties."

"She's faring all right?"

"Appetite returning and improving every day." The lovely Italian's eyes displayed relief.

"Our church community has prayed for her recovery every morning at matins."

"For which we are grateful." The contessa held up her demitasse cup filled with the caramel colored brew. "Do you mind?"

"Please, help yourself."

The contessa took a light sip with her satiny pink

lips.

"Please, sit." She motioned towards a wooden chair at the ample oak farm table nearby.

Berdie obliged. "I'll get straight to it then." She was firm yet kind. "My husband told you that I have some inquiries to make of you?"

The contessa nodded, moved to the range stove, and took another swallow of her java. She stirred a wooden spoon through the boiling contents of a saucepan.

"Have you considered who may have wanted to do you harm, contessa?"

"Yes, I've considered it and have not one person in mind." The contessa sat her demitasse on the table and returned to stirring the pot more vigorously.

"I see." Berdie could hardly settle for that answer. "Contessa Santolio, where did you say your family was from?"

"Our relatives live in Milan."

"Yes, I understand your husband's people are from there, and yours?"

The woman lifted her chin. "If you're trying to establish if my own family was wealthy…"

"No, that's not my inquiry," Berdie interrupted and proceeded. "You and your husband seemed to have been well suited. How did you meet him?"

The contessa raised a brow. Even with the swath of powdered blush over her cheeks, Berdie could make out a light pink tinge across the tan face.

"Is that important?" Mrs. Santolio asked.

"Why don't you tell me?" Berdie urged with a firm tone.

The lovely woman spooned the contents of the saucepan into a bowl that sat near the stove. "If you must know, I came into the Santolio home when the count was still married."

"Came into his home. You mean you worked for the Santolios?"

"An aide, yes." There was a slight chill in her voice. She knocked the spoon hard against the edge of the awaiting bowl, loosening the last of the sticky gruel. "As time went on the count became fond of me."

Berdie watched the contessa closely as the woman placed the empty saucepan in the sink and turned the water full-on, filling the pan to overflowing.

"When his wife died, he asked me to marry him." The contessa continued matter-of-factly. "It was not well received by his family, but none of them would really benefit by my death. That is what you're interested in, yes?"

"You're sure of that, no one?"

The woman turned the water off, grabbed a tea towel, and wiped her hands. "The summer house in Monterosso al Mare became mine along with a comfortable monthly stipend. I'll never worry for money. The rest of the estate, the business, and all assets, went to his children, and rightly so. I didn't want his fortune."

"I see." Berdie took a deep breath. "Now, Contessa, will you tell me why you're really here?"

"What do you mean?" Delicately, Mrs. Santolio picked up the cup of her demitasse from the table and brought it to her lips.

Berdie pulled the torn photo of the muddy twins and the domestic, which she had taped on the backside, from her bag. She handed it to the contessa.

The woman gazed at the photo in her hand. She caught her breath. "Where did you get this?" Her voice choked.

"You don't know?"

"I've never seen this picture before," she avowed.

"You are the domestic serving the girls fizzy water in that old photo."

The contessa carelessly returned her demitasse to the table. The cup rocked spilling drops of cappuccino.

She handed the snap back to Berdie, a sense of culpability played across her sea green eyes. She moved to the large kitchen window and turned her back to Berdie as she looked out upon the view to Swithy Hall.

"Yes," she said, her voice shaky. "I am the maid in the snap." She spun round dramatically and looked intently into Berdie's face. "And, no, I'm not. Charlotte Grainger, the mousey Lollie you see there in that photo, no longer exists."

Nor did the contessa's light Italian accent exist, Berdie observed.

The woman before Berdie stood her full height and collected herself; poised, yet self-protective. "The moment I married my Alberto, I became Contessa Carlotta Santolio, and no one can take that from me."

"Does someone want to take that from you?" Berdie asked bluntly.

The contessa exhaled. "I should think not."

"Well, I certainly don't. But I do want to know just what you're doing here in Aidan Kirkwood."

"What a hash of things," came from the lips of Carlotta Santolio, but sounded more like Lollie Grainger. "Very well, but please, don't spread it about, I beg of you."

"Go on then." Berdie still held the returned snap.

Mrs. Santolio sat in the chair next to Berdie.

"Yes, I was in the Preswood employ twenty years ago, my first job. I lived in Timsley with my family. I was young, but I did my job well." She swallowed. "Suddenly, I was sacked, just like that, on false grounds. I had no opportunity to defend myself, sent on my way with a 'don't let the door hit you on the way out,' and a ruined reputation." Her face lighted with the anger of unjust dues. "Do you have any idea what that feels like?"

"Just what was the accusation?"

The contessa stood and moved to the window again. "I was accused of stealing an expensive piece of foreign glassware by Mrs. Preswood's sister, Mrs. Darbyshire. She had only been in the house three days." She faced Berdie squarely. "If you ask me, she needed to look a little closer to home at that dodgy husband of hers."

"John Darbyshire was with Rose and the girls?" Berdie was getting a broad picture.

"Oh, Colonel Preswood wouldn't have allowed it, but he wasn't about when they arrived, nor Mrs. Preswood for that matter."

"Was Rose's husband given to domestic violence?" Berdie leaned forward in her chair.

The contessa paused for a moment. "He and the missus had rows, raging, but never any slapping about or that. Quite frankly, he gave me shivers. He was secretive, furtive. And he certainly didn't spare the gin." The contessa shook her dark hair. "You know the very day that glass came up missing, so, too, did her rangy husband."

"Rose's state of mind?" Berdie had a spade and she was digging.

"She was temperamental at the best of times. That

day she was half mad."

"Did she explain her husband's absence?"

"He and the children were off to London to visit relatives and she was to follow." Mrs. Santolio furrowed her brow. "They could off to China for all I cared. I rue the day."

"A very difficult situation, I can see that." Berdie was delicate. "Back to my original question, Mrs. Santolio, why are you here now?"

The contessa returned to the chair. She folded her hands in her lap.

"All I said previously about Alberto and I visiting Aidan Kirkwood is true. We strolled the High Street to the church. He noted to me that it would be most lovely to have flowers and a fountain in the church garden. When he died, I thought of what he had said and contacted the parish council president, Mr. Webb. That is all true."

"But there's more." Berdie took in every word the maid-cum-contessa spoke.

"I know it sounds terrible, but I wanted to rub the Preswood's face in my good fortune. Embarrass them. I'm the one with a real title." She unfolded her hands. "But when all this horrible business with the spider took place, the prospect of losing Ortensia, well." The contessa sighed heavily. "My need to settle old scores paled."

"You went up to the big house to visit just after the spider ordeal. Why?"

"I thought to reveal myself to the Preswoods, to clear the air. But when it came to it, I lost my bottle and didn't go through with it."

"Did they recognize you?"

The contessa became almost melancholy. "Not

even a remote glimmer of awareness." She straightened herself. "I made some excuse and came back to the lodge."

She looked at Berdie with eyes that now reflected the calm of a Mediterranean sunset. "It all suddenly felt a bit hollow."

"Revenge, for all its appearance of sweetness, only sours the soul," Berdie proffered in a gentle but solid tone.

"The bile I wished for another came upon my own house in the form of a Wandering Brazilian spider."

"Ah, yes. Well, in due time, I believe that will be rectified." Berdie placed her free hand on the contessa's. "Now that is justice yet to be settled and the information you've given me will help us get there."

"Does anyone need to know all this?" Mrs. Santolio's lovely face wore a plea.

Berdie brought her hand back. "I see no reason to make it known. In fact, I believe there is still danger lurking about. I should let sleeping dogs lie and be very careful. When the whole affair is brought to rest, it's your decision if you wish to make your former tie with the community known."

Berdie returned the photo to her bag. "I'll inform the authorities if needed, discreetly of course."

"Yes, I see." The woman, sitting there in her lovely clothing covered by an old servant's pinny, responded without any pretense.

"Thank you for being candid and telling the truth, Mrs. Santolio. It's been most insightful. Berdie gathered herself and leaned forward. "I'm afraid I really must push on."

"No, I need to thank you, Mrs. Elliott. I feel confident that you'll do what's best."

"Yes," Berdie assured.

"And I want to present a more formal thank you. Ortensia and I will be returning to Italy as soon as she is able to travel. So, I'm planning a tea to celebrate her recovery. I've invited Mrs. Preswood and the girls. I'd like it very much if you and Lillie would attend."

"We'd love to." Berdie stood.

"Tomorrow afternoon, two o'clock." The contessa smiled.

"We'll, see you then. Oh, and I should think Ortensia's porridge has cooled." She pointed to the neglected bowl. "I can see myself out."

Berdie left Swithy Lodge armed with new facts. "If Mrs. Santolio didn't tear that photo, who did? And just as importantly, why?"

As she watched the Hall and Lodge retreat into the distance in her rear view mirror, something in her stirred. "There's a menacing sense about, Lord. Protect those at risk and bring evil to its knees, sooner rather than later," she prayed.

14

Berdie eyed herself in the undulating mirror of her antique dressing table. Getting dressed for a formal tea was never one of her favorite things to do. Not that she had to impress Contessa Santolio or the Preswood contingent; she just wanted to be casual without appearing uninterested.

"This could be pleasant and insightful." She prodded herself. "I shouldn't think it will carry on too long."

Berdie decided on her light gray linen trousers and a salmon colored poet's blouse. Yes, that was just the right balance. She scanned her shoes and decided on the sturdy black flats. A bit of polish and they looked quite suitable while still offering buckets of comfort.

By the time Lillie rang the door chime, Berdie was ready. Well, she was dressed. She felt a reserved misgiving concerning this tea, but she couldn't pinpoint just why.

After meeting Lillie at the door, they went straight way to the car, down the vicarage drive, and off to Swithy Lodge.

The sun was running its course, and a fresh drift of daffodils waved their showy heads near the edge of the road.

"I am looking forward to this." Lillie nearly purred. "It fits the day to have a lovely tea."

"Perhaps," was all Berdie offered as that tickle of

doubt still played itself in her head.

At that exact moment Berdie's mobile, lying between her and Lillie, played its loud tone.

"Do you mind getting that please, Lillie?"

"Mrs. Elliott's mobile." Lillie answered the phone with a chipper greeting. "Oh, dear. Now?" Her words after listening to the caller took a more somber note.

Berdie glanced at Lillie whose expression became downcast.

Lillie turned her gaze to her dear friend. "Berdie, it's the hospital in Timsley. Mary Gordon was rushed in. She's taken a bad turn, and she's asking for you."

"Mary?" Berdie blinked. "Yes, of course I'll be there straight way."

"She'll be there as quickly as possible," Lillie said into the phone. "Good-bye." Lillie laid the mobile down. "Bang goes the tea."

"I must get there sharpish. She made a quick U-turn. "I thought Mary was improving."

"Yes, well one never knows with debilitating diseases."

"Can you call the contessa to tell her of the development?"

Lillie was already dialing her mobile. "Contessa? Lillie Foxworth here."

Berdie accelerated.

"Fine, thank you. I'm sad to tell you that Berdie has been called to an emergency and neither of us is able to come to tea. I'm dreadfully sorry."

There was a prolonged silence.

"Oh," Lillie said with some surprise. "Yes, what a day."

"Tell her I'll ring this evening," Berdie relayed.

"Berdie will be in touch this evening. Yes, good-bye, Contessa."

Lillie rang off then shrugged. "None the worse I s'pose, since it seems the whole tea's gone pear shaped anyway."

"What?"

"Mrs. Preswood was called to an unexpected meeting of the Family Heritage Circle, and Rosalie is in Timsley with a broken car."

"Really?" Berdie lifted her brow. "Rosalie's car, that's odd. It was just serviced at the garage."

Berdie turned the car onto the High Street. "I should call Hugh."

She pulled to the curb near Bearden's Creamery and grabbed her mobile.

"Look," Lillie spouted. She pointed towards the creamery.

There, big as life, stood Wilkie Gordon with a bulging carrier bag. He looked up and down the High Street, then gave a whistle.

Berdie put down her window. "Mr. Gordon?" she called. "What are you doing here?"

"Hello, Mrs. Elliott. Why I'm buying ice cream of course." He held the bag up and grinned. "It's orange sherbet actually, Mary's favorite." Wilkie squinted. "Say, have you seen Fritz? He's done a runner while I was inside the shop, little beggar."

Lillie leaned forward. "Shouldn't you be at the hospital, Mr. Gordon?"

"Hospital?" Wilkie laughed. "Why would I want to be there?"

Berdie tapped the steering wheel. *What is going on?*

"Come to the house and join Mary and me for a bowl of orange…"

"Orange!" Berdie all but yelled. She felt heat rise to

her cheeks. "Snap! Tea and fruit baskets." Like a rush of water over a dry plain, the little puzzle pieces of this whole business suddenly fitted together. "Shoes, Pitts, herbs. Oh my word, Lillie, how could I have missed it?"

"Hey?" Wilkie piped.

"Mr. Gordon, when you worked at the Preswood estate, did you keep your woodsman hat in the paddock area?" Berdie was in full flow.

"What are you going on about?" Lillie appeared as bewildered as poor Wilkie.

"Yes," he clipped, "but…"

"Sorry Wilkie, must be off." Berdie nodded to the confused gentleman.

"Lillie hold on," she commanded.

The tires screamed as Berdie rocketed away from the curb, made a hard U-turn that sent Lillie on a sail, and pointed the car back in the direction from which they came.

"What on earth?" Lillie squealed as she grabbed the dash.

"Call Goodnight," Berdie instructed. "Tell him to meet us at Swithy Lodge, now."

Berdie turned off the High Street and onto the road that went to Bampkingswith Hall.

Lillie punched nine, nine, nine.

Her foot steady, Berdie pushed the gas pedal full-on, making the car speed down the road. "I just hope we're not too late." The daffodils near the road became a blur.

"I just hope we get there at all." Lillie grasped the dash with white knuckles.

Upon their arrival, gravel from the Swithy Lodge drive scattered like so much popcorn as Berdie raced the car up the drive and stopped on a dime.

After being certain it was locked, she shot from the vehicle with Lillie just behind her.

"Go up to Ortensia's room, Lillie," Berdie commanded. "No matter what you hear happening downstairs, keep her still and in place."

"What's she going to hear?" Lillie called after Berdie.

"I'm not sure."

She twisted the handle of the front door. It was unlocked. "Thank God." Without hesitation, she was in the hall and motioned Lillie upstairs.

Berdie could hear voices in the drawing room. Steeling herself, she briskly stepped into the room.

"Mrs. Elliott." The contessa's face registered surprise. "I didn't hear you ring."

"No, Contessa, you didn't."

The royal and a guest stood near a side table laden with cups and saucers. In Mrs. Santolio's hands was a small gift, from which she was peeling back the gift wrap paper, a bow on the table.

"I thought you were detained." Mrs. Santolio smiled at Berdie. "You've arrived just in time to see the hostess gift Robin has brought me."

"Don't open it," Berdie insisted. "Please, Contessa, put the box down, now."

Despite the attractiveness of her trendy clothing and matching stiletto-heeled shoes, Robin Darbyshire's face went sour. "Mrs. Elliott, what a silly bird you are." Her voice was stilted. "It's my gift to the contessa." She leaned towards Mrs. Santolio. "Go ahead. Open it. Mrs. Elliott may enjoy the surprise as well."

"No, I won't enjoy the surprise." Berdie could feel her heart pound. "Contessa, please, put it down."

The hostess blinked with confusion.

"If I'm wrong," Berdie continued, "I'll deeply apologize."

Robin shoved the box more firmly into the contessa's hand.

In an act of desperation, Berdie lunged forward and grabbed the gift from the contessa's grasp.

Robin stretched to snag the box from Berdie, a fruitless gesture. "Mrs. Elliott, this is entirely irrational and absurd behavior." Robin's face reddened. "Give it back to the contessa. Now."

Berdie carefully put her hand on the bottom of the box and tipped it upward. "Yes," she said and returned it to its proper position. "Why don't you open the gift, Robin?"

"You're mad." Robin swallowed hard.

Berdie, with great care, loosened the lid.

"Give it to the contessa," Robin commanded.

The lid was nearly off.

"Here, Roberta, you open it." With great vigor, Berdie hurled the box forward towards the impertinent girl.

"Move Contessa," Berdie ordered, but the hostess barely edged.

"You stupid woman," Robin Darbyshire screamed and shot backward as the box tumbled to the floor near her feet, the lid flying through the air.

And there it was, as it had been before in this place, a deadly Brazilian Wandering Spider.

The contessa drew her hands to her face and shrieked.

The creature appeared stunned. Then Berdie recognized it, that evil stretch of the legs, the onslaught of the unearthly sway of death.

In a breath, Robin had removed her shoe. With great precision and a laden howl, she drove the stiletto heel, like a spike, into the spider.

The arachnid lay motionless. Then, with eerie resilience, its legs began to stir.

Robin blithely removed her other shoe and forcefully slammed it into the creature again and again and again, as if the vehemence of the spider itself drove Robin's stabs.

The young woman staggered back and dropped the shoe. Her tussled black hair hung across the aqua blue eyes. She gasped for air and her face went dark.

It was then Berdie became truly aware of Robin's petite stature. Those five-inch heels were deceptive, indeed, and only confirmed what Berdie had suspected. She crept towards Robin.

In one furious movement, Robin grabbed a porcelain saucer and smashed it against the table. Chinaware flew and scattered across the floor. She gripped what was left of the saucer, a large pointed shard. With startling accuracy, she wheeled the point of it to the stunned Contessa's throat. Robin grabbed Mrs. Santolio's arm and screwed it behind the captured woman's back.

A faint scream seeped from the hostage's lips, fright making her body sway.

"You escaped before, but this time you're going to die," Robin seethed.

"No," Berdie shouted. "The contessa's not your problem."

Oh Lord, protect, Berdie prayed, *I'll distract!* "Let her go, Robin. Or should I say, Evergreen?"

The young woman's eyes flared. Her face revealed astonishment.

"Oh yes, I know. But the contessa is unaware."

Robin stiffened. Her eyes narrowed. "She was there."

"Yes, she was there, and you weren't. That is the problem, isn't it? But she's not aware."

"You miserable, old hag." Robin sneered.

Berdie observed Robin's eyes dart beyond the sitting room to the door in the hallway. Carefully, Berdie positioned herself between Robin and the exit.

"Now put the shard down," Berdie coaxed. "It will do no good to eliminate Mrs. Santolio."

"She's nothing more than a common house maid," Robin screamed.

"And you're the daughter of the misguided Wanda Pitts."

A corner of Robin's mouth curved downward. "Misguided? She was a debauched, manipulative, blackmailing witch."

"She threatened to reveal all, once she found you, so she had to be disposed of." Berdie took a tiny step forward. "I know your little secret. Lillie knows, too. And Goodnight is on his way."

Robin lifted her chin. She released a bit of pressure from the shard, revealing the red imprint on the frightened captive's neck.

"Perhaps you're right," Robin breathed.

She appeared to be relenting.

Then with the strength of ten, Robin withdrew the shard, twisted the contessa round, and thrust the noble woman's body with its full weight directly into Berdie. The force of it tumbled Berdie and Carlotta headlong. Down with a crash, both sprawled across the floor.

Robin instantly vaulted the two of them and made for the door, her unshod feet thumping as she raced across the room.

Berdie felt pain all through her body as she attempted to get to her feet. She was suddenly grateful for the extra padding of her backside, which took the brunt of the fall.

"Contessa, can you cope?" Berdie asked.

Lying on her back, gasping for air, the contessa nodded.

Like a hound on the fox, Berdie gathered herself, flew to the hallway, and lit out the door.

"You're not getting away," Berdie yelled as she breeched the drive and desperately raced after Robin, who was well ahead of her.

Robin sped across the grounds of Swithy Lodge, onto the green that stretched to Swithy Hall.

Berdie thought she saw Goodnight's car come to a hasty stop in the road at the Lodge.

Good lot that would do. He'd be even further afield from Robin.

"You can't out run the law," Berdie cried in Robin's direction. *What am I thinking? In Goodnight's case, she's probably counting on out running it.*

Berdie continued her rapid pace still able to keep Robin in sight, no doubt due in part to the fact that the young woman had no proper shoes.

A distant voice fell upon Berdie's ears. It trailed behind her.

"Bloomin' monkeys," came in the panting tone of Albert Goodnight, who, by the sound of it, had joined in the chase.

Robin took a hard right, sprinting into the Hall's back gardens. Beyond laid the woods.

The need for justice fueled Berdie's drive, but the shortage of oxygen began to take its toll. Berdie had a moment of regret for all the Devonshire cream heaped on her afternoon scones for all those years.

"Dear God" — Berdie heaved — "stop her."

A bush just ahead made a jostle. Like a giant red bullet, a fast moving sausage with legs shot from under the vegetation, joined by a bouncy white Highland Terrier.

One quick lift of the nose and Fritz seemed to recognize the scent of one who fed him meat pies.

With energy to spare, the wee dog and his furry friend joined in the chase, running ahead of Berdie as in a merry game. They clipped off gleeful barks as if challenging one another to take part in a jolly good contest of speed.

Berdie felt a sharp momentary pain in her side. *Keep going, old girl.*

The dogs espied the escapee ahead of them and must have decided she was a part of the game: a very large squirrel to be tracked down and dominated.

Robin halted for a brief second. Berdie drew in large gulps of air, but she kept moving.

"Stop in the name of the law," Goodnight, still trailing Berdie, was just audible.

The policeman's call appeared to only fuel Robin's energy. One look in the constable's direction and the woman sprinted off again.

By now, the rollicking dogs had gained on her.

Berdie dug deeply. "Lord," she breathed.

A figure emerged from out the distant woods. Berdie recognized the strong figure of Jamie Donovan. She heard him whistle for Snowdrop, the Highland Terrier and beloved Donovan family dog.

"Stop" — pant — "her." Berdie tried with what breath she could muster to alert Jamie.

He made a quick study of what was happening and stood directly in the middle of Robin's flight path.

Little Snowdrop now raced near Robin's feet, dashing for her master.

Berdie heard foul words from Robin's lips, then the yip of the little white canine that was at the receiving end of Robin's swift kick. A blur of white toppled across the greenery, and Jamie Donovan was on the move.

The trapped woman made a hard left and ran alongside the old, dilapidated, estate greenhouse.

Fritz was at full bore. He reached Robin, and as if in defiance of her treatment of his wee friend, and in allegiance to his pie-making cohort, the sausage nipped at Robin's heels.

She tried to maneuver another well-placed kick, but Fritz dodged her.

The relentless and stout-hearted dog landed a precision nip that sent Robin into a howl and threw her off balance.

Arms extended and screaming, her legs flew out from under her. Robin's body smashed into the neglected greenhouse and penetrated the panes of aged glass. Shards and wood flew all around the woman. She came to rest on her back, the degenerating structure completely smashed.

Fritz continued to yelp. He danced about the scene keeping his giant squirrel at bay.

Jamie, speed his gift, was now where Robin lay. Berdie saw him bend down to check her pulse. She was near enough now to hear a mournful groan from Robin's lips.

"She'll survive," Jamie called. "More's the pity."

Berdie soon stood where Robin was now

immobilized. A bit of glass protruded from the downed woman's forehead, creating a trickle of life-giving red liquid across her ivory skin.

"Are you OK, Mrs. Elliott?" Jamie asked.

"Out"—pant—"of breath"—pant—"but fine." Berdie bent over placing her hands on her knees and took in buckets of air.

"She's not going anywhere." Jamie glared at Robin. "I'll see to Snowdrop."

Fritz came to rest at Berdie's feet, panting heavily himself.

"Good lad." Berdie praised him, and breathed in more fresh oxygen.

Albert Goodnight, at a crawl, arrived. He gasped and grunted like a clapped-out steam tractor on its final plow.

"Robin Darbyshire," he breathed as he extended his upper body over the groaning woman.

"Evergreen Pitts," Berdie corrected.

"Huh?" the constable's face was bright red. He took a gulp of air and continued, "I'm arresting you for," he paused and looked at Berdie.

"The attempted murder"—pant—"of Carlotta"—pant—"Santolio."

"The attempted," he drew in a large swallow of air, "murder of Carlotta Santolio."

"And"—Berdie stood straight—"the murder of Wanda Pitts."

Constable Goodnight gazed at Berdie, frowned, and then leaned into Robin's face. "And for the murder of"—he yanked his thumb in Berdie's direction—"who she said."

Jamie approached holding the humbled but unscathed Snowdrop in his muscular arms. "And for kicking my dog," he snapped.

"We'll get a medical and then she's nicked." The perspiring Goodnight panted, still bent over the body.

"You were quite something," Jaime directed to Berdie.

"All in a day's job, my lad," Goodnight answered. He stood wearing a certain smugness.

Jaime smiled at Berdie who grinned back.

"Now, about the bones." Goodnight grunted in Berdie's direction.

"I dare say that's sorted as well." She nodded.

"How's that?"

"That, constable, is a subject that can be discussed over a cup of tea. And I"—Berdie ran the back of her hand across her forehead—"am certainly ready for a nice cuppa. Aren't you?"

అంశం

A touch of blue peeked through the voluminous grey clouds and faded. Berdie prayed it wouldn't rain. The garden blessing was taking place momentarily in the newly completed water feature in St. Aidan's back garden where she, and many from the village, stood.

There were more people than Berdie expected at the garden blessing. Many whispered to one another about her exploits. But here, at this moment, it was neither the time nor place for her to satisfy their curiosity. After what had happened at the sod turning, she expected low attendance. But many in the village considered the gathering today a kind of full circle. Closure.

Berdie inhaled the aroma of flowers whose lovely blooms encircled a humble fountain that looked more a birdbath in the middle of a small pool. It spouted water that created an enchanting trickle, as in a brook: unassuming and peace-inducing. Berdie admired the chiseled stone bench where The Late Count Alberto Santolio Garden Patron was inscribed on the upper edge. The handsome seat welcomed all to take their ease amongst the beauty. A small sculpted lamb sat atop a plinth amongst the flowers, a sweet memorial to a small boy.

There was no choir, no floral arrangements, no chairs. There were no curious coach tour visitors or flash appearances. Mrs. Santolio looked very much the contessa, but she no longer had a need to impress. Mr. Webb, at her side, kept well away from the spotlight.

Ortensia beamed, her broken "Tank you" given to all who inquired about her health.

Loren and Lillie, hand in hand, approached Berdie. "It's lovely." Lillie smiled.

"Anyone due to rail or pass out?" Loren's inquiry was quiet yet held an edge of banter.

"A much more subdued gathering." Berdie raised a brow. "God willing."

Hugh stepped near the bench. He called for everyone's attention.

"We're here to dedicate this feature to our divine Creator and to the people of our parish."

He went on to thank the contessa, applaud the landscape artist, and then offered a short but sincere eulogy for the little lad whose bones were now at rest with his rightful family who had gone before. He prayed for solace, joy, and blessing to all who visited the feature. Hugh then invited any whom so wished to enjoy light refreshments at the vicarage. Mr. Webb declared the area officially opened for the enjoyment of the entire village. Young Dave Exton took some snaps for the newspaper.

"There we are. Bob's your uncle," Berdie commented in a low tone. "All done quickly and peacefully without a hint of malice in sight."

"Indeed." Loren's jest turned to relaxed agreement.

As the grey clouds tumbled away, people admired the structures and flowers then dispersed quietly. Some gathered at Oak Leaf Cottage, others trooped home.

For those who came to the vicarage, Berdie was at work in the kitchen. She filled pastel-colored trays with little bits of canapés from Villette Horn's shop.

Lillie entered just as the hall telephone rang.

"Someone will get it," Berdie asserted to Lillie who had spun on her heel.

"You mean Hugh will get it," Lillie teased. And she joined Berdie at her task.

"I think today's do went quite well."

"I'm surprised the Preswoods weren't in attendance."

"They are in profound grief." Berdie was matter-of-fact. "I shouldn't wonder if it's a long time before they join village life again."

"If you consider it, they've lost two loved ones." Lillie sighed.

"In an odd sort of way, they've also added a family member, although I'm not sure they're very keen."

"Ah yes, the so called John Smith." Lillie placed the last bit on the full-to-the-brim tray.

Hugh swung through the kitchen door. "Love, that was Wilkie Gordon ringing up. He's invited us for

Easter lunch on Sunday."

He looked at Lillie. "You and Loren as well."

"Lovely." Berdie smiled. But she noted Hugh didn't appear so keen.

"He mentioned that he wants to hear all the details of how you cracked the case."

"Oh." Berdie was reserved. "We'll see."

"He also asked that you bring a meat pie." Hugh took one of the canapés from the tray. "I was hoping for lamb."

Berdie and Lillie laughed.

"I shouldn't wonder that the pie's for Fritz." Berdie shook her head.

Hugh brightened. "Oh, that's all right then. I'll tell him we'll be there."

Berdie put her hands on her hips. "Really," she declared.

15

Berdie loved the way the brilliance of the Easter sun poured through the church windows. It gave cheerful witness, just as it had two thousand years ago, to the celebration of the Lord's resurrection. And Saint Aidan of the Wood Parish Church regaled in its affirming warmth and beauty.

The faithful were joined by many new faces Berdie had not seen at the church previously. But she recognized Bobby, Milton Butz's little friend from the science outing, and greeted him. In a gentlemanly manner, Bobby introduced his parents and sister.

"So glad you came today," Berdie welcomed.

"Yeah, well, it is one of the big two." Bobby fingered his tie.

"Big two?"

"I mean Christmas and Easter. We always go to church for the big two. Besides, my parents wanted to see the lady who chased down that girl."

Berdie chuckled, but Bobby's parents, with a touch of Easter pink in their cheeks, excused themselves and directed the family to a pew near the back of the church.

Many women wore their new hats. Mrs. Plinkerton's was extremely ostentatious, while Ivy Butz's was an eye-jolting lime green. The young women wore dainty Fascinators, little bundles of feathery things that clipped on to well-groomed hair, made popular by Princess Kate. Cara Donovan's pink one was especially admired, and little daughter, Katy, had a matching bow.

Men adjusted their ties and little girls showed off their fresh sunny-colored dresses. Young boys made an art of scuffing their new shoes, and fresh-washed aromas filtered through the pews.

But gathering together for Easter service was far more than welcoming a warm season or adorning the body with new apparel. It was a time to let go of the old and embrace the hope of the future.

The revelation of Robin Darbyshire as the murderous Evergreen Pitts sent shock waves throughout the parish. But there was also the sense of resolution. The little garden child was given a proper family farewell and burial. It was as if the village was free to move on, to begin afresh.

When Berdie arose with the rest of the congregants to sing a beloved Easter hymn, the words of it seemed to come alive. *This joyful Eastertide, Away with sin and sorrow! My Love the Crucified, Hath sprung to life this morrow.*

Berdie could sense it. Hugh's wish for the village to get back to humming along again was set in motion.

When the church service was finished, all the children hunted colored eggs in the front garden, Ivy in full flow. After tiffs about who got which egg first were sorted and everyone departed for their homes, the doors of the church closed upon a now silent edifice.

Loren and Lillie joined Berdie and Hugh in the quick walk to Wilkie Gordon's cottage.

When they neared the terraced home, Berdie saw Albert Goodnight on the pavement. In uniform. He was entertaining Milton Butz with tales of his exploits and capture in the recent case.

"Hello Albert," Loren called to the constable.

"Afternoon all."

"Constable," Hugh addressed, "are you joining us inside?"

"In due time."

"He'll put me off my food," Berdie whispered to her husband.

"Berdie." Hugh scolded in a quiet manner.

Milton ran ahead to open the door and escorted Berdie, Hugh, Loren, and Lillie inside to the sitting room.

Wilkie Gordon, Jeff Lawler, and Edsel Butz stood from the chairs where they were seated, a simple courtesy for female guests entering a room.

"Welcome," Wilkie greeted. Baby Dotty Butz cooed in his arms.

"Hello," Jeffry Lawler lifted a glass in Berdie's direction.

"The reverend's come and all," Edsel Butz trumpeted towards the kitchen door.

"We're delighted to be here." Hugh offered a gracious grin.

"Please, sit down," Berdie consented.

"Milty," Edsel directed, "take Mrs. Elliott's meat pie to the kitchen. And, Lucy love, please move."

While Milton took the pie, well made-up teenager, Lucy, blinked her heavily mascaraed lashes and continued her conversation on a mobile, an iPod ear bud firmly entrenched in the other orifice. How she heard anything Berdie couldn't reckon. But the teen removed herself from the sofa to the bottom step of the stairway where Martha Butz sat reading a book.

"Thank you," Berdie offered, but it was barely heard over Lucy and Martha's discussion about who was taking too much room on the stairwell and who ought to move or stay.

"Ivy's in the kitchen preparing the meal," Wilkie offered as Berdie and Hugh sat on the emptied spot.

"And Cherry's stuck in as well," Jeff amended.

Loren and Lillie seated themselves on two small dining chairs pulled near the sofa.

"Family life," Lillie commented quietly to Loren who smiled.

Four-year-old Duncan sat on the floor, a large basket of colorful eggs and Easter sweeties beside him. With sticky cream all about his mouth, and presumably his hands, Fritz licked the child's fingers rapidly and made him giggle.

Lila Butz, in a pink dress, looked a bit of an Easter egg as she entered the sitting room from the kitchen, Milton behind her. She held a tray of glasses filled with fizzy water.

"Mum says to quiet down, Dad," she said softly to Edsel. She mutely distributed the liquid refreshment all round. "Mum and Cherry will be right in."

The words no sooner left her mouth than the two jovial women burst through the door.

"Happy Easter, all." Ivy's rotund figure was alive with goodwill, dressed in green polka dots. "Lamb's in the oven. Who's the hungry one then?"

The room erupted with responses from all quarters, and Berdie noticed Hugh's eyes became especially bright.

Ivy seated herself in a dining chair while Cherry rested on the arm of Jeff's armchair. He sweetly put his hand on the knee of his petite wife.

When it quieted, Milton Butz, seated near Duncan on the floor, raised the question everyone was hoping to have answered at today's gathering.

"So, Mrs. Elliott, how did you sort everything, the spider, the bones, and all?"

"I want to know how you figured out who that little boy was." Martha came to attention and put her book down.

"Yeah, and all from bones." Milton glowed.

"That's really Doctor Meredith's expertise." Berdie glanced at Loren.

"I don't want to bore everyone with endless dull details." Loren tipped his head. "And, really, we want to hear about Mrs. Elliott's exploits."

"Well," Berdie began, "the information that Dr. Meredith uncovered was invaluable, the lodged shard of glass was absolutely key. Very rare glass, and to be found in a collection at the Preswood home, was too much of a coincidence."

"But that didn't implicate the Preswoods," Lila reasoned.

"No, you're right, Lila, but it was a shadow over the entire household. Bampkingswith Hall became a suspected 'where' in the child's death."

"Do you know how he died?" Cherry asked.

"The how." Berdie took a deep breath. "I had bits and pieces, but it was my conversation with Mrs. Santolio that was of greatest help."

"She's a fake." Lucy deposited her mobile in a convenient pocket. "All posh, but she was a maid."

"No, she's not fake," Lillie corrected. "She really did marry a count and she really is a contessa.

"Her station in life changed, Lucy," Ivy explained. "For the better. Only in Italy."

"There was something in the paper about that." Wilkie recalled. "Young Dave Exton interviewed her just a few days ago. As a youth, she was in service at Swithy Hall, but I don't recall her."

"Nobody did," Edsel agreed.

"Not quite true, Edsel," Berdie exacted. "The contessa arrived, a paying guest, at Swithy Lodge. Robin, Evergreen Pitts, settled the contessa into the lodge the evening we were there for dinner."

"Cauliflower soup." Lillie wrinkled her nose.

"The young woman recognized the contessa from a dated photo of the twins. It was taken at Swithy Hall before Robin, Evergreen, entered the household."

"The snap of the two three-year-olds was Rosalie and the real Robin," Lillie informed.

"Thus the spider," Lila declared.

"Well sorted, Lila," Berdie praised.

"What did the contessa tell you that helped?" Edsel brought his fizzy water to his lips.

"She informed me that when Rose and the girls came to Swithy Hall, Mr. John Darbyshire her husband, was with them. Mind you, they were there for only three days in full. John Darbyshire was, by all accounts, a man in hiding. He was given to drink, not violent, but none settled either."

"Colonel Preswood wouldn't let him in the house." Wilkie scowled.

"The colonel wasn't there, nor Mrs. Preswood." Berdie went on. "I genuinely believe the child's death may have been an accident."

"How's that?" Cherry asked.

"John Darbyshire was a dandy, not a killer. However, neglect entered in. Full of drink and rowing with his wife, he knocked into the child and sent the small boy tumbling. The lad hit the rare glass that crashed to the marble floor below where he landed."

"He would have died instantly," Loren assured. "Mrs. Elliott's scenario fits with forensic evidence."

"Poor lad." Ivy ran her hand along the edge of her pinny.

"If it was an accident, why not bury the child properly?" Jeff had fire in his voice.

"Darbyshire was on the run." Hugh spoke up. "He couldn't chance the questions that would arise at such a death, the publicity, or the law getting involved. What we gather, goons from defrauded enterprises in Venezuela were hunting him."

"Still," Jeff said, "he was a coward."

"When Mrs. Santolio told me that Darbyshire scrambled to London the very day the rare glass was discovered missing, well…"

"Shameful." Wilkie gently rocked the dozing Dotty.

"Darbyshire hastily buried his son, Rosalie's twin, Robert, the night before he fled to London. He planted a Lenten rose at the grave." Berdie raised her eyebrows. "A floral memorial and criminal neglect. Strange bedfellows, but there it is."

"He planted the Lenten rose, the one we identified?" Milton's eyes were wide.

"As attested to by John Darbyshire's brother."

"How could he not be seen?" Cherry leaned against her husband's shoulder.

"Someone did, actually." Berdie nodded. "He was seen in the woods that night, but not entirely recognized."

Berdie glanced quickly at Hugh who went coy.

"The account given was that Darbyshire carried a

spade and wore the hat identified with another person, an estate worker, to throw off his own identity."

Wilkie's face became a light-turned-on. "That scoundrel!"

"Scoundrel," Duncan echoed Wilkie's words in his cherub voice.

As several chuckled, Duncan climbed into Milton's lap and fingered the colorful eggs in the basket. Fritz lay next to the boys, but kept astute for possible edible morsels.

"So Rosalie's twin was really a little boy." Martha cocked her head. "That's weird. I mean wouldn't someone notice when boy, Robin, was suddenly a little girl?"

"Apart from mom and dad, no," Berdie answered. "The Preswoods knew only that Rose had twins, born in Venezuela."

"Mrs. Santolio, as the domestic, had to see the twins. And she didn't know?" Loren's tone was skeptical.

"She was a kitchen maid. She never changed nappies or had a great deal of contact, and children that young aren't immediately recognizable as male or female."

Lucy snapped her fingers. "Robin tried to kill the contessa for no good reason. Mrs. Santolio didn't know that Robin wasn't Robin."

"Hello," Lila responded loudly, "I already said that."

"Well, I didn't hear you," Lucy protested.

"Well, you wouldn't."

"Girls, we're with guests, mind," Edsel corrected his daughters.

Cherry tapped her finger on her knee. "So Rose

Darbyshire replaced, if you can use that word, boy Robin with girl Robin to protect her husband. Yeah?"

"Yes." Berdie put forth what she had placed-like-a-puzzle together. "We must assume that in trying to find enough physical resemblance to Rosalie, there were no boys so she chose a girl. Hugh actually made a critical discovery in all this, too."

"Yes," Hugh sighed. "Though not until late in the game. Christening certificates: Robin's had been altered. Not apparent at first, but close examination showed that an *A* had been added to Robert, so it became Roberta. The same with Daniel, which became Daniela. I dare say Rose Darbyshire altered the original."

"So, where did the pretend Robin come from?" Milty looked a bit confused.

"Ah, well," Berdie tipped her head toward her friend, "Lillie helped there."

"Rather inadvertently I'm afraid." Lillie smiled.

"But Lillie's mention of the village of St. Erts created a thread."

Now everyone in the room looked a bit confused as they searched out Berdie's face.

"Well, it was after I, well we, took a trip to London to learn more about a previous spider death. That's where we learned of Wanda Pitts. Her demise was done much in the same way as the attempt on Mrs. Santolio's life."

"She's Robin's, Evergreen's, birth mother." Lillie sounded somewhat precocious as she filled in the details.

"It took some difficult work by a professional friend, Mr. Beaton, to uncover it all. Mrs. Pitts, unable to keep her own at the best of times, gave up her child to an institution, St. Erts Home for Children in London."

"So Rose Darbyshire adopted Evergreen Pitts." Ivy stated the next step of deduction.

"Indeed." Berdie folded her hands in her lap. "Then, when Evergreen reached the age of eighteen, Wanda made contact with the girl, as was a provision of the home's adoption plan. When Mrs. Pitts found out her daughter had been taken into the wealthy Preswood family, she threatened to reveal all unless Evergreen paid her large sums of money."

"Blackmail." Jeff furrowed his brows.

"Her mother did that?" Martha sounded horrified.

"When everyone thought Robin was going through teenage angst about being a twin; changing her eye color, hair, trendy style, even moving away to a new school, it was instead her reaction to a new identity. Lucy and Lila helped me to glimpse that."

"Get over, Mrs. Elliott." Lucy laughed.

"Lucy," Ivy corrected then looked at Berdie. "How did my girls possibly do that?"

"Girls Hockey uniforms," Berdie replied.

"The day we went to Ivy's for a meeting." Lillie raised her index and third finger. "Two very different young ladies, albeit sisters, dressed in the same clothing, I remember that."

"I certainly won't forget it soon either." Lila pursed her lips. "I hate hockey."

"Yeah, well I'm still changing nappies." Lucy wrinkled her nose.

"Girls, enough." Ivy squalled like a North Sea gull, then quietly turned to Berdie. "Go on Mrs. Elliott, please."

"When the girls were in the same uniform, their

differences, though easily discerned, became far more revealed. In Evergreen's case, creating differences distracted from the whole idea of similarities, making it more plausible for her to carry on as Robin Darbyshire."

"Well, I thought her black hair looked a bit naff," Cherry said.

"Naff, perhaps, and rather desperate." Loren put his arm on the back of Lillie's chair. "Eventually, Evergreen had to do-in Wanda Pitts to maintain her established Preswood identity and all it held for her."

"Money." Jeff shook his head.

"Charles was an attempt to marry money, too, a backup plan to move into an entirely new identity: Mrs. Roberta Swindon-Pierce." Hugh ran his finger over his collar.

Ivy shifted her weight in the chair. "Money or not, I can imagine the poor bloke's shattered."

Little Dotty, still in Wilkie's arms, made a cooing sound while drifting in and out of dreamland.

"I have to ask you, Mrs. Elliott." Wilkie spoke softly. "What is it about orange sherbet that sets you going?"

Lillie had a good laugh.

"Ah you, Wilkie, put the final puzzle piece in place for me. Orange. More specifically, chocolate truffles infused with orange blossom water."

"Those from the French place in Timsley?" Ivy ran her tongue over her lips. "They're so moorish. Edsel brought some home. They lasted about three minutes."

Milton thrust his thumb towards Edsel. "Dad ate all of them."

"No, sir, you did," Martha interjected.

"Put a sock in," Edsel warned his twins. "Let Mrs.

Elliott tell us how orange truffles solved everything."

"It wasn't the truffles themselves. It was that Robin, Evergreen, ate them without effect. And that dovetails with John Smith, who is, as we all now know, an alias. He is the uncle to Rosalie Darbyshire. Robert Darbyshire is the dead lad's namesake.

The room buzzed.

"He revealed himself as a Darbyshire kinsman, so he could attend the private family burial of his nephew," Hugh informed. "I conducted the service. Robert related that he was aware of his nephew's demise and committal. His long estranged brother, John, called Robert to his death bed in Canada to confess before he died, though not in complete detail."

"But what was a problem for Robert." — Berdie took the lead — "He was asked to pass on John Darbyshire's legacy to the one remaining Darbyshire twin, a daughter. When he arrived here, presumably on a coach tour, there were two Darbyshire girls. They both held enough resemblance to confuse. He had no idea who was the real niece."

"He was trying to find the truth while living a sham." Lillie raised her brows. "That's certainly not a combination for success."

"I have to put my oar in, Mrs. Elliott." Jeff was intent. "When Smith, Darbyshire, absently drank from the teacup of another guest one breakfast at the B and B, he became covered in red lumps. An allergic reaction to citrus that vexed his family he said."

"Yes," Cherry agreed. "The poor fellow really suffered. And just from one tiny sip."

"I saw him in the Upland Arms car park that same morning. I can attest to the bumps." Berdie ran her finger across her neck. "Robert Darbyshire sent citrus gifts, some covert, to the Preswoods to see if the spots would reveal themselves on the real Darbyshire daughter. It didn't work. But it was that morning I saw those lumps that I began to consider the allergic problem in relation to identity. It wasn't until bumping into Wilkie that I remembered. We saw Robin shortly after she had eaten orange infused chocolate truffles at Le Petit Chaumier, and not a bump in sight."

"Oh yes, *that* night," Loren said in a low voice.

Lillie smiled uneasily.

Berdie gazed at Wilkie. "So then, when you said orange sherbet, it all suddenly fit together."

Wilkie grinned. "I wonder if Sherlock Holmes needs another Watson."

"There you are, Granddad, you could go into the detecting business." Cherry giggled.

"A divine reality," Berdie remarked, "is that the resolution to the whole mystery was given to us at the burial site, right there in the back garden. She looked to Milton. "Remember the wild geranium?"

"Herb Robert I think." Milton's eyes widened. "Herb Robert!"

"Forgotten by some, unknown to most, God remembered little Robert with a simple flower where he laid in that cold earth." Berdie sighed. "And right near was where John Darbyshire planted the Lenten Rose."

"An evergreen," Milton exclaimed with a sense of wonder.

"Sometimes the things most difficult to see are the things right before us," Berdie expounded.

"How tender is our God." Wilkie rocked little Dotty in his arms.

A knock came at the door. Fritz burst from his spot

and went into a barking frenzy.

"They're here." Ivy jumped from her seat and answered the door.

It was Mr. Webb and Constable Goodnight, followed by Dave Exton.

"Please come in." Ivy, arms waving like Easter bunting in a spring breeze, could barely get the words out for her excitement. "Now, Mr. Webb, explain to all what this is about."

"Thank you, Mrs. Butz." The well-dressed gentleman tipped his head. "I won't keep you from your Easter lunch or rest on ceremony. Constable Goodnight and I are here with the reward I sponsored. It is, as I stated when announced, to go to the individual who was instrumental in bringing down those responsible for Mrs. Santolio's attempted murder. One in this room will receive five hundred pounds. Would you all be upstanding?"

Everyone got to their feet and flutters of surprise circulated the room like a bouncing rabbit. Many eyes went to Berdie, others to Goodnight.

"Constable Goodnight," Mr. Webb's voice resounded, "please come forward."

Goodnight had the glow of fresh daffodils as he stepped to the right of the parish council chairman.

Mr. Webb gave Albert an envelope.

A hush came over the household.

Berdie merely grinned.

Mr. Webb addressed those present as if announcing the arrival of the Prime Minister. "This award goes to one of great courage, one who went beyond the call, a genuine hero to us all." Mr. Webb paused and Goodnight glowed. "As the law in Aidan Kirkwood, Constable Goodnight," the room froze, "I'd like you to present the five hundred pound reward to Fritz, beloved pet of Wilkie and Mary Gordon."

Goodnight blinked. He swallowed then furrowed his brow. His jaw tightened.

The whole household broke into a resounding cheer, which sent the award-winning sausage into a barking serenade.

"Yea, Fritzi," Milton yelled.

"Good boy." Martha and Lila clapped their hands.

Duncan stood to his feet and did a little dance and Fritz joined in.

Dotty, who was half-asleep, was jarred awake and began a howl. Ivy rescued her from Wilkie's arms and the elder scooped the dancing Fritz into his grasp.

Little Fritz seemed to know he was the center of attention, and he looked absolutely regal.

"I'm givin' this to a flea-bite dog?" Goodnight went red.

Mr. Webb bent towards the humiliated constable. "Don't be a git, Albert. Give it to Wilkie."

Albert Goodnight took a deep breath, twitched his broom of a mustache and thrust the envelope towards Wilkie Gordon who grabbed it with one hand, and held on to the squirming canine in the other. Dave Exton took several snaps.

Goodnight pursed his lips. "Not the newspaper."

"Congratulations," Berdie nearly sang. Since going straight and having been forgiven by Randal Preswood in a merciful moment, Wilkie needed every penny.

Mr. Webb, across the room, smiled broadly at Berdie. Just last week he had notified her that she was due the reward, but Berdie asked that he give it to the Gordons, to Fritz—the real hero.

Wilkie waved a hand for silence. "Thank you, Mr.

Webb. And I'll try to keep the little rascal out of your rubbish on dustbin day."

Everyone went back to the tumult of a joyful celebration.

Goodnight slipped out the door faster than a fox fleeing a pack of hounds. Mr. Webb and Dave Exton courteously dismissed themselves.

Fritz pranced about, being patted and basking in the cheers.

Then Berdie caught a glimpse of Wilkie Gordon. His celebratory laughter halted. Awe spread across his aged face as he looked to the stairwell.

Berdie, and all present, turned to the stairs. Adorned in a lavender dress, silver white hair neatly arranged, and a smile of rosy lipstick brightening her renewed facial glow, Mary Gordon steadied herself against the banister.

"Grandma?" Cherry called.

"Sounds a party down here." Mary's voice was just audible. "And I'm hungry for Easter lunch."

"Aunt Mary." Lila stood from her stair step and went to her great aunt's aid, Lucy directly behind her.

"Aunt Mary,"—Milton wore surprise—"you're about."

Wilkie, still silent, gazed. Moisture gathered in the corner of his eye. "Indeed, she is," he spoke hoarsely.

When the brave woman who had weathered so much illness reached the bottom of the stairs, Martha gave her Great Aunt Mary a giant hug and Duncan offered her a bright yellow egg from his treasure trove.

As Wilkie gathered the woman, with Edsel's assistance, to the armchair in which he had been seated, Hugh put his arm around Berdie's shoulder and bent closely to her ear.

"It seems we have a resurrection of our own today, right here in Aidan Kirkwood," he whispered.

"Indeed." Berdie nodded. "Indeed."

"Aunt Mary"—Ivy raised baby Dotty near the elder's face—"our Dotty would like an Easter kiss."

The great-great-aunt ran a wrinkled finger across the baby's cheek. She placed her aged lips upon the child's forehead. "Bless you, Dotty, love."

"Now, Aunt Mary," Ivy rabbited on as she passed Dotty off to Edsel, "Cherry and I have made you the best roast lamb ever."

Hugh raised his glass of fizzy water. "Let us be upstanding."

Everyone, less Mary, rose to their feet.

"A toast. Happy Easter and to Mary's good health."

"To Mary's good health." The group responded a little out of sync. "Happy Easter." Glasses clinked round the room.

Ivy and Cherry buzzed into the kitchen.

"What a day." Lillie moved next to Berdie. "And you cracked another case." She touched her glass to Berdie's. "Not rusty anymore, then?"

"Oh, well oiled."

Lillie clinked her glass again on Berdie's.

"What's that for?

"That's for the next opportunity that waits out there, yet unknown."

"Yes, well, for my husband's sake, let's hope it doesn't become known to him," Berdie gurgled.

"What's that?" Hugh questioned, Loren peering over his shoulder.

"Just discussing rust, my love." Berdie winked at Lillie and took Hugh's hand.

Ivy appeared from out the kitchen again. "It's laid on. Come you hungry lot, tuck in."

And all of Aidan Kirkwood, filled with a sense of well-being, sat down to Easter lunch.

Author's Note

In this Lenten mystery novel, "This Joyful Easter Tide" was sung by Berdie and the congregation of St. Aidan in the Woods Church on Easter morning. It is sung in churches all cross England on that special day. Here is a bit about it. George Radcliff Woodward (December 27, 1848 – March 3, 1934) is accredited for the blissful Easter hymn, though officially anonymous, with George Wood the composer. It was in the collection of hymns Mr. Woodward published in 1894: *Carols for Easter and Ascension-tide*. He grew up in Hertfordshire, England and graduated from Caius College Cambridge. He became an ordained clergyman in the Anglican Church. He was noted for his religious verse and enjoyed setting his work to Renaissance tunes. An avid beekeeper, it was also said that he took pleasure in playing cello or euphonium in church processions. Besides other hymn publications, he's the author of the Christmas carol, "Ding Dong Merrily on High."

This Joyful Easter Tide
This joyful Easter tide,
Away with sin and sorrow!
My love, the crucified,
Hath sprung to life this morrow.

Refrain: Had Christ, who once was slain,
Ne'er burst His three day prison,
Our faith had been in vain:
But now hath Christ arisen,
Arisen, arisen, arisen.

My flesh in hope shall rest,
And for a season slumber.
Till trump from east to west,
Shall wake the dead in number.

Refrain

Death's flood hath lost his chill,
Since Jesus cross'd the river.
Lover of souls, from ill,
My passing soul deliver.

Refrain